HAVOC

NINA LEVINE

Copyright © 2016 Nina Levine
Published by Nina Levine

All rights reserved. No part of this publication may be reproduced, distributed or transmitted in any form or by any means, including photocopying, recording, or other electronic or mechanical methods, without the prior written permission of the author, except in the case of brief quotations embodied in critical reviews and certain other noncommercial uses permitted by copyright law. For permission requests, write to the author at the email address below.

authorninalevine@gmail.com
www.ninalevinebooks.com

This is a work of fiction. Names, characters, places, and incidents are a product of the author's imagination. Locales and public names are sometimes used for atmospheric purposes. Any resemblance to actual people, living or dead, or to businesses, companies, events, institutions, or locales is completely coincidental.

Editing by Hot Tree Editing
Cover Design ©2016 by Romantic Book Affair Designs
Cover Photography by Sara Eirew
Cover Models: Mike Chabot and Carolyn Seguin

Dedication

This book is dedicated to the perfect life we think exists.
It doesn't.

Sometimes life works out differently to the plan in our head, and that's not always a bad thing.

Sometimes the one journey we don't want to take is the one journey our soul *needs* to take.

"The past has no power over the present moment."
~ Eckhart Tolle

If you're going through the daily grind and shit's getting too fucking real and you get to that point where you start to doubt yourself, just remember—

You've got this, girl.

Chapter One
Havoc

She had to be fucking kidding me. Rubbing her hand against my crotch, she begged, "Come on, baby, take me back to your place and show me how well you can use this."

No way was I fucking this crazy bitch. I knew women like her. They were always on the lookout for a man to pay their bills. I would never be that man again.

Her hot breath on my ear turned me way the fuck off. Pushing her hand away from my body, I muttered, "I can use it really fuckin' well, just not with you."

She took a step away from me, eyes wide, stunned at my refusal. Her face clouded over in anger. "Well, aren't you a prick," she spat. "Leading me on like that and then telling me no. I've wasted my time on you, time I could have spent finding a man who knows a good thing when he sees it."

Fuck, bitches like her pissed me off. Usually, I wouldn't waste my breath, but I'd had a shit of a day, and she'd just pushed me that bit too far. "Let's get something straight. I didn't fuckin' lead you on. I didn't buy you a drink, didn't do much talking and I sure as hell never gave you the impression I wanted to fuck you. I've met too many women like you, so I know what you're after, and there's no way you're ever getting it from me. Been burnt once in my life, not going back for seconds. So move the fuck on and leave me the hell alone."

She stiffened as her mouth fell open. She recovered quickly though, and narrowed her eyes at me. "Fucking asshole," she snapped, before giving me one last glare and stalking off. I pitied the poor bastard she latched onto next.

Turning back to the bar, I motioned to the bartender to bring me another scotch, and contemplated why the hell I was back in Brisbane. It had been six months since I'd been home, and a year before that. It was never long enough between visits as far as I was concerned, but my sister had her own way of bringing me back every now and then. When she'd called to tell me our father wasn't well, I hadn't hesitated to return home. However, as much as I wanted to check on him, I didn't intend to stick around for long; too many bad memories lived in Brisbane.

The bartender brought my scotch over and as I threw it back, a woman settled onto the stool next to me at the bar. I didn't look at her, but I knew it was a woman by her smell. *Balenciaga*. The same fucking perfume my ex-fiancée had worn. I loved it, and yet I hated it, simply because it reminded me of her. Raising my chin at the bartender, I indicated my desire for more scotch. I'd knock myself out with alcohol before I'd dredge memories of that bitch up.

"So you're with Storm, are you?"

I turned and scowled at her. The cut I wore had a tendency to attract women but tonight I just wanted a quiet drink. "I'm not interested. I just want to have a drink in peace. You think that's possible?"

She didn't flinch, just raised a brow at me, and returned my scowl. "Hate to break it to you, Romeo, but I'm not interested either. I was just asking a question."

I'd fully intended on turning away from her and minding my own business, but her smoky voice stopped me. It was the kind of voice that commanded a man's attention, and it got mine. My gaze lingered on her face for a good while. It was her green eyes that did it; there was something there that called to me. Sadness perhaps. Definitely pain of some sort. Whatever the hell it was, I wanted to know more about her and that was without even taking a look at the rest of her.

"Yeah, I'm with Storm," I answered, my gaze steady on hers.

She nodded, and then broke eye contact to ask the bartender for a drink. I let my gaze drop to her chest and then lower. She wasn't my usual type; her breasts were smaller than I liked them and she wasn't as curvy as I preferred. And she was a brunette; I always went for blondes. But fuck, she had something that made my dick get hard and I needed to know what it was.

Turning back to me after she'd ordered her drink, she asked, "You know where the ladies' room is?"

I nodded in the direction. "Over that way."

She moved off her stool and slid her bag along the bar towards me. "You watch that. I'll be right back." Without waiting for my response, she took off in the direction I'd indicated. I watched her go, finding something about her that was definitely my type. Her ass. It had to be one of the best I'd ever seen. Desire slammed into me. I wanted to hold that ass in my hands before the night was over.

"You want another drink, buddy?" the bartender asked.

I dragged my gaze from her ass and answered, "Just keep 'em coming." I retrieved some cash from my wallet and placed it on the bar. "Keep hers coming too, until that runs out."

She surprised the hell out of me by only taking a couple of minutes. I raised my brow at her while she settled herself back on the stool. "That was quick."

Reaching for her drink, she said, "I did what I needed to do. Besides, I needed this drink so there was no time to waste." Her words had barely left her lips when she sculled her drink.

"I've never known a woman who didn't fuck about when they went to the ladies'."

She placed her drink on the bar and slid it towards the bartender who nodded and began making her another. "Yeah, well today, I couldn't give a shit about my hair or makeup. And that's saying something because if you knew me, you'd know I normally spend hours on my appearance. You know what, though? Today I realised what complete asses some people can be, and I just want to sit here and stew in my own misery." She paused for a moment before continuing, "And drink. I want to fucking drink until I can't remember his fucking name. And then tomorrow, I might go around to his place and trash it and fuck his car up. That'll serve the asshole right." Again, she paused before her face lit up and a wicked grin crossed it. "Fuck, and then I'll send my brother over to finish the prick off. He won't know what fucking hit him." She raised her glass at me. "Cheers!" She lifted the glass to her lips and grinned at me before throwing it back.

I returned her smile. "Remind me to never piss you off." The hostility she displayed towards whoever had screwed her over caused desire to coil in my gut. I wanted to help her fuck the asshole up. "What did he do?"

A frustrated sigh escaped her lips, and she ran a hand through her long hair. "What they all do. He cheated on me." She leant forward and pinned me with a hard stare. "Do all men cheat? Is it like an impulse they can't control or something, because I gotta tell you, just about every guy I've dated has cheated on me."

"You're dating the wrong men, darlin'. I've never cheated, and never contemplated it. Sure, I don't miss a beautiful woman when she walks past, but my dick stays firmly where it belongs."

She assessed me for a few moments before leaning back away from me. "I actually believe you because there's no reason for you to lie to me. But you're fucking hot, so I'm kinda struggling to believe women don't throw themselves at you."

"Just because a woman is up for it doesn't mean a man has to go there."

"Out of all the relationships I've had, I think only three of them didn't cheat on me."

"Like I said, you need to look for different men."

She shook her head. "No, I'm swearing off men for awhile."

I couldn't help but smile at the dirty thoughts running through my head at her declaration. Fuck, she'd managed to pull me from my foul mood, something not many people could do. "You gonna try pussy for awhile, darlin'?"

Another drink had been placed in front of her and she was just taking a sip when I asked her that question. She almost spat it out. "Who's to say I haven't already tried it?" She shifted on her stool to face me, and levelled a sexy grin on me, waiting for my comeback.

This conversation was just warming up and my day was taking a turn for the better. I hadn't flirted with a woman in a long time; it was almost like the art of it was dying. The women I met simply threw themselves at me. There was no challenge anymore and I fucking missed it, missed the chase. I let my gaze drop to her lap and then slowly lifted it back up to her eyes before saying, "Nothing like the taste of a woman on your tongue, is there?"

She didn't miss a beat. "The only thing better is a man's cum sliding down your throat while your lips are wrapped around his cock and you're holding his balls in your hand."

Jesus Fuck. She was a dirty bitch and my dick ached for that mouth of hers. I leant towards her, our faces close. Tracing her lips with my finger, I murmured, "Anytime you want to wrap these lips around my cock, you just say the word."

She stared at me for a couple of moments in a trancelike state before finally smiling lazily and reminding me, "I've sworn off cock, remember?"

I laughed, and drank some of my scotch. "I remember, darlin', but I'm not suggesting a long term thing here. I only want your mouth for one night."

She raised her glass in the air before taking a sip of it and saying, "The night is young, Romeo. I'm not easy though. You want me, you have to work for me."

"The name's Havoc," I informed her as the thrill of the chase kicked in at her words. If she wanted me to work for it, I was gonna fucking work her hard once I got it.

Frowning, she muttered, "You bikers have weird names sometimes. Where did you get that one from?"

Dark images flooded my mind—shit she didn't need to know and shit I didn't want to think about. "Not going there with you," I rumbled.

She shrugged. "Suit yourself." As the words left her mouth, someone pressed play on the jukebox in the corner and she turned to the sound of the music. "What the hell is this?"

"That's a classic. You don't like the Eagles?"

Turning back to me, she answered, "I could do without them." She jumped off her stool and muttered something about checking out what other music was on the jukebox as she stalked across the room towards it.

I watched her ass again and enjoyed the anticipation running through me. She would be mine tonight, and that pretty little mouth of hers would be sucking my dick while her hands worked their magic on my balls. No fucking way was she getting away with teasing me like that.

She spent some time at the jukebox and when the Eagles finished, she selected a song and then made her way back to me. I didn't know the song, but I didn't care. My attention was on her tits now. Even though they weren't the handful I usually preferred, they were still tits, and a man would take what he could get. And fuck, I wasn't complaining; between her ass, and her dirty mouth, I couldn't care less how big her tits were.

Once she settled back on her stool, I asked, "Do you always leave your bag with complete strangers?"

"No, but there's something about you, Havoc. Something I think I can trust."

"Jesus, woman, you give your trust too fuckin' easily."

"So you're saying I shouldn't trust you? Cause I gotta admit, I don't fuck men that I don't trust."

She was playing with me now, and fuck if I didn't like it. "Baby, you can trust me with your pussy. I know how to take care of that real well." I watched her closely, noting the rapid rise and fall of her chest as her breathing picked up. She was just as turned on as I was.

Her mouth parted slightly, and her tongue swept across her bottom lip before she bit it. When she spoke, her voice was low and huskier than before. My gut tightened with want, the need to get inside her strong. "I bet you've got mad skills with that dirty mouth of yours, but I'm not sure about your cock yet. Is it as talented as your mouth?"

I grabbed her hand and guided it to my crotch. Pressing it against the bulge there, I growled, "My dick will worship your pussy in ways you've never even imagined, darlin'."

She ran her hand over me, and moved her face to mine so that our lips were close. "I said you'd have to work for it, but I think I've changed my mind. I'm ready to sample this cock of yours, Havoc."

I resisted the urge to throw her over my shoulder and leave straight away. Instead, I kept my movements and voice controlled. "You sure about that? Once we leave here, I'm not letting you go, so be clear on what you want."

As she continued to tease my dick, she reached for her bag with her free hand, and said, "I've never been more sure of a man. Sexy as sin, dirty mouth and a dick to die for—what else could a girl want?"

Feral desire coursed through me, and I was done. Done waiting and done checking to make sure this was what she wanted. I stood and reached for her hand, gripping her wrist tightly. I led her out of the bar without a word exchanged.

When we made it to my bike, I shoved a helmet at her and waited for her to climb on behind me. She wrapped her hands around my waist and held on tight as we sped off into the night. I was staying at a motel not far from the bar, thank fuck, and we quickly reached our destination. Pulling up outside my room, I cut the engine and got her inside fast.

I needed to have her under me. Everything about her consumed every one of my senses.

Her eyes communicated her want.

Her voice dripped sex, weaving a spell over my cock.

Her touch shot heat through my body.

I couldn't remember the last time a woman had gotten to me like this.

Once inside, I kicked the door shut behind us, slid my hand around her waist and pulled her to me. "You're mine to do what I want with tonight," I growled in her ear.

One of her hands moved to my ass and the other tangled in my hair, pulling my face down to hers. "So long as you fuck me long and hard, I'll do whatever you say," she promised on a soft moan.

Fuck. I dropped my mouth to hers, and claimed her with a savage kiss. There would be nothing gentle about tonight and I fucking hoped she was up for it because I was ready to fuck the ever-loving shit out of her.

She kissed me back—hard, demanding. Urgency drove us forward, forcing our kiss to spiral into a frenzied attack, with lips and tongues pushing for more. Our need was fierce, unrivalled. Our hands began searching and grabbing at clothes. *Christ, she has too many fucking clothes on.* Without restraint, I began tearing them off. She kicked her shoes off and I stripped her of everything but her panties. When I had her how I wanted, I stood back and admired her body. She was fucking tiny; there wasn't an ounce of fat on her and not a lot of muscle either. My dick screamed at me to hurry the fuck up and bang her. I eyed those panties and moved my hand in their direction, ready to remove the last barrier between me and her pussy.

Her hand shot out and stopped me. My eyes flicked straight to hers in question. Shaking her head, she chastised me. "Havoc, it's rude to shoot for heaven when you haven't even stopped to ask a girl her name."

I fought the grin forming on my lips. *Fuck, she was sexy.* I traced her mouth. "What's your name, darlin'?"

She caught my finger in her hand and held it in place as she sucked it. Her eyes didn't stray from mine. When she was finished with my finger, she let it go and answered, "Carla."

Carla.

Her name would be burned in my memory forever; how could it not? But this was the last time she had any control over tonight. My hand gripped her neck, and I forced her to understand how the night was going to go down. "Carla, when I fuck a woman, she does what I say. She submits to me, totally. Do we have an understanding?"

She only hesitated for a moment before nodding. Her eyes betrayed her excitement though; she was fucking up for this.

I kept my hand around her neck and drew her closer. "And, I don't fuckin' shoot for heaven. I bring it to your goddamn door," I rasped.

Her lips brushed over mine and she gently bit my lip while her hand stroked my dick through my jeans. "Well, hurry the hell up. I'm way past ready."

I let her go, and pulled my T-shirt over my head. She undid my belt and removed my jeans and boxers faster than I'd ever seen a woman do it. Her gaze narrowed on my dick before moving over my body, and I slowed my movements to give her the time to take it all in. I liked her eyes on me.

When she finally looked up, she said, "You weren't joking about your cock, were you?"

"I don't joke about anything, least of all my cock," I promised.

"I'm working that out about you."

It was time to move this along. Taking her hand, I guided it to my dick, and demanded, "Stroke it until I tell you to stop."

She panted with desire as she followed my instruction. Her grip was firm, and she moved it up and down my hard length with a confidence I liked in a woman. Carla knew what the fuck she was doing and that pleased me no fucking end. I closed my eyes as I breathed through the urge to bend her over and just take her rather than restraining myself and drawing every last drop of pleasure from this. My mind wanted one thing while my body craved another, and as the desire ran through my spine and out along every nerve ending, I forced one heavy breath out after the other.

Pure, raw instinct clouded my thinking.

I need to be inside her.

When she picked up speed, I barked, "Stop." My eyes opened and I trained them on her. She'd immediately followed my order and let me go. Her gaze held mine and shallow breaths left her parted lips in rapid succession as she waited patiently for my next command.

Fuck.

She'd taken in what I'd told her about submitting to me, and that knowledge shot more need through me. I didn't know her, but what I'd seen of her at the bar told me she had a mind of her own and wasn't afraid of using it, so I'd half expected her to fight me for control. I fucking loved that she wasn't. I had no doubt that being with her was going to bring me the motherfucking orgasm of all orgasms.

"Lie on the bed and spread your legs. I want to taste you, want to run my tongue from one end of your pussy to the other and make you scream for my dick," I ordered, and watched as she obeyed. When she'd settled on the bed and opened her legs for me, I positioned myself between them. With bent legs, she planted her feet on the bed. I moved my hands to her knees and pushed them wider apart. My gaze zeroed in on her bare pussy, and I dipped my head for my first taste.

I had only planned to lick her, but a force I was unable to control took over.

I need more

Carla moaned as my tongue entered her, and her ass lifted off the bed as she tried to push herself into my mouth. My hands slid under her and I greedily pulled her even closer, swirling my tongue and sucking her.

"Havoc... more... fuck, I need your cock..." Her words were disjointed as she lost herself in the pleasure.

I ignored her and continued to work her over with my tongue. She was so fucking wet, and it took all my restraint not to give her what she'd begged for. My dick wanted what she wanted. It wanted nothing more than to slide into her wetness and fuck her hard, but I was a master of denial and control; I could go all night without succumbing to my need.

As I brought her closer to orgasm, her hands fisted in my hair and she gripped me hard. I growled my approval and used my teeth lightly on her clit, which only caused her to writhe even more in pleasure. The fact she got off on me biting her was another turn on; this woman was ticking all my fucking boxes.

I moved my mouth away from her pussy, and licked and bit my way up her body until I hit her breasts. Making eye contact with her, I asked, "How much do you like my teeth on you?"

She graced me with a sexy smile, and lightly trailed her fingers over my shoulder. "I love your teeth on me," she murmured.

I didn't wait for further encouragement. I lowered my face to her tits and took a nipple into my mouth, sucking and lightly biting as I went. Letting it go, I wrapped my lips around her other nipple and treated it to my teeth as well. She moaned her approval and fuck if that didn't cause my dick to harden even more.

Her hands had moved from my hair to my shoulders and then to my back, but I needed control over them. I grabbed hold of them, and pushed her arms above her head while I continued to suck and bite her breasts and then her neck.

"Havoc, I need my hands. I want to touch you," she insisted, struggling against my hold over her.

I lifted my head so I could look at her. "You'll have your hands when I say. Not before," I asserted.

"But don't you want me—" she started before I cut her off.

"What I want is for you to do as you're told," I growled, my eyes not leaving hers. She sucked in a breath, but didn't say anything. Her silence was my answer, and I nodded once. "Good girl." I ground myself against her as I moved further up her body and caught her mouth in a kiss. When I pulled away, I pushed her hands against the headboard and let go so I could take hold of her jaw with one hand and her neck with the other as I moved to straddle her. "I want my balls in this mouth," I said, letting my thumb graze her lips while I kept a firm hold on her jaw. "You ever had a guy sit on your face, darlin'?"

Shaking her head, she said, "No, but when I said I'm yours to do what you want with, I meant it."

My balls tightened at the fucking thought. Hell, Carla was fast becoming my perfect fuck. I shifted to kneel over her, and stroked my dick while I positioned my balls over her mouth. Her mouth instantly opened and took hold of them, and I shut my eyes while I savoured the feel of her wet warmth. She knew what she was doing, and worked me like a fucking expert until I reached the point where I had to rein it in if I didn't want to blow over her face. I reluctantly stopped her and moved away from her mouth, shifting back on the bed.

Our eyes met and she licked her lips. Smiling at me, she said, "As much as I love this whole control thing you've got going on, I really want to use my hands. Your cock would feel good in my hands."

"Baby, my cock is gonna feel good in your pussy. Forget your fuckin' hands." My usual preference was to fuck women in silence—get in, get out and move on—and to have full control of it. Carla's preference to talk and be involved was testing me; however, it was also arousing as fuck. I trailed my fingers over her breasts and circled her nipples before reaching for her neck and roughly pulling her to a sitting position. It was time to fuck her.

Leaning in to kiss her, I took in the expression on her face; she was so fucking ready for me. The knowledge hit me in the gut. My desire to have her warred with my love of drawing this shit out. A part of me wanted to make this last all night long, but I knew there was no way I could wait. "Gonna fuck you now, darlin', and it's gonna be rough. I hope you're up for that," I said, my eyes searching hers. Even though I demanded control, I never took what wasn't offered.

She pressed her lips to mine, and kissed me hard, giving me what I needed. "I'm up for that. I want your cock and I want it rough."

My movements were fast. I slid off the bed, taking her with me. Standing at the edge of the mattress, I positioned her so she lay on the bed in front of me, her legs raised to my chest. I wanted to watch my cock pump into her, wanted to see her pussy take it. Gripping her ankles, I bent her legs at her knees. My gaze was firmly on her entrance; she was swollen, wet and ready, and I was having trouble concentrating. My usual level of control of the situation had slipped as I chased my release.

I thrust in hard and grunted loudly at how fucking good it felt. Carla took me all the way and her pussy contracted around my cock. She wasn't far off an orgasm, and fuck, neither was I. Keeping hold of her ankles, I withdrew and thrust hard again. Her eyes rolled closed and she lost herself to it while I pounded into her. I shifted my gaze back to watch my cock slamming in and out of her. My balls tightened, and my breathing picked up as the familiar sensation rushed through me.

"Fuck!" I roared as it hit, and I thrust into her one last time. I stilled and let the pleasure take over. I'd been right; she'd given me one motherfucking good orgasm. My senses drowned in it, and my mind and body exploded from the pleasure. I was lost to the world in that moment, nothing and no-one could have dragged me from its grip.

As I came to, I realised Carla was moaning and grinding herself into me. I released her ankles from my hold and let them rest against my shoulders as I leant down to her. Grasping her neck, I pulled her face to mine and kissed her. My lips were demanding and she responded with her own exacting kiss. Her hands came up around my neck and she clung to me as she continued grinding into me.

"Havoc...need your fingers in me...fuck me," she panted between kisses.

I knew exactly what she wanted and didn't hesitate to give it to her. Moving my hand down her body, I worked her clit to bring her to orgasm. My dick was still inside her and I felt her pulse around me as she frantically fought for what she wanted. When she came, she didn't scream out like most of the women I fucked. Her eyes squeezed shut and her teeth bit down on her lip as her face fell to the side. I couldn't be sure, but it looked like she stopped breathing for a moment before finally expelling a long, satisfied breath. When she turned her head back to face me, she opened her eyes and gave me a slow, sexy smile. And then she simply said, "Fuck."

Shit, she was beautiful, but in that moment, she was fucking glorious.

I pulled out and lowered her legs. She stood and curled her hand around my neck, pulling me close for a kiss. "I've gotta use the bathroom to clean up your cum because you fucked me without a condom," she murmured in my ear.

Fuck.

I'd been so distracted that I'd forgotten the fucking condom. "Shit," I muttered, eyeing her. "I'm clean, but fuck, I'm sorry."

"I'm clean too, and on the pill so no worries there. Guess we got a little carried away," she said before leaving me to sort herself out.

I took a minute and watched her go before sitting on the bed and dropping my head into my hands. Christ, I hadn't had sex that good in fuck knows how long. But it had gone way too fast. I hadn't been able to stop myself from having her straight away, and already I wanted to take her again. Running my fingers through my hair, I stood. The night was young, and she hadn't taken my cock in her mouth yet. She'd promised me submission, and I intended to have it. I intended to fuck my need for her out of my system.

Chapter Two
Havoc

Two Weeks Later

"Get the fuck up, motherfucker," I demanded, keeping my eyes trained on the asshole on the floor in front of me, vigilant of his sidekick standing to my right. Any lapse in concentration on my behalf, and his friend would take me down and fuck my agenda to buggery.

The guy on the floor slowly began to move. He clutched his ribs where he'd taken a good beating from me. But he was taking his sweet-ass time—time I didn't have to waste.

Reaching down, I yanked him up hard by his shirt collar and yelled at him, "For fuck's sake, what are you? A fuckin' pussy who can't cop a punch?" Once he was standing, I shoved him back against the brick wall, and pulled my phone out. Looking at the guy to my right, I said, "Move the fuck next to your friend while I make a call."

He scowled at me but did what I said, and I put my phone to my ear while it rang.

"You got them?" Griff snapped into the phone.

"Yeah," I answered.

"Be there in a minute," Griff said before hanging up on me.

I slid the phone back into my pocket and eyed the two idiots in front of me. Dickhead Number One had ripped off King, the President of the Sydney Storm chapter for more than $20,000. A clear example of a man without a brain. Dickhead Number Two was in for a lot less, but had pledged allegiance to Dickhead Number One, which made him just as much of a fuckwit.

"Why the hell are you doing King's dirty work?" Dickhead Number One piped up.

I wondered at the intelligence of the human race sometimes. Were we really as stupid as we sometimes appeared? And then as I thought back on my life, I was reminded that, yes, sometimes we were. Sometimes we were blind to what was right in front of us. I met his gaze and replied, "You'd be surprised at the dirty work I do for

King. But this time, I'm doing it for my president, Marcus. And he's told me to do whatever it takes to get that twenty grand out of you."

He opened his mouth and uttered another string of stupidity, "I'll pay you off to let me go. How much do you want?"

I cracked my knuckles and then shrugged. "I'd rather take my frustrations out on your face, asshole. In fact, I kinda hope you don't come up with the money today. That way I can do what I do best."

Dickhead Number Two's eyes widened a touch. He had more brains than I gave him credit for. "What the fuck?"

I stepped closer to them, and said, "Yeah, that's what I was gonna ask you. What the actual fuck were you thinking ripping a club president off?"

"We were going to pay him back." Number One was almost pleading; well, his eyes were and I knew from experience his mouth would be soon, too.

I was just about to reply when Griff entered the alley. We were behind the bar where I'd found these two, and I was keen to get this over with because it fucking stunk from all the rubbish littering it.

Griff jerked his chin at me. "Which one owes the most?" he asked, his voice clear that he intended to carry out King's wishes. Griff was the Vice President of the Brisbane Storm chapter and not a man to ever fuck with. In fact, he'd only just assumed this role after pushing out the prior VP. And that VP was the son of the president and I thought, a friend of Griff's, so the ruthlessness of Griff's actions was pretty fucking evident. Personally, I didn't bother with friends and allies anymore, so it didn't concern me either way. I simply trusted no-one. It seemed to be the best way to live.

I pointed at Dickhead Number One, and Griff moved towards him. Speaking in a low, menacing tone, he asked, "How's this gonna play out, motherfucker?"

"I ain't got the money if that's what you're asking."

Griff didn't waste time; his knuckles collided with the guy's cheek a moment later. "Shall we begin again?"

Number One glared at Griff, and spat at his feet before saying, "You can't get fucking blood out of a stone, asshole. Tell King he'll get his money when I have it."

My fist itched to be used but I waited for Griff's signal. He'd been clear in his directions for this job; he wanted to have first go at these idiots before letting me loose. So I watched him, and I waited, because sure as fuck, these dickheads would need me to encourage them to pay up.

Griff's hands latched onto Number One's shirt, and he pulled the idiot towards him before spinning him around, letting him go, and punching him so hard in the face that the guy fell to the ground. Standing over him, Griff bent at the waist and bellowed in his face, "You ever fucking spit on me again, and you might not have a mouth left to fucking produce spit." He straightened, and indicated for the guy to get up before turning to Dickhead Number Two. Pointing at him, he ordered, "You start thinking seriously about your next move. King wants the money you owe him too." Turning back to Number One, he was pissed to find the guy still trying to get up. He shook his head and raised his fist, but I was surprised to see him lower it almost straight away, and turn to walk my way.

I gave him a questioning look but didn't say anything; Griff wasn't a big talker so I usually tried to keep communication with him to a minimum.

He shook his head in annoyance. Jerking his thumb in the guys' direction, he muttered, "Fucked if I could be bothered. They're all yours. I don't have the fucking inclination to deal with this shit today."

I nodded, thankful that Griff passed the job to me. It had been a shit week so far and I needed to get rid of my pent-up anger and frustration; these motherfuckers would help me with that. Griff pulled out his phone and made a call, leaving me to it.

Adrenaline coursed through me. This was the best part of my job, and I was fucking good at it. The results spoke for themselves and the club often called me in to take care of their shit around the country. I took a step towards Dickhead Number One, my gaze glued to his. Fear lurked in the depths of his eyes, and rightly so. I lifted my chin at him, and asked, "You got the money or do we have to find another way to settle this?"

He laid on the bullshit and I dug deep for the patience needed to deal with him. "I can probably come up with half of it by tomorrow," he said.

Failing to find any patience, I took one last stride in his direction, pulled my arm back, and smashed my fist into his face. I welcomed the blood that flew at me; I fucking lived for that blood. Not giving him time to catch a breath, I backed the first punch up with another one to his gut. He doubled over in agony, expletives streaming from his mouth. My mind wasn't even processing his words; it was intently focused on delivering more pain to him. I continued to land punches on his face and body until he collapsed onto the ground and curled himself up into a ball, trying desperately to shelter himself from me.

"Stop!" he screamed, drawing me from my violent haze.

I pulled back, caught my breath and demanded, "You got the money now, motherfucker?"

"Not all of it, but—"

I didn't give him time to finish that sentence. Bending down, I reefed him up, and slammed him backwards against the wall. Moving close, I snarled, "There will be no negotiations. Either you've got the fucking money or you don't."

"And if I don't? What happens then?"

Narrowing my eyes on him, I asked, "This the first time you've ever owed King money?"

"Yeah, why?" He was doing a damn good job at appearing unaffected, but his tells were there and I could read them all.

"I just thought I'd educate you a little, because it seemed to me like you were under the impression there are options here. When you owe King that kind of money, you pay." I paused for a moment to let that sink in. When he showed no signs of understanding, I elaborated. "You either pay up or King finds another way to encourage payment."

His brow furrowed. "Not sure I'm following," he said.

Fuck me.

"Jesus fucking Christ, you're a dumb cunt, aren't you?" I muttered. Seriously, how this fucker managed to get through life astounded me. I reached for the back of his head, grabbed a handful of his hair, and pulled his head back. Leaning close to his face, I asked, "You like breathing, motherfucker? You like your family members breathing? 'Cause if you fuckin' do, you better pay King his fuckin' money." I let his hair go and smacked the back of his head. "You following now?"

Before he could reply, his friend cut in. "Whatever he's short, I can put in."

I turned to face him. "Someone with some fuckin' brains. And what about the money you owe?"

Nodding furiously, he agreed to pay up. "I can cover it all. Just leave our families out of this."

I could smell his fear. That got my blood pumping almost as much as using my fists. "Your friend can't come up with his money till tomorrow, but I'm not waiting till then. You good to cover him in the meantime?"

"Yes," he said. "No problem. I'll go now and get it. Should I meet you back here?"

I chuckled. "Not fuckin' likely, dickhead. We'll all get the money."

Resignation crossed his face, and he nodded.

Griff ended his phone call and joined back in on the conversation. "We good to go, brother?" he asked me.

"We are."

"Thank fuck, because we have more shit that's just come up and you're needed on that."

My happy levels spiked at the thought. Looked like my week was taking a turn for the better. If I had to be in Brisbane, at least I would be having some fun during my stay.

As I entered the bar of the clubhouse, I took in the familiar surroundings. It was still the same as it had been six months earlier, and wasn't much different from two years ago when I walked away from it all for the peacefulness of the nomad life. It was a Wednesday afternoon, and most of the boys were at work, so the bar was fairly empty. Even the pool table in the back corner was empty. I liked the quiet and the lack of people.

"Havoc," Nash grinned as he came towards me. Slapping me on the back, he said, "I heard you were in town. It's been awhile, asshole. How the fuck you been?"

I'd been back for two weeks and had met with Marcus at a local bar where he'd detailed some jobs he had for me. This was the first time I'd seen anyone else. My preference was to take care of shit on my own and Marcus had no issues with that.

"Same old shit, different day," I said, thinking that nothing much changed in my life anymore. I spent my days either dealing with assholes, or on my bike. Both were enjoyable, but lately it had started feeling a little empty. I didn't want to think about what that meant so I did my best to avoid thinking. Easier said than fucking done.

"You ready to come home yet?" Nash asked the question that my father and sister kept pestering me with—the question that irritated the fuck out of me.

"No."

Nash didn't push it. "Fair enough, brother." He paused for a moment, his gaze travelling to my shirt. "You been dealing with some shit today?"

I looked down at the blood on my shirt. "Yeah." Looking back up at him, I said, "I hear you've got something else for me to sort out."

"We do," he started, but was interrupted.

"Fucking Havoc," came a deep voice behind me.

I turned to find Jason Reilly walking towards me with a huge shit-eating grin on his face. Unable to stop myself, I grinned back. J had been like a true brother to me before I left, and although I'd pretty much cut ties with everyone, I still counted him as a friend. "How's your sorry ass?" I asked.

He pulled me into a hug and slapped me on the back. Hugging was not something I did, not even with women, but J had a way of getting shit out of me that I didn't want to give, and so I let him at it. When he let me go, he answered, "I'm fucking brilliant."

Nash groaned. "Don't get him started, brother. Madison finally got that ring on her finger and the fucker's been walking around with a grin full of pussy ever since."

I wasn't surprised at this news; J and Madison married was something I'd always seen coming. "Happy for you, J. Surprised as fuck that you and Nash are in the same room though." These two had never gotten on, so to see them under friendly circumstances was a shock.

"One word for you, Havoc: Madison," Nash said. He jabbed his finger at J, and added, "She's sorted him out."

"Well she must be a fuckin' miracle worker to get you two talking," I said, shaking my head.

J scowled and muttered, "Let's just say she has her ways of making me do what she wants."

I had to laugh at that. "A woman finally grabbed you by the balls, huh?"

"Laugh all you want, dickhead. It happens to the best of us."

Nash cut in, changing the subject. "As much as I'd like to stand around counting the ways that Madison has him by the balls, we need to hurry this along. Did Griff give you any info on what's going on?"

I detected a change in his tone when he mentioned Griff. "No, but first, what's going on with Griff? You pissed that he challenged Scott?" Scott Cole was the previous vice president, and from memory, he had Nash's support so I had to wonder about how Griff's challenge for the VP role had affected club dynamics.

Anger clouded his face. "Yes, I'm fuckin' pissed. Griff played us all for fools when he betrayed Scott."

That was a feeling I knew well. Betrayal by a friend was the worst kind. "Yeah, I get that," I murmured, lost in my thoughts for a moment.

Nash moved back to the topic at hand. "We've got a problem with one of the strip club clients harassing one of the strippers at Indigo. Need you to deal with him so he leaves her alone. She's one of our best, and we don't want to lose her."

Storm owned the strip club, Indigo, and from what I knew, it was one of their more profitable businesses. The Brisbane chapter kept its nose clean so relied on various business ventures for income. "You got an address?"

J handed me a piece of paper with the information. "He's an out-of-towner, staying at that hotel."

I shoved it in my pocket. "No problem, I'll deal with him tomorrow. I've got some family shit to take care of this afternoon."

J raised an eyebrow. "Everything okay?"

"Yeah." I didn't want to get into it, but he continued to stare at me, his gaze demanding further information. "Dad's not well so I'm in town for him."

J nodded slowly. "Let us know if you need anything, yeah?"

Calling on anyone for help was not something I planned on doing, but I agreed so he wouldn't push the point. "Will do."

"Right, I'm out of here. Got a hot date, and if I'm late, she'll withhold sex," Nash said as he made to leave.

"What the fuck?" I asked, stunned that Nash had a date. As far as I knew, he never dated.

"I'm a changed man, brother. It's about time *you* found a pussy to stick with," he threw over his shoulder.

"Keep fuckin' walking, Nash. Me and pussy don't play so nice these days. Unless of course, it's new pussy, and then I'm all over that shit."

He shook his head and kept walking. J said his goodbyes too and left me alone to contemplate the afternoon ahead. Yvette, my sister, had texted me about half an hour earlier to let me know Dad had been taken to hospital, so that was where I was headed. He'd had a heart attack about three weeks earlier, which was why I was back in Brisbane, and it seemed he'd had another one. Fuck, if it wasn't one thing messing with my family, it was another.

I started heading outside when a familiar laugh slammed into me, jolting my senses. The woman it belonged to was a woman I did not want to see, but her voice rang out as she caught sight of me. "Havoc," she called out, and I heard the tap of her heels across the floor as she came closer.

For fuck's sake, why can't I have some peace and fucking quiet in my life?

Her hand landed on my shoulder, and I spun around and shrugged it off. My hard glare landed on her. "Don't fuckin' touch me, bitch," I snarled.

She flinched, but quickly recovered. "Baby, I didn't know you were back," she said in that breathy voice of hers. That voice used to make my dick jump to attention but not anymore. All it wanted to do now was shrivel up and pretend she didn't exist.

"Let's get one fuckin' thing straight, Kelly. I'm not your fuckin' baby, so cut that shit right now."

"There's no need to be such a bastard," she complained, still trying to move closer.

I reached out and gripped her shoulder, halting her progress. "Stop whatever the fuck it is you're doing, and leave me the fuck alone. We haven't been together for two years, and if you think I'd ever go there with you again, you're seriously mistaken. You fucked *me* over, remember?"

Her eyes widened, and she took a step back. She hadn't expected that reaction from me. Probably because for the five years we'd been together, she'd had me wrapped around her little fucking finger. Her voice was soft when she spoke. "I made a mistake, Havoc, and I know that now. Let me show you how sorry I am."

I raked my fingers through my hair as tension punched through my body. She was a piece of fucking work. "Letting you show me anything is the furthest thing from my mind. I'm leaving now, and I'm telling you for the first and the last time, don't fuckin' come near me again. You've no fuckin' idea how close I am to losing it with you, and I can promise you, that is something neither of us want to happen."

I turned to leave the club, relieved she didn't follow. She'd managed to drag me closer to the edge that threatened to rip every last piece of sanity from me if I stumbled over it. I lived precariously on that verge, but after seeing her, I needed to get my shit under control so I could find my way back from it.

Fuck.

Chapter Three
Carla

I stared at my teacher in alarm. He'd just given me the choice between sleeping with him or failing my subject. And I had to decide right that moment, because he had to report my grade for the semester tomorrow. "You're fucking kidding me, right?" I demanded to know as my mind flicked through options. Surely he couldn't get away with this.

He leant back against his table, and gave me a creepy smile. "I never kid, Carla," he answered me smoothly. In that instant, I knew he'd done this before, probably many times and gotten away with it. There was just something about his demeanour and the confidence with which he spoke.

Shit.

I was far from a prude, but I wasn't the type of woman to sleep my way to anything. And I knew there was no way in hell I would ever give my body to this prick. I made my decision. "Fail me if you must. I'm not fucking you, asshole," I snapped. Slinging my bag over my shoulder, I made him a promise. "If you do fail me though, just know that I won't let it rest. I will find a way to fuck you over."

He laughed. "I'm shaking in my boots, baby."

"Yeah, well you should be. You've no idea what connections I have," I muttered as I walked out of his classroom.

He yelled out after me, "What, are you friends with the local gang or something?"

I turned and gave him one last filthy glare. "No, you fucking prick, worse than that... a lot fucking worse."

I didn't wait for his response before I stalked out of the room. My blood boiled at the audacity of his demand, and I had to get out of there before I punched him. As I walked to my car, my mind conjured up all the ways I could inflict harm on his body. Just because I was a female didn't mean I couldn't make him hurt; I damn well could because my brother had taught me how.

"Fucker," I muttered as I opened my car door and slid into the seat. Shit, he'd really riled me up. If he did fail me, I would make good on my threat to fuck him up. Passing my fashion design course was a major part of my life plan, and I was almost finished; to fail a semester would mean extra time and money, and that time and money wasn't in my fucking plan.

I shoved the gear stick into reverse and squealed out of the car park. Ten minutes later, I was stuck in bloody bumper-to-bumper traffic. *Shit.* I didn't have time for this; I had to be at work in an hour. My waitressing job paid for my course, and I'd missed a lot of shifts lately so I could spend time studying. My boss was getting shitty about it, and I sensed that if I missed too many more, he would start looking for someone to replace me. So this traffic was the last thing I needed, and after my run-in with my teacher, it only served to put me in a worse mood.

I tapped my fingers on the steering wheel and searched for good music on the radio. All three stations I tried were playing shit music. I turned it off in disgust. I really needed to get my CD player fixed in my car, but it was an old bomb of a vehicle so I was reluctant to spend money on it. And besides, it was money I didn't really have.

A loud honk caught my attention. I'd been so engrossed in my search for music that I hadn't noticed the black ute in front had moved. My eyes flicked to the driver behind, and I gave him the finger. Sure, I hadn't moved forward, but hell, it wasn't like I'd be moving very far. God, I hated impatient drivers.

I inched my car forward, and then sat idling again waiting for the traffic to move. My gaze shifted to the clock. Shit, I really was going to be late if we didn't start moving faster. As I contemplated this, my phone rang, and I reached to check who it was. I had no intention of answering it while driving, but in this traffic, it couldn't hurt to see who it was.

Fuck. My boss. I dropped it back onto the seat next to me, and commenced panicking. And then the asshole behind me honked again. Jesus fucking Christ! I looked in the rearview mirror at him again. He was making rude hand gestures at me so I flipped him the bird again, and at the same time, I pressed my foot to the pedal. I didn't mean to press it hard but my foot slipped and I jerked forward and hit the ute in front.

Fuck me!

This was so not my fucking day.

I sat still for a moment waiting to see what the driver would do. When he left his ute and headed in my direction, my belly fluttered. He was built, and damn, he was sexy. I couldn't make out his face due to the glare from the afternoon sun, but the rest of him had me drooling. But he was pissed off; his rigid posture made that clear as he stalked toward me. When he got to my door, I finally managed a good look at him, and my belly did more than flutter. And damn, the desire ricocheting through me caused me to feel things I didn't want to feel.

Havoc.

Tall, olive skin, unruly dark hair, inked muscles to die for. It was the guy I'd slept with a couple of weeks ago. The guy who'd fulfilled his promise and brought heaven to my fucking door.

"What the fuck?" were the first words out of his mouth. Then he squinted his eyes, and dropped his face down to look at me through the window. "Carla?"

Had to give him points for remembering my name. "Yeah. Ah, sorry about that," I offered an apology he wasn't likely to accept, going by his pissed-off state.

He held onto his angry glare. "How the hell does someone have a fuckin' car accident in this kind of traffic?"

I scrambled to offer an explanation. "It was the guy behind me. He was honking and giving me the finger."

He shook his head once, in a I-can't-fucking-believe-what-I'm-hearing gesture. "So it was his fault that your foot hit the accelerator?"

I didn't like his tone. Sure, I was at fault, but there was no need for his attitude. I tried to open the door but he was blocking it. I eyed him. "Can you move so I can open the door?"

"What the fuck for?" He continued to lean against the door, eyeing me through the window. And I hadn't failed to notice his gaze roaming over my chest.

"Because I want to get out to talk to you."

The driver behind honked again, multiple times. Havoc scowled before straightening and glaring at the driver. I took the opportunity to open the door and get out. Another honk came from behind and Havoc stalked to the other car. I watched as he had words with the driver—angry words by the look of it. I then watched as he stalked back to me. His jeans hugged his legs, and his grey T-shirt clung to his chest. I couldn't help but stare. I knew that body, and I knew what it was capable of giving me.

Shit, get yourself together, Carla. The last thing I needed was to want this man again. We'd had our night together, and that was all it would ever be. I didn't have a biker in my life plan. No, my plan involved stability, not a man who raised his middle finger at society.

"Get back in your car, Carla. We're done here, but you need to be more careful," he muttered, treating me like a fucking child.

"We're not finished here, Havoc. We need to swap details for the insurance." I stood my ground, not letting his dismissive attitude scare me off.

"No need. I won't be claiming it."

I raised my eyebrows at him. I actually had no idea how insurance companies worked because I'd never had an accident, but his attitude made me pursue this. No fucking way was I giving in. He was treating me like the little woman and I wasn't having a bar of it. "Well, I might be, so give me your details anyway," I said.

His gaze flicked to my car, my old-as-fuck bomb of a car. When he shifted his gaze back to me, he failed to hide his amusement. "Seriously? You've got insurance on this?"

I placed my hands on my hips. "Yes, I do. Now give me your goddamn details," I snapped.

It was his turn to raise his brows at me, and then he slowly nodded. "You got a pen? Paper?"

"Yes," I said, and reached into my car to retrieve them.

A couple of minutes later, we'd exchanged details, and he gave me one last look before leaving. It was the kind of look that gave a woman goose bumps; good goose bumps, and it didn't fail to cause that reaction in me. He was still annoyed, but something else seemed to pass between us as well. It was a sexy something that curled itself deliciously around me, and begged me to pursue it. But I refused. And I let him go without another word.

Fuck. He'd left me with a need I couldn't get satisfied anywhere else. The kind that only one man I'd been with had been able to take care of. And that man was him. Fuck, it really was a shit day.

Chapter Four
Havoc

I scrubbed my hand over my face as I listened to Yvette. My sister could be a cranky bitch sometimes, and tonight was no exception. She was giving me her opinion on my choice of lifestyle and the fact it was taking me away from our family at a time she felt I was needed.

When she stopped speaking, I asked, "You finished?"

"That depends. You listening?"

I checked the time on the kitchen clock. It was nearly 10:00 p.m. and we'd just arrived back at Dad's house where I was staying. Dad had been admitted to hospital with more chest pain. The doctors were concerned he was at risk of another heart attack and wanted to monitor him. So we'd left him there and finally come home. I was tired and ready for bed, so having Yvette rant at me about moving back to Brisbane really was the last thing I needed after the long day I'd had. "I'm always listening, sis, but it doesn't mean I'm gonna do what you want. There's a reason I left Brisbane, and I can't say I'm in a hurry to come back permanently."

She blew out a long, angry breath. "I hate that bitch for driving you out of town."

"Yeah, well it was more than just her, and you know that."

My phone rang, interrupting us, not that I minded. It wasn't a number I knew, and normally I wouldn't answer it, but my desire to get out of this conversation made me hit answer. "What?" I snapped into the phone.

The smoky female voice that came through was one etched into my memory. "I am *not* a bad driver." Her words were slurred, and I could barely hear her over the noise in the background. I assumed she was at a pub, drunk.

"I'll have to take your word for it, babe, because you were this afternoon." I walked to my bedroom, ignoring Yvette's questioning stare.

"Yeah, well I was having a really bad fucking afternoon. My teacher threatened to fail me if I didn't screw him, and then I was running late for work, and the guy behind me kept honking at me, and... and, I just need you to know I'm normally a good driver. A really fucking excellent fucking driver." I listened with amusement as she worked herself up, which surprised the hell out of me. Usually women who rambled annoyed the shit out of me. "So you can take your judgemental attitude and shove it where the sun don't shine, Mr Perfect Biker who must never have a bad day."

I lay on my bed, stretched my aching body, and responded to her bullshit. "A couple of things, darlin'. Number one, I am far from perfect and have bad days all the fuckin' time. Number two, I hope you told your teacher to go fuck himself, and number three, how the fuck old are you if you're still in school?" I hoped to Christ she wasn't a teenager. I'd thought she was closer to my age.

"Pffftt... I'm twenty-three. Why, how old are you?"

Thank fuck for that. "Thirty-one."

"And I did tell him to go fuck himself. And I also told him I'd fuck him over if he messed with me. Shit, can you believe he did that?"

I didn't doubt for a minute that she'd mess with him if he failed her. "Babe, I've met worse men so yeah, I can believe it."

She sighed a long breath into the phone, and I enjoyed the effect it had on me. I rubbed my hand over my hard dick, and closed my eyes. I hadn't fucked anyone since her, and I wanted back in her sweet pussy. Since that was unlikely to happen, I decided to keep her talking while I jacked off.

"Havoc, I need sex, and there's not a man in this club who I want to have it with."

"You want me to talk dirty to you?" I squeezed myself and groaned, enjoying the new direction of our conversation. What I really fucking wanted was for her to talk dirty to me, and knowing her mouth, I had no doubt she'd be good at it.

"No, I want you to fuck me."

"Not gonna happen tonight, darlin'. I'm too damn tired to move, let alone fuck." I couldn't believe the shit coming out of my mouth, but it was true. I was done for the day.

"That's a shame. I loved having your cock in my mouth, and really fucking loved sucking your balls." She breathed the words into the phone, causing my dick to throb with need.

A male voice filtered through the line. "Sweetheart, you can have my balls in your mouth anytime."

My eyes shot open, and I sat up, waiting for her reply.

"Fuck off, asshole," she muttered, still slurring her words.

His voice was angry when he spoke again. "Don't fucking tell me to fuck off, bitch."

She didn't say anything back to him. All I heard was the noise of the people in the background. And then she said, "Shit!"

"Carla, what the fuck is happening?" I demanded to know; I was wide-awake now.

"He fucking groped my tit, but I think he's gone now."

"Tell me where you are. I'm coming to get you," I said as I grabbed the keys to Dad's ute and headed outside. I wasn't sure why the hell I was doing this, but I kept moving anyway.

She rattled off the name of the club as I started the car. Putting my phone on speakerphone, I ordered, "Keep talking to me while I drive."

The bar was a ten-minute drive from where I was, and she prattled on about God knows what the whole time. Fuck, I could probably listen to her voice for hours and stay hard the whole time. And thank Christ that dickhead seemed to have left her alone.

I parked the ute, ended the call and made my way inside. The beat of the music and the noise of the crowd assaulted me as I entered. I fucking hated these types of clubs that played this dance music shit. Give me a pub with a live band any day over this crap. Spotting her at the bar, I headed in her direction.

She saw me, and sent a drunken smile my way. In the time since we'd ended our call, she'd started talking to another guy, and he didn't look too pleased to see her watching me approach. "Who's this?" he asked when I stopped in front of her.

"I'm with her, dickhead," I muttered while curling my arm around her waist and pulling her to me. She smelt fucking amazing and felt even better as I pushed my hand up under the bottom of her top and found skin.

Her hand snaked around my waist too, and she murmured, "Yeah, he's with me. He's got magic ways with his cock and I really hope he'll show me them again tonight."

I bent my mouth to her ear. "Jesus fuck, woman, you've got a dirty mouth that's gonna get you into trouble one day," I said while trying to ignore the begging my dick was doing.

She turned to me, her eyes full of lust. "Can it get me into trouble tonight, Havoc?" As she said this, her free hand landed on my dick and she rubbed me.

Fuck.

"Trouble's your middle fuckin' name, isn't it?" I growled, reaching for her hand and pulling it off my crotch. "You keep that shit up, and I'll be banging you on the fuckin' bar."

She pouted. "You keep talking but all I'm hearing is a whole lot of grumbling. I've never known a man who didn't jump at the chance of sex."

The idiot she'd been talking to cut in. "Baby, if you want sex, I'll give it to you."

My head snapped in his direction. "Back the fuck off, asshole. The only man she's gonna be fucking tonight is me." He scowled but got the message and left.

As I watched him go, Carla placed her hand back on my crotch, and said, "Halle-fucking-lujah! Now can we hurry—"

I cut her off and yanked her hand off my dick again. "Stop talking, darlin', and start fuckin' walking. And if you touch my dick again before I say you can, I'm gonna make your ass red."

Her eyes widened and a sexy grin formed on her lips. "I like the way you think, and I might just be tempted to break that command before you get me home."

I bent to her ear again. "Who the fuck said anything about getting you home? If you think I can wait that long to get my dick in you, you're fuckin' dreaming."

She licked her lips. "Hell to the fucking yes!" And then she did as I said, and walked out of the club, her ass swaying from side to side, teasing the hell out of me as she went.

I followed her out, and then led the way to the ute. She eyed it and asked, "Why do you drive this instead of your bike? I kinda wanted to see what sex on a bike was like."

"I'm not putting your drunk ass on the back of my bike," I responded as I opened the door for her and helped her in.

She began rambling about something but I tuned it out as I headed around to the driver side. I was sure she'd still be talking when I got in the car, and I was right. I let her get all her words out before asking, "Do you always talk this much?"

Her filthy glare was the only answer I received, but she stopped talking.

I started the car and asked her, "What's your address?"

She frowned. "I'm not telling you my address until after you screw me. You made promises and I need you to make good on them."

I let my gaze dip to take in her skirt and top, and then I looked back at her face. She was a sexy woman, but in her drunken state with her pout and her demands for sex, she was off the fucking charts hot. In that moment, if she were next to a woman with the tits and curves I would have preferred, I would still have chosen Carla. There was an indescribable something to her that was making me act in ways I never did with a woman.

"Darlin', I'm making good on those promises. On the way to your house. So give me the goddamn address and then rest your mouth for what I have planned for it."

She sucked in a breath, and then her address tumbled out before she finally shut the hell up. We drove in silence until I pulled off the road and into a park. I found a dark, secluded spot and cut the engine. Turning to her, I wrapped my hand around her neck, and pulled her face to mine. My eyes bore into hers, and for a moment, we just stared at each other as the electricity hummed between us. Her breathing grew shallow, almost to a pant. Mine did too. I wanted this woman, and fought the desire to take her hard and fast. Because what I really wanted was to drag the pleasure out; let the anticipation build until her pussy was so wet that my dick would fucking drown in it.

Eventually, her voice cut through the silence. "Havoc, I don't think I can wait any longer," she said, her voice pleading with me, silently promising me a hell of a fuck. Women who were in touch with their sexual side like Carla was didn't come along very often. A lot of women had hang ups a mile fucking long that got in the way of good sex. I'd found one that didn't.

Ah, fuck. I wanted to take my time but she wasn't going to let me. As much as I wanted to control this, she had me. By the fucking balls. When her lips met mine in a kiss, and her tongue forced its way into my mouth, I knew for sure this wasn't going to go down the way I wanted. This was going to be hard and fast after all.

She moved onto my lap in what seemed like one swift movement. Her size and agility allowed her to do this. In the next minute, she clawed at my jeans, undoing them and then lifted her top over her head. Her hands then gripped onto my jaw and pulled my mouth back to hers for another searing kiss. Hot fucking damn, she was wild. I moved my hands under her skirt and slid my hand into her panties. Her wetness welcomed me, and I slid two fingers inside her, working her towards what she wanted.

As my fingers worked harder, she ground herself against me, and threw her head back, moaning my name. I dipped my mouth to her neck and sucked it while moving my free hand to her bra. Pushing it to the side, I covered one of her tits with my hand and rolled her nipple between my fingers.

"Oh, my God, Havoc... Fuck... Shit.... Fuuuck!"

I reached my hand up to her face and pulled it back to mine. Her eyes were shut but she opened them and found my gaze. "As much as I want to fuck you slowly, it's not gonna happen tonight. I will make you come though, one way or another."

She smiled lazily, and murmured, "Havoc, a woman doesn't need your cock in her to come; your fingers and your mouth are enough to get me off. Hell, just looking at your sexy ass and listening to your dirty mouth is enough to get me close and I'd even be happy to finish the job myself if I were treated to those."

I pulled her hair gently, and growled, "How long does it take you to get yourself off, baby?"

Her eyes danced at that question, and she whispered, "I can blow my own damn mind in five minutes, Havoc, but I bet with your help it could be done in two."

Fuck me.

My cock was more than ready to get this done. "No need, darlin', I'm gonna take care of you tonight, but I'm thinking I'd like to see those fingers of yours blowing your mind another time."

She reached into my jeans and grabbed hold of my dick. Licking her lips, she asked, "You got a condom this time?"

I nodded and searched in my wallet. Handing it to her, I indicated for her to take care of it, which she did while I pulled her panties down. Once we were ready to go, I slid my hands around her ass and pulled her into position. We held eye contact as she sunk her pussy down over my dick. The moment she'd taken me all the way, she let out a long breath, and whispered, "Holy fuck, you're huge. Feels so good." And then she took charge, and for once, I found myself enjoying a woman being in control. She slid up and down my dick, picking her pace up as she went. I knew it wouldn't take long for me to orgasm, but she brought me to it faster than any woman before. As I felt it hit, I gripped onto her hips and groaned out, "Fuck!"

Her fingers dug into my arms as she held onto me while I came, and a moment later she came too. Watching her in the throes of an orgasm was a beautiful sight, one I could watch over and over. Her head lolled back and she bit her lip as she rode the wave. When she'd wrung it for all it was worth, she dropped her head forward and grinned. Bending her face to mine, she whispered, "No man has ever made me come as fast or as good as you. You've got talents, baby."

I liked to give credit where it was due. "The same can be said for you, darlin'."

Her grin spread further across her face. I liked that I'd put that there, and then wondered where the fuck that thought had come from. Making women happy was not on my agenda anymore. The only thing I wanted to make women do was fuck me. I couldn't care less what they did after that.

I smacked her ass. "Time to get you home," I muttered, pushing her to let her know the night had ended. The thing I liked about Carla the most was that she didn't seem to have any problems understanding that what happened between us wasn't and wouldn't be anything more than sex. When I'd fucked her two weeks ago, she'd been more than happy to leave the next morning without asking for my number or a follow up. She happily crawled off my lap and waited to be dropped home. When I pulled up outside her house, she grabbed her bag, gave me one last drunken smile and exited the car without another word. I watched her walk inside, and decided she could well be the perfect lay.

Chapter Five
Carla

As I weaved through the afternoon traffic, I let my mind drift to thoughts of last night. I'd ended up drunk after having a run-in with my boss about being late to work. He refused to listen to my explanation about being stuck in traffic and involved in a car accident, and sent me home after three hours. That meant I'd missed out on five hours of pay so I'd hit the club to dance my aggression out. Men kept buying drinks for me, so a few hours later I was drunk, and that was when I'd had the bright idea to call Havoc. I'd wanted to set him straight about my driving skills. That was what I'd told myself anyway.

Truth be told, the man fascinated me. I had so many questions for him, ones I knew he'd never answer. Like, why did he have blood splatter on his T-shirt when I'd hit his car, and how did he get the nickname, Havoc? He was far from the kind of man I usually went for, but he was also the man who turned me on more than any other I'd come across.

I was torn about him. I wanted to have sex with him again; hell, I wanted a *lot* more sex with him. But I was the kind of woman who fell too easily for a man once I was sleeping with him. And Havoc was not the kind of man I wanted to ever fall for. I didn't believe he could give me the stability I craved. Plus, it was clear he didn't want anything from me except sex. I was good with this. For now. But if I kept sleeping with him, I knew myself and I was pretty damn sure I wouldn't be good with it after awhile. So, it was probably best not to see him again. But fuck, I couldn't stop thinking about him.

I hit the steering wheel in frustration. And that was when I saw him. He was exiting the hotel I was passing, and I made a snap decision to pull over. I didn't know why, but I couldn't have stopped myself if I tried. My sunglasses shielded my eyes from the burning afternoon sun; for winter, it was unusually warm, and I regretted wearing jeans and a long-sleeved top. His sunglasses hid his eyes from me, so I had no way to know if he was pleased to see me or not as I walked towards him.

He stalked right up to me, grabbed me roughly by the elbow, and demanded, "What the fuck are you doing here, Carla?"

Well shit. Not the reaction I was expecting. And not a reaction that impressed me. I tried to shake myself from his grip but he held firm. Looking up at his face, I answered him angrily, "I was driving by, saw you and thought I'd stop and say hi. Gotta admit I'm regretting that decision now."

His anger matched mine. "I'm regretting that decision too, babe."

He began to pull me back towards my car. I didn't appreciate being manhandled, and resisted. That only annoyed him further and he grasped me tighter in an effort to pull me. "Stop!" I yelled.

He stopped and bent his face to mine. He hissed at me, "Trust me when I say this is not a place you want to be. You need to leave right fuckin' now."

"Why?"

He resumed dragging me in the direction of my car, and muttered, "I don't have fuckin' time to detail it for you. I just wish to hell that you didn't have to argue with me about every-fuckin'-thing."

Fine. If he wanted me gone, I was going. He wasn't making any sense, and he'd upset and pissed me off so there really was no point in sticking around. Obviously, he'd had enough of me, and whatever we'd had going was finished. I finally found the strength to break free of his hold. Throwing my arms in the air, I yelled, "Fine, I'm going. You don't have to drag me anymore."

"Keep your fuckin' voice down," he hissed again. His hand landed on my lower back and he continued to guide me to my car.

I unlocked my door, glared at him one last time, and said, "I don't know what the hell is up your ass today, but I get the message. I won't bug you again. But let's just get one thing clear, Havoc. There are much nicer ways of telling a girl you want nothing more to do with her. You really need to learn them." Without further ado, I got in my car and sped off without a backwards glance.

What an asshole.

★★★

I arrived home half an hour later. I lived with my mother while I was finishing my course, but she was out for the day. Thank God, because I needed some time to myself to calm down. I loved my mother but she always knew when something was bugging me and I didn't want to discuss Havoc with her. Instead, I ran a bath, poured a wine and sank into the warm bubbles, letting them wash over me. I hoped they would ease the tension from my body.

I'd brought my mail in to read, and quickly worked my way through the five letters. The last letter caused me to sit upright in the bath and shout out expletives. My fucking teacher had failed me after all.

Motherfucker.

I stood and grabbed a towel. After I'd dried off, I hurriedly got dressed again in preparation to go down to the college and give him a piece of my mind. I was walking out the door when my phone rang.

"Hello," I snapped at whoever it was without checking caller ID.

"Shit, girl. You having a bad day?"

It was Velvet, my brother's girlfriend. I sighed. "Sorry. And yes, I'm having a bad afternoon."

"What's happened?" she asked, and I knew she genuinely wanted to know. Velvet had a heart of gold, and we'd grown close since she'd come into our family a couple of months ago.

"I just found out I failed my semester at school because I wouldn't sleep with my teacher. And on top of that, a guy I've been sleeping with was the biggest asshole to me earlier. Ugh, men."

"Your teacher can't fucking do that!" she exclaimed, her anger at the situation matching mine.

"Well, he has."

She was quiet for a moment, but then came out with the big guns. "Nash will take care of him for you."

I smiled. Nash was my brother, and was a biker with the Storm Motorcycle Club; he would definitely take care of my teacher for me. He had a violent streak in him and wasn't afraid to use it. I didn't know much about his club or his role in it but I sure as hell knew he wasn't a man to be messed with. And he always looked after those he loved. My teacher was fucked.

"Now to this guy you've been sleeping with. What did he do? And who is he? You never told me about him!"

I laughed at her; I told Velvet pretty much everything, but I hadn't told her about Havoc. I wasn't entirely sure why not. "It doesn't matter what he did because he was only a two-night stand. I shouldn't let him get to me."

It was her turn to laugh now. "A two-night stand? Only you could dream up something like that."

"Shut up!" I mentally poked my tongue at her.

She was still laughing. "Oh, God, I do love you, Carla. No wonder you give Nash grey hairs."

"Well, he shouldn't worry about me like he does." Nash was twelve years older than I was and had always been something of a father figure, along with my other brother, Jamison. My sister, Erika, also looked out for me. Our father had left when our mother was pregnant with me and we'd never heard from him since.

"You know he's never going to stop worrying, don't you?"

I sighed. "I know." I had to smile; she'd helped calm me down, and I decided not to go and confront my teacher. "Thank you, Velvet," I said softly.

"What for?"

"For being you, and for calling at the exact right moment. You're always there for me when I need you."

I could hear the smile in her voice. "Well, it was a fluke this time, but I'm glad I could help."

"What did you actually call for?"

"Shit, I'd nearly forgotten about that! I was ringing to see if you wanted a girls' night out tomorrow night?"

I grinned. Nights out with Velvet were the best thing, and I wasn't turning that down. "Hell yes!"

"Good. Meet me at my house and we can get Nash to drop us off at the club."

We said goodbye and hung up. My mood had lifted a little, and I decided to go dancing at the club by myself again that night. Dancing always made me feel better, and it would help me forget my shitty teacher for a few hours.

★★★

The bartender passed me a glass of water and I drank it all in one go. I'd been dancing for the last two hours and was sweaty and thirsty. I was also on a high, and felt like nothing could shake my good mood. How wrong I was.

My phone buzzed in my bag, and I pulled it out and pressed it to my ear. "Hello?"

"Carla, where are you?"

Shit, it was Havoc. I didn't want to see him so I tried to fob him off. "Why are you calling me, Havoc? Didn't you say everything you had to say to me this afternoon?"

His frustration was clear in his tone. "You've got no idea what this afternoon was about and I want to explain it to you. Tell me where you are so I can come and see you."

"There's no need. I don't want to see you again."

"Babe, you will be seeing me again. We've got shit to clear up."

It was my turn to get frustrated. "Look, we had a two-night stand. It's done, so let's just move on. I really don't need to know whatever the hell it is you think I need to know."

"Fuckin' hell, woman. Are you this argumentative with every man you meet, or am I the only one blessed with your arguing?"

"Fuck you," I yelled into my phone, and hung up on him. *Bloody men.*

The bartender raised his brows at me and I shook my head. "Don't ask. Men!"

He grinned. "Gotcha."

I moved back out onto the dance floor and attempted to lose myself in the music again. The time passed and I was unsure how long I'd been dancing for when strong hands slid around my waist, and warm breath tickled my neck. Havoc's voice filtered through the music into my ear. "Time to talk, babe."

I spun around to face him, and his hands landed on my ass and pulled me to him. Our faces were close, eyes searching the others'. "Why did you come?" I asked as I placed my hands against his chest.

"I really don't fuckin' know," he admitted.

The anger from our phone call was gone, and in its place was a sexual tension I was convinced we were both feeling. How this man managed to make me want him even when I knew I didn't was beyond me. But the pull to him was undeniable, and my belly fluttered with desire.

"You shouldn't have come," I said, my eyes still firmly on his. "We had sex, and neither of us want anything more out of it, so I don't need to know why you were a prick to me this afternoon."

"You're right. But the thing is that for once in my life, I feel the need to clear up a misunderstanding. I need you to not think of me as that prick."

I listened closely to his words, and watched his eyes and his face. He was fighting this. It was as if he was torn between not wanting to be anywhere near me, and wanting desperately to tell me his reasons. I couldn't work him out. And that right there made me want to take the time to do just that. I wanted to know what made Havoc tick.

Pushing gently against his chest, I moved out of his embrace. "Okay, let's talk," I agreed, indicating for us to go outside where we could hear each other.

When we were outside, I asked, "How did you find me?"

He shrugged. "Took a guess you'd be at the same club as last time. It was right."

"Okay, so talk. Why were you such an ass to me?"

His shoulders tensed up, and he raked his hand through his hair. "You know I'm with Storm, right?"

I nodded, giving him the confirmation he needed to move on.

"Part of my job with them is to sort out dickheads who threaten the club or the people close to the club. This afternoon I was dealing with a situation when you turned up. The guy involved is a nasty piece of work and I didn't want him to see you there. That's why I was trying to get you to leave."

Shit, that was so far from what I'd expected; it made me stop and think. I cocked my head to the side. "So you do have some warmth in that heart of yours, Havoc?"

"Let's not get carried away, darlin'," he muttered.

My annoyance with him faded, but I wasn't about to let him off the hook that easily. "You know, there was no need for you to be so damn rude to me. You could have just said that to me this afternoon and I would have left."

His glare was piercing. Again, I couldn't read him. After staring at me for what felt like an eternity, he agreed, "Yeah, I could have, but in the heat of the moment, I went with my gut, and my gut told me to get you the hell out of there fast. I didn't have time for all the questions I knew you'd ask if I tried to explain it to you."

Clarity hit me, and fuck, it wasn't what I'd ever have thought about him. I leant closer to him, and said softly, "You were worried about me. You cared what happened to me." My heart beat faster at the thought. I didn't know what to do with it, wasn't even sure why I'd said it aloud to him.

Scowling, he said, "The only thing I care about right now is getting back inside of you." His hands hit my ass and he pulled my body to his. "You think we can take care of that?" he growled.

With his erection pressing against me, and his earthy scent invading my senses, I struggled to say no. I was caught in that in between where I didn't want anything further to do with him, but on the other hand, I wanted and craved only him. Havoc was demanding, bossy, crude and unpredictable—all the things I didn't want in a man. And yet, those qualities of his turned me on and drove me wild. He excited me and just the thought of him got my heart racing. I knew nothing about him, but I desperately wanted... no, needed to know everything.

Fuck.

He stared at me, and pushed for an answer. Trailing his finger down my cheek, neck and over my breasts, he said, "I want these tits in my mouth again, baby. And I sure as fuck want my cock between your lips. Tell me you want the same."

Oh, God, I did want that. The ability to play games with men was not in me, and so I went with pure honesty. "Havoc, I am so wet for you right now that I doubt I could say no even if I wanted to. But I don't want your cock in my mouth. I want it in my damn pussy. You think you can take care of that?"

He made a grunting noise I'd never heard any man make, but shit, it was the hottest noise I'd ever heard. Grabbing me by the wrist, he began walking and dragged me along with him. I stumbled a little but managed to quickly right myself. When I saw he was heading towards a bike, my insides buzzed with desire. I wanted to fuck him on that bike.

He gave me a helmet, and I murmured, "I've been dreaming of sex on your bike."

His forehead creased slightly. "Babe, the shit I want to do to you cannot be done on a fuckin' bike, so get that fantasy out of your mind."

"Really? It would be so hot though."

His lips crashed down onto mine, and he took my mouth forcefully before letting me go and growling, "No. What would be hot would be me spending all night using my mouth and dick in ways you can only imagine, ways that you can't fuckin' do on a bike." He smacked my ass and ordered, "Now get on."

My body tingled all over. He hadn't convinced me that sex on a bike wasn't all I thought it would be, but I did as he said, and held on tight because the one thing I did know for sure was that Havoc didn't make promises he couldn't fulfil.

Chapter Six
Havoc

I ran my hand over the curve of Carla's hip and over her waist. She was asleep on her side, back to me, and the sight of her ass was the best view to wake up to in the morning. We'd fucked all night and had only fallen asleep about four hours ago. Carla was as insatiable as I was when it came to sex. I was ready for more and I reached my hand over her to drag my fingers through her pussy in an effort to wake her up. She moaned in her sleep, parted her legs and rolled onto her back.

Dropping my lips to her chest, I continued to stroke her pussy while sucking on her nipple. As I sucked, I kept an eye on her face, waiting for her to give me her gaze. It didn't happen so I pushed two fingers inside her and bit her nipple. Finally, she cracked her eyes open and looked at me. Smiling. Fuck, that smile made my dick twitch. I let her nipple go and murmured, "Mornin'."

Her hands came down onto my head and she ran her fingers through my hair as she lifted her ass off the bed slightly so she could push herself into my hand. "Morning. What havoc are you gonna cause today?"

I shifted so I could brush my lips over hers. "Funny," I whispered, and then more loudly, "I thought I'd start my day off with my tongue in your pussy. Yeah?"

She pushed her pussy up again, and pulled my hair. "I'd say that's the best way for a woman to wake up."

I nodded and made my way down her body. My tongue had just entered her when a loud knock on the front door sounded. I ignored it and swirled my tongue inside her, but the knocking continued and grew louder, more insistent.

I pushed up off the bed. "Motherfucker!" I yelled, and then said to Carla, "You stay there. I'm gonna get rid of whoever the fuck it is and be right back to eat you."

She grinned at me from hooded eyes, and flicked her hands at me. "Go. Hurry the fuck back though."

I stalked to the front door and ripped it open with a, "What the fuck do you want?"

My eyes hurt at the sight in front of me.

My fucking ex-fiancée.

She raised her brows and her gaze roamed over my body, landing on my naked body with my erect dick. "Do you always answer the door like that these days, Havoc?"

"Only when I'm interrupted in the middle of eating pussy. What the hell are you doing here?"

"I came to see if you were okay because I heard your dad was in hospital." She took a step forward in an effort to enter the house.

I placed my hand firmly on her shoulder and halted her. "Don't take another step. And don't give me that fuckin' bullshit. You couldn't care less about my dad."

She appeared upset at my words, but I knew her better than that. Kelly was good at acting; hell she'd acted her way through our fucking relationship. "God, you can be so mean, and distrustful. I do care about your dad."

"I'm distrustful because you made me that way. And the only thing you care about is that when he dies, I'll inherit half of his fuckin' money."

The air was tense around us as we battled. I was under no illusion here; she was going in to battle hard. Kelly was a money hungry bitch, and she had her eye on my inheritance. No fucking way was I falling for her lies again.

Carla, who appeared next to me, interrupted us. I eyed her; she was dressed and looked like she was leaving. I frowned at her. "What are you doing, babe?"

She looked from me to Kelly, and back to me. "I'm going to head off. Looks like you've got stuff to take care of here."

"Fuck no. Kelly was just leaving," I said. Carla going was the last thing I wanted; my dick needed her attention.

And then Kelly did what she did fucking best; she convinced Carla there was shit going on where there actually wasn't. She rubbed her hand up my arm, and purred, "Thanks for understanding. Havoc and I have a lot of things to discuss and work out, so it means a lot to me that you're leaving us to do that."

Carla's gaze latched onto Kelly's hand on my arm, and she pushed past us to leave. "See you, Havoc."

"Babe, how you gonna get home? You don't have your car here."

"I'll catch a bus, no worries," she threw over her shoulder and kept walking.

I let her go. As much as I wanted her to stay so I could get my hard-on taken care of, I didn't have the patience to deal with female drama, and I could sense it happening. I'd rather take care of myself than deal with bullshit from a woman. But first, I needed to set Kelly straight.

I directed my attention back to her. "Let me make something clear," I barked. "The day you fucked me over was the day my dick decided not to dance with you again. You need to take your bony-ass home and never fuckin' set foot near me again. Whatever you think is gonna happen between us, isn't."

"But—"

I cut her off. "But fuckin' nothing, Kelly. You had your shot at me and you fucked it. Now fuck off before I do something I'll regret." My tone was feral; she brought out the worst in me and I was helpless to control it. I slammed the door in her face and stalked back into the house. When I hit the kitchen, I punched my fist down onto the kitchen bench.

"Fuck!" I bellowed to the empty room. "Fuck!"

★★★

Four hours later, I was roaming around Dad's house at a loss. I couldn't fucking get Carla out of my head.

Jesus.

Not since Kelly had a woman consumed my thoughts like she did. In honesty, she consumed my thoughts more. I didn't want this, but I had to see her. My sanity was at risk if I didn't.

I called her and was surprised she answered on the second ring. "What do you want, Havoc?" She sounded resigned, defeated.

"What's wrong?" Even my concern for her was a foreign feeling to me, but I couldn't stop the words falling out of my mouth.

"I'm at work and I'm having a shitty day with my boss. And you and I really need to stop whatever this is. You obviously have something going on with that other woman and I'm not interested in getting between that."

"Fuck, babe. If you'd just let me explain this morning, you'd know that woman is my ex and not a woman I ever want to see again. As for your boss, what's he doing?"

She was quiet for a moment before responding, "Oh."

"Yeah, oh."

"Sorry, I should have waited." Her voice was quiet, hesitant.

"Yeah, you should have. But it's done now." I was shocked as shit. I'd expected her to drag this out like women tended to do. The fact she didn't made me want her even more.

"I'm on my lunch break and it's just about to end so I've gotta go."

"Tell me where you work. I'll come and see you at the end of your shift."

"Gossip Café. You know it?"

"Yes, what time do you finish?"

"Three."

"I'll be there," I promised and hung up.

★★★

Two hours later, I entered Gossip Café, and my gut tightened when I caught sight of Carla at a table in the back. I was an hour early but I couldn't stay away any longer. She finished with her customers and walked my way. When she saw me, she faltered, and slowed. I didn't take my eyes off her. Even surrounded by the busy hum of a full café and distractions everywhere, all I saw was her. She was fucking beautiful. Dressed in black pants and top with flour marks down them, her long brunette hair pulled back in a ponytail with strands falling out, and a frazzled look on her face, she was perfect in her imperfection.

She kept walking my way, her focus solely on me, but suddenly her attention diverted to some customers and she ceased movement. I narrowed my eyes to take it all in.

"Sir, what is the matter here?" she asked a guy who glared at a woman who sat on her own.

His angry eyes shifted to Carla, and he jerked his thumb at the lone woman. "This dyke is making my woman uncomfortable by staring at her, and I've had enough."

The lone woman stood up, anger etched on her face also, but before she could respond, Carla spoke. "I think it's pretty damn rude of you to use language like that," she said to the guy.

"I don't give a shit what you think, bitch. I just want this fucking lesbian to take her eyes off my woman."

This dickhead had overstepped all boundaries now, and I moved towards them, ready to kick his ass. Carla kept talking, impressing the shit out of me. "Number one, you don't call me a bitch and get away with it, asshole. Number two, you don't diss lesbians and get away with it.

And number three, did you ever stop to consider that perhaps this lady wasn't looking at your woman? Perhaps she was looking past your woman."

The woman he was referring to as a lesbian piped up. "Thanks, but I can stand up for myself," she said to Carla, and then looked at the asshole. "I wasn't looking at your woman. I was actually checking out the chick behind her, dude. Your woman isn't my type."

Carla grinned. "Great." She turned to the guy. "So you can sit your judgemental ass down and leave this lady in peace."

He glared at her. "Not before I complain to your boss."

Carla waved her hand in the air at him. "Do what the fuck you want, dickhead. If he listens to you, then he's not the kind of man I want to work for anyway."

With that, she turned and headed over to where I stood. She didn't look happy.

"I'll probably get fired for that," she said, dropping her head down and shaking it before looking back up at me. Tiredness lurked in her eyes.

"Maybe you'd be better off not working for him if he fires you over that."

Nodding, she agreed. "Only problem is that I need the money."

I shrugged. "I'm sure you could get another waitressing gig."

Her lips pursed together and she sighed. Running her hand through her hair, she asked, "Why does life have to be so damn hard sometimes?"

Before I could answer that, her boss bellowed out, "Carla! My office now."

"Fuck," she muttered, and then added, "Yep, he's gonna get rid of me. I'll see you in a minute."

I figured she knew what she was on about so I waited outside for her. She didn't take long, joining me a couple of minutes later. Disappointment was etched on her face as she said, "Get me out of here, Havoc. Take me far, far away."

In that moment, the barriers I had built began to wash away. I'd decided a long time ago that I didn't want any fucker getting close to me anymore; didn't want them to have any power over me and I certainly didn't want to help them deal with the shit in their lives. After wanting so much in life, and losing everything I'd worked hard for years ago, all I wanted these days was the shirt on my back and my bike. Yet, Carla standing before me, with a wearied and beaten aura to her, threatened to rip my barriers down.

Against all my better judgements, and against the voice screaming out *No* in my mind, I nodded, got on my bike and told her to get on behind me. Pulling her hands around my waist tightly, I said, 'Hope you're up for a long ride, darlin', because that's the only way I know to get rid of the shit in your head."

Chapter Seven
Carla

We'd been riding for probably close to an hour and a half when Havoc pulled off the road and cut the engine. We were somewhere in the Sunshine Coast hinterland, and the café he'd stopped at looked inviting. I was a little cold because I hadn't dressed for the cooler air in the mountains, so the warmth that hit me as we entered was welcome.

"What do you want to drink?" Havoc asked.

"Coffee, white with one please. And cake. I need cake." I was firm. Cake always made me feel better.

He chuckled. "What kind of cake, babe?"

I licked my lips thinking about it. "White chocolate mud cake if they have it. But if not, anything will do so long as there are no sultanas or fruit in it." I pointed at him sternly. "If you bring me back fruit cake of any kind, there will be hell to pay."

His face broke out in a huge grin and my stomach did somersaults. I'd never seen Havoc smile. Not once. In fact, until that moment, I'd never heard him laugh or even chuckle. I liked it, a lot. He turned me around and smacked me on the ass before placing his hands on my shoulders and whispering in my ear, "Go and sit this gorgeous ass down and I will bring you cake that doesn't contain any fuckin' fruit. Trust me, sweetheart, the last thing I want to do is incur your wrath."

Warmth spread through me. This was a side of Havoc that I really liked. I did what he said, and checked out the café while I waited patiently for him. It was a country-style café with lots of wood, and a potbelly fire burning in the corner. No wonder it was so warm inside. Nearly every table was occupied and people were laughing and enjoying themselves. The staff seemed chirpy too. I bet they had a brilliant boss.

Just as I was about to wallow in self-pity about the turn my life had taken this week, Havoc pulled up a seat and sat with me. I looked at him, and enjoyed the thrill that ran through me at the sight. "Fuck, you're gorgeous," I said, the words spilling out of me before I could censor them. Censoring and me didn't really go hand-in-hand so I was used to saying shit I shouldn't, and rarely got embarrassed because of it.

He laid a sexy grin on me. "You just say what you're thinking, don't you?"

I shrugged. "Yeah, one of my many good traits," I said with a wink.

His grin turned into a laugh. "I'd have to agree with you there, babe. Nothing sexier than a woman who knows what she believes and isn't afraid to say it."

I leant forward and asked, "What cake did you get me?"

"Well, it sure as shit wasn't fruitcake, but I think I'll make you wait until they bring it out."

"You're playing with me now, aren't you?"

"Maybe," he agreed. He then leant forward too, and added, "Playing with you is fast becoming one of my favourite activities."

Fuck.

Talk about desire hitting all points in my body at once. This man had it going on, and I was sure I might burst into flames from the heat surrounding us.

I gathered my wits and said, "You're a smooth talker, Havoc. I bet you have no trouble scoring wherever you go."

He shifted back in his chair, his gaze stuck on mine. The depth in his eyes got to me. Havoc was not a shallow man—of this I was sure. He nodded slowly, contemplating what I'd said. "You're right. I have no trouble in that department. But, babe, I don't say yes very often."

I wasn't able to hide my surprise. "What? You knock back sex?"

"Yeah."

I settled into my chair, enjoying this conversation because it was giving me a small glimpse at who he was. "Okay, so how often do you have sex?"

"I don't fuckin' count it, Carla. My point is that it takes a lot for a woman to interest me. I don't just fuck someone because they've got a good set of tits or a hot ass. There has to be something more for me. Something *to* the woman."

I let his words settle over me and soaked them in. Because what he'd just given me was a huge compliment. It made me feel good about myself, and I desperately needed that after this week.

While I processed that, he changed the subject. "Tell me why you're so down."

I expelled a long breath. "Do we have to talk about me? I'd rather talk about you. That's so much more interesting."

The waitress brought our coffee and cake at that moment, and I smiled at him when I saw what he'd ordered. "Wow, and you project such a badass image, Havoc. Who would have thought?" He'd ordered me a small piece of every type of cake they had except for fruitcake. There must have been six different mini cakes sitting in front of me.

"Shut up and eat, woman," he muttered, clearly uncomfortable with my backhanded compliment.

I laughed, but did as he said. My mind spun in a million different directions. He'd managed to confuse me all over again. I'd kind of been relieved when his ex had turned up. I'd thought it was a woman he had something going on with and that thought helped me at the time to make a decision to cut and run. It was the decision I'd been trying to make where he was concerned, but I'd been having trouble following through. Since knowing who she was, and after he'd treated me to this other side of him, I was back to being confused.

We ate and drank in silence for a few moments. The cakes were so damn delicious, and I devoured them quickly. He smirked at that, and said, "I take it they were good?"

As I finished the last piece, I looked up at him, and answered, "They were divine. This café needs to be added to my 'favourite places to visit' list. Thank you."

"Now you owe me."

I raised my eyebrows. "I can only imagine how you plan to exact payment."

Pinning me with his stare, he said, "As payment, I want to hear what's causing you grief."

I took a deep breath. "Fine. If you must know, I failed my semester at college, so when you add that to the fact I lost my job, it's been a shit week."

"The teacher you refused to sleep with actually failed you?"

"Yes."

His face clouded over with anger. "What's his name?"

I didn't know Havoc well, but I knew it would be a bad idea to give him my teacher's name. Nash would just hurt him a little if I let him loose on the guy. I hazarded a guess that Havoc would do a lot worse than that. If the club sent him to take care of problems, I could only imagine what that entailed.

Shaking my head, I said, "No, I'm not giving you that."

I watched as his chest rose and fell in a pissed-off, jerky movement. It appeared as if he was fighting to control his anger. "I'll get that name, sweetheart. It'd just be a lot easier if you gave it to me."

I scowled. "No, Havoc, I don't need you to fight my battles. Do not pursue this." My voice was firm, but I doubted he was the kind of man to listen.

"That asshole needs to learn a lesson. Manipulating women into sex is disgusting. I hope you've reported him."

There was no way he was letting this go; I knew that in my gut. "Havoc, I'm being dead serious when I say I don't want you anywhere near this. I'll get my brother to sort him out."

He stood abruptly. "We need to go," he commanded in that domineering voice of his that I hated to love.

Without waiting for me, he stalked out to his bike. I followed him, annoyed. When I caught up with him, I demanded, "What the hell's gotten into you? I still had coffee to drink."

Pulling me close, he rasped, "Listening to you try to boss me around turns me on. And, babe, what I want to do to you will give you more fuckin' pleasure than coffee, but if you still want coffee once I'm finished, I'll damn well go out and buy it for you." He stopped for a moment and stared at me. "Now, are we good to go?"

Damn, I liked the way he thought. "Yes, Havoc, we're good to go."

Chapter Eight
Havoc

It had been four days since Dad came home from hospital and he was finally starting to get on my nerves. This was how our relationship had always been though, so I'd been waiting for it. He was feeling better so that was a plus. The doctors had given him a stent and I was hoping there wouldn't be a repeat of this because staying in Brisbane for an extended time wasn't high on my list of things to look forward to. On the other hand, staying meant seeing Carla again and that ranked highly on my list. Sex with her was the best sex I'd ever had, and I'd miss it when I left.

I was helping Dad sort out his medication when my phone rang. Checking the caller ID, I was surprised to see it was King. The President of Sydney Storm. Not a man I dealt with often, but when he called, I answered.

"King," I said into the phone, leaving Dad to his medicine. This wasn't a call he needed to hear. The kind of jobs King called on me for weren't jobs anyone needed to know about.

"Havoc. Got a problem and we need you to take care of it."

"Figured, brother. Where?"

"Sydney. It's that idiot you dealt with two weeks ago."

"What? He owes you more money?"

"No, turns out the asshole is cousins with one of our suppliers who is now threatening to cut us off. It's Jackson Jones. The boys tell me you know him well so I thought you might be able to help us out."

I did know Jackson. Psycho drug dealer. "Fuck, King. Jackson's a crazy motherfucker."

He sighed. "You're telling me, brother. Can you be here in a couple of days or sooner?"

"Yeah, I'll leave tonight, and ride straight through. See you tomorrow."

"Good," he said, and hung up.

I shoved my phone in my pocket, and then pulled it straight back out to send Carla a text.

Me: You home?

Carla: Yeah.
Me: See you in an hour.
Carla: Fuck yeah.

I smiled and put my phone back away, not sure I could last an hour. The bulge that seemed to live in my pants thanks to her might well cause me to head over sooner.

★★★

Carla

"Carla!" Nash yelled out from the front door.

Bloody hell, I had the headache of all headaches, and his yelling was only going to make it worse. Velvet and I had gone out drinking last night, and I'd ended up with a hangover from hell. Thankfully the headache had eased somewhat but it still lingered.

I didn't bother answering him; he'd find me.

A minute later, he appeared in the kitchen, a scowl covering his face.

I frowned. "What's wrong?"

"Havoc fuckin' Caldwell. That's what's wrong," he thundered.

Shit.

I figured he'd be pissed if he found out. Hence, I hadn't told him, but the anger rolling off him was far worse than

I'd imagined. I put down the dish I was washing up, and gave him my full attention. "He told you?"

"No he fuckin' didn't. Velvet spilled it by accident when she got home drunk last night. You've got no clue who you're dealing with there, and you need to call whatever it is you've got going, off."

I raised my brows. "Oh, really? Do I? And what gives you the right to dictate how I live my life?" This was a common argument with us; Nash had spent my entire life telling me how to live it and I was sick of him interfering.

He jabbed a finger in the air at me. "I know Havoc, and I know he is not the man for you. Fuck, Carla, how the hell did you even get mixed up with him?"

"I met him at a bar. The rest is history." I wasn't going to detail it for him.

"And so you're dating him now? I didn't think Havoc was the kind of man to date after all the shit that went down with his ex."

I was clueless about his ex; it wasn't something we'd ever discussed. It wasn't something I was interested to know. And we sure as hell weren't dating. "Nash, we're not dating. It's just sex."

His eyes were wild. "Good. So you will stop seeing him then?"

"Give me one good reason why I should," I challenged him even though I really had no intention of giving up sex with Havoc; it was too damn good to give it up.

He glared at me. It looked like he was weighing something up in his mind. "Havoc has a violent side. It's not safe for you to be around him."

His words should have scared the shit out of me, but they didn't. I'd sensed that about Havoc; knew there was something dark lurking inside him. Yet, he didn't scare me. I felt the opposite when I was with him. I felt safe.

The world stilled as I locked eyes with my brother. We were about to take part in the biggest battle we'd ever had. I wasn't giving Havoc up, not yet. Eventually I would, when he left town, but not until then. "I'm not going to stop seeing him, Nash," I declared.

His eyes bulged out of his head and the veins in his neck popped. "Fuck!" He turned, and hit the wall behind him. When he looked back at me, it was with determination. "You *will* fuckin' stop seeing him. I will make sure of it one way or another," he roared, and then stalked out of the house, slamming the front door on his way.

Shit.

Nash had a temper, but I hadn't seen him that angry for a long time. I had no idea what he planned to do to stop me seeing Havoc, but it pissed me off that he was going to interfere.

My phone rang and I snatched it up, hoping it was Havoc; I needed to hear a friendly voice. "Hello?"

"Hello. Carla?"

I didn't recognise the voice. "Speaking."

"Hi, it's Justin from the Coffee Club calling back about the interview you attended yesterday. I just wanted to let you know you were unsuccessful. And we wish you all the best in your job hunting."

"Thanks for letting me know." I hung up and slumped into the chair at the kitchen table.

It was the fifth interview I'd gone to in the last week and they'd all rejected me. I was beginning to think I'd never get another job. Perhaps I could just block the world out and pretend my life wasn't falling to bits. And perhaps pigs would fucking fly.

"Carla!"

More banging on the front door, only this time I was happy to hear Havoc's voice.

"Come in," I yelled out, not moving out of my seat. Nope, I'd decided to stay in my own little pity party bubble.

I heard his heavy boots coming down the hall, and my body tingled with anticipation. Hell yes, Havoc would make it all better, make me forget for a couple of hours at least. When he stopped in the kitchen doorway a moment later, his words caused my stomach to sink.

"We need to talk," he said.

I took a deep breath. Without moving out of my chair, I said, "Sure. Why not. You may as well add to the bad in my life," I muttered.

Frowning at me, he asked, "What's happened now?"

I was drunk on disappointment and didn't hold back. "Well, my brother's trying to control my life, telling me what I can and can't do, and then I found out I didn't get yet another fucking job. Add those to the other shit happening in my life, and let's just say, I'm over it. Out. Had e-fucking-nough. So hit me, Havoc. Tell me your news." I gestured with my hands for him to carry on.

He stood, staring at me, not saying a word.

I returned his stare, waiting.

Nothing. He said nothing. But the air in the room had changed. Something new thrummed between us.

A need.

A want.

It vibrated around us, pulling at us to acknowledge it.

"I've got to go to Sydney for awhile," he said, and then added, "Come with me." His eyes betrayed him. He wasn't sure of what he was saying.

My breathing sped up. I didn't want to admit even to myself that I wanted this. I shook my head at him. "You don't want me tagging along, Havoc."

"I wouldn't have suggested it if I didn't want it."

My mind felt like it was spinning inside my head. I was going to do this. After living my life up until now to a plan, I was going to throw it all out the window and pursue this. I was going to see where it took me. I was going to follow a fucking biker to another city, to hell with the consequences.

Havoc

What the fuck was coming out of my mouth? *Come with me?*

Fuck.

But I couldn't deny this pull to Carla any longer. I wanted her, simple as that. I didn't know where the hell this would lead, if anywhere, but I fucking wanted her. That truth was inescapable.

She stood and smiled at me. "Okay, I'll go with you. One condition though."

Of course she had a fucking condition; she wouldn't be her without that. "I don't do conditions, Carla. Either you're coming or you're not."

That fucking sexy grin of hers spread across her lips. That grin would be the death of my dick. "Oh, you're gonna love this condition, Havoc."

"Jesus, woman. Just fuckin' spit it out."

She moved into my personal space, curled her hand around the back of my neck, and pulled my face close so she could whisper in my ear. "Somewhere between Brisbane and Sydney, you're going to fuck me on your bike. Otherwise, I'm not going."

My hand shot straight out and roughly gripped her neck. "It's a fuckin' deal, baby."

As I agreed to her condition, I prayed to a God I didn't believe in that this decision and this woman wouldn't ruin me in the same way the last woman I'd let in had.

Chapter Nine
Havoc

How long does a woman need to go to the bathroom?

I checked my watch again.

Fuck.

We were at some shitty little service station near Port Macquarie and Carla had left me nearly ten minutes earlier, so I pushed off from my bike and headed towards the bathrooms.

The darkness of the night and lack of lighting around caused me to tread carefully and I cursed under my breath when I realised the lone light that usually lit the area near the restrooms was broken.

My pace quickened when I heard a male's voice. I couldn't discern his words, but I sure as fuck wasn't taking any chances.

"If you change your mind, doll, I've always got a free seat in my truck." As I drew closer, the guy made his offer and I let out a long breath of relief.

Raking my fingers through my hair, I muttered, "Jesus."

When did this woman become someone I cared about to this level?

The truck driver passed me a moment later just outside the restrooms and I scowled at him through the darkness, even though he wouldn't be able to see.

"Havoc," Carla murmured when I reached her. I heard the confusion in her voice and it matched the confusion I felt.

This is just sex.

"I was coming," she added, wobbling on the cracks in the cement path that connected the restrooms to the car park.

My hand slid around her waist to steady her and I pulled her body close to mine. "Taking your time in a place like this is not a smart move." My eyes had adjusted to the darkness and I could make out her features. Those lips of hers pursed together for a second and I imagined the irritation brewing in her mind. Carla was a feisty woman—it was one of the things that turned me on—but fuck, she had her moments that tested me, and this could well be one of them. I'd seen too many women put themselves in dangerous situations and have to deal with the consequences. I had zero patience for stupidity.

When she finally spoke, her words surprised me. "Sorry for worrying you. I was done, but as I was leaving, I ran smack bang into that guy and fell over. I twisted my ankle and he stopped to help me up. We got talking for a bit and I lost track of time." The irritation I'd expected to hear in her voice didn't surface, and as a result, my frustration subsided. Yet, the tension still punched through my body.

She's gotten under your skin.

We watched each other for a few moments before I let her go and nodded. "You ready to go or do you want to grab something to eat and stretch your legs for a bit longer?" We'd been on the road for about seven hours and had only stopped to stretch once so I imagined she might want some more time before jumping back on the bike.

Her bottom lip curled in as she bit it, right before she reached for my T-shirt. Snaking her hand under it and around my waist, she said, "I'm not ready to go anywhere until you make good on your promise."

She closed the tiny distance between us and before I could form a reply, she stood on her toes and kissed me. Her tongue found mine and I groaned as my hands took hold of her ass.

I can't get enough of her.

"Havoc..." Her voice was breathy as her fingers frantically tried to undo my jeans.

Backing her up against the wall behind her, I helped free my cock, and exhaled my pleasure when she wrapped her hand around me. My eyes squeezed shut for a beat and my body relaxed against hers.

Yes.

Fuck yes.

Her hand moved faster and I gripped her ass harder. The desire to take her tits into my mouth fought with my need to just stand still and experience every ounce of bliss pulsing through me.

Bliss won out and I let her work me towards an orgasm without laying my mouth on her.

Carla's hands worked their magic fast and when I was close to coming, I opened my eyes as I stilled her hand. Bending so my mouth was near her ear, I ordered, "Undo your pants and slide your fingers through your pussy. I need to see how wet you are for me."

The moan that fell from her lips told me how turned on she was, and I loved the way her hands worked fast to obey me. My gaze dropped and I greedily tracked her fingers as they glided through her wetness.

When her eyes found mine, she murmured, "Do you want to taste me?"

Fuck, yes, I want to taste you.

I held her gaze as I reached for her hand. Holding it in front of my mouth, I ran my tongue along her finger before sucking it into my mouth. Having her on my tongue only caused my dick to harden more. I focused on breathing through the desire to sink myself deep inside her.

All in good time.

As I let her finger slide out of my mouth, she said, "I guess that was a yes." Her sass upped my need to get inside her and I fought to control myself.

Spinning her around so she faced the wall, I ground my dick against her ass, and growled into her ear, "That was a *hell fuckin'* yes. And for the record, one taste wasn't enough. If we weren't standing on the side of the highway, in the dark of night, with trucks flying past us, I'd lay you out and spend hours eating you. Putting you on the back of my bike for this many hours, with your pussy against my ass was not the best move I've ever made. Seven hours of that and all I can fuckin' think about is getting inside of you."

Her body sagged against the wall and she moaned again. "I want you to fuck me on your bike."

I reached into my back pocket for my wallet and grabbed a condom. When I had it in place, I pushed her jeans and panties down. "Not this time. My dick will fuckin' disown me if I wait any longer."

She grumbled something under her breath that I didn't quite catch, but I ignored that while I slid one hand around her waist to hold her in place while my other hand positioned her, getting her ready for me.

As I pushed inside, her sweet cunt welcomed me and I knew this was going to be a quick fuck. My ability to control my orgasms was put to the test by Carla. When I was inside her, all I could think about was how fucking good it felt to have her pussy around my dick. Any attempt at slowing my release was futile. It was as if my brain short-circuited and the connection between my mind and my dick was cut. All that was important was fucking her senseless and experiencing the pleasure I'd only ever known with her.

"Fuck... Havoc, I'm going to come..." She had one hand pressed against the wall while her other hand reached up and gripped onto my neck, pulling my face down to nuzzle against her neck. She was working as hard as I was for her orgasm. The sounds of our bodies and grunts were drowned out by the noise from the highway, and when she came, her cries of pleasure bled into the night, only to be heard by me.

I grasped her as I came, growling her name as it coursed through my body. She gripped my neck tighter, her fingers digging in hard. Just the way I liked it. Our breaths were coming fast, and we didn't move for a couple of minutes while we came down from the high.

When I eventually pulled out of her, she turned and found my gaze. "That was good, but it would have been better on your bike."

I watched as she bent to pull her panties and jeans up. "Babe, I don't need to fuck you on a bike to make it good."

Her eyes found mine again as she did her jeans up, and at the raise of her brows, I stepped closer and moved her hand away from her button. I undid her zip and slid my hand inside her panties. When my finger moved over her clit and through her wet pussy, I growled, "Does *that* feel good?"

Her eyelids fluttered closed and she bit her lip, but she didn't answer me.

I moved my free hand to her ass and gripped her hard while pushing two fingers inside her. Lowering my face to hers, I caught her lips in a bruising kiss. Carla loved rough as much as I did. Her body melted against mine and a low moan fell from her lips.

"Answer me," I demanded. "Does that feel good?"

Her eyes opened and she nodded. Placing a hand on my chest, she gave me what I wanted. "Yes."

My fingers moved inside her, finding a rhythm that her pussy loved. I'd thought she was wet already, but her arousal intensified as I pushed deeper and harder. I kissed her again and lightly bit her lip as I ended the kiss. "I'll fuck you on my bike when *I* decide." As her mouth opened to say something, I shook my head. "This is non-negotiable. You don't like it, I can drop you at a bus stop and you can go back to Brisbane."

Fuck.

I knew I was being an asshole, but years of building my defences dictated my behaviour. Even though I'd told her I would, there was no fucking way I was screwing her on my bike. I refused to open those wounds inside my soul, and even thinking about it had scratched and burned those wounds. I'd been in preservation mode for the last couple of years and it was a place I liked. Taking a step outside of that wasn't something I would even contemplate.

My words hurt her. I knew that by the look that flitted across her face. It had only been there for a moment before her usual mask of strength returned, but I'd seen it. Even the darkness couldn't hide her bruise of pain.

A fleeting bruise I'd caused.

Jesus, why the fuck are you even thinking about this shit?

I pressed my fingers deeper inside her while at the same time, I circled her clit with my thumb. She was so damn wet and her pussy pulsed around my fingers; this wouldn't take long.

Her orgasm hit and she was silent as it moved through her. She closed her eyes and bit her lip for a few moments before letting out a long breath. When she opened her eyes again, she held my gaze for a while before finally saying, "You can be an asshole, Havoc, but you sure do know your way around a pussy."

With that, she gently pushed me out of her way before leaving to go back in the ladies' restroom. I stared after her for a beat. She confused the fuck out of me. Indecision rooted me to the spot.

I wanted her as far from me as possible in that moment. Yet, I didn't want her anywhere else *but* with me.

You swore off women a long time ago for a good fucking reason.

Remember that the next time you've got your cock deep inside her and your head is a mess of bewilderment and need.

I headed into the restroom opposite to the one she entered so I could dispose of the condom. It was time to get my head together and remind myself this was just sex. Nothing more.

Chapter Ten
Carla

This is just sex.

I placed my hands on the basin and stared into the mirror of the dingy, little restroom. Havoc's declaration that he would happily leave me at a bus stop reminded me not to let my heart take over from what my head told me to do. Not that I'd even realised it had, but as soon as those words had left his lips, I'd known I was in trouble. Disappointment had sliced through me at the ease with which he could switch between showing care and then nothing at all except a desire to fuck me.

You don't want a biker, anyway.

Taking a deep breath, I straightened.

I definitely do not want a biker.

I just want some good sex until I find the right man for me.

And good God did Havoc know how to fuck. I'd never had sex as good.

Turning the tap on, I washed my hands and then my face. As I reached for some paper towels to dry off, I glanced at my reflection in the mirror again. I had that just-fucked glow, but lurking underneath, there was still a tinge of disappointment.

Shit.

"Carla."

Havoc's voice snapped me back to attention and I turned to find him staring at me from the doorway of the restroom.

When I didn't reply, he continued. "We need to get going."

His voice dripped with that gruff, take-charge tone I'd grown to know him for.

I nodded and finished drying my hands and face. Moving towards him, I said, "I just need to buy a chocolate and then I'm ready."

He frowned. "A chocolate?" There was something off about him that I couldn't quite put my finger on. While he had his take-charge voice on, he seemed distracted.

I cocked my head. "Are you okay?"

"Yeah. Why?" His gaze pierced mine and a hard look settled on his face.

"I don't know. You just seem off."

"I'm fine," he threw out and I knew he was lying by the way his eyes avoided mine, but I also knew this was not the time to challenge him on it. He took a step back and muttered, "Can we just get your chocolate and get back on the road?"

"No need to get your grumpy pants on," I said as I passed him and headed in the direction of the service station shop. I didn't wait for him, but the sound of his boots crunching on the gravel told me he was close behind.

He followed me into the shop, which surprised me. I'd figured he would wait at his bike. When I placed a Snickers bar on the counter, he handed over five dollars to pay for it. I said nothing and allowed him to guide me back outside to his bike. Something had definitely rattled him and I wanted to know what it was. Havoc was a mystery I wanted to solve.

★★★

"I've gotta head out," Havoc said as he did up his belt.

We checked into a Sydney motel about five hours ago and after some mind-blowing sex that I'd been surprised either of us had been capable of after about thirteen hours of travel, we'd both passed out.

I rolled and swung my legs over the edge of the bed so I could stand. Pressing my naked body to his, I wrapped my arms around his neck, grinning when his hands landed on my ass and pulled me tight against him. "How long do you think you will be? Not that I'm nagging, but I want to make sure I'm ready for you."

His brows arched. "You got plans, darlin'?" As he asked this, one of his hands moved up my back and around to my front so he could cup one of my boobs. Lust bloomed in my belly when he traced lazy circles around my nipple.

Choosing to ignore the fact I hadn't cleaned my teeth, I kissed him. He didn't seem to mind my morning breath and deepened our kiss, his tongue quickly finding mine.

Oh, God.

I want him so bad.

Groaning, I ended the kiss. "If we don't stop that, there's no way you're leaving any time soon. And to answer your question, I always have plans where you and your cock are concerned."

He let me end the kiss, but he tightened his hold on me so I couldn't move away from him. His finger continued to tease my nipple. "I'd like to see a video of you making plans for my cock," he growled against my ear.

The lust in my belly shot straight to my core.

"As in I should write it all out and video the list and then send you the video?" I played with him, wanting to work him up a little before he left. However, if I was honest with myself, I was delaying his departure. I craved all of his time and attention.

He chuckled against my ear before pulling back to find my gaze. I loved the desire I saw there. "While a list could be hot, I'd prefer to see a video of you getting that sweet pussy ready for me."

Another rush of lust coursed through my body.

I grinned. If a video was what Havoc wanted, a video he would get. Slapping his hand away from me, I said, "You need to go. I've got a video to prepare for."

He took a step back, letting his gaze drop to my breasts. Silence consumed us while he lingered there. My breaths quickened as the anticipation of what he would do to me later filled my mind.

When he finally gave me his eyes again, his voice was thick with desire. "I don't know how long I'll be, but when I get back, I want that pussy swollen and wet for me. I'll text you when I'm on my way so you can be naked and waiting on the bed. And, Carla?" I nodded while swallowing back my excitement. "Be ready to take it hard."

My mind almost exploded with bliss just at his words. So much so that I had trouble forming a reply.

I watched as he turned and exited the motel room. Once the door closed behind him, I sunk down onto the bed.

This is just sex.
This is just sex.

This is just sex.

Chapter Eleven
Havoc

"King's about fifteen minutes away," Hyde advised after he greeted me at the clubhouse about half an hour after I'd left Carla.

I followed him into the clubhouse bar. It was quiet at that time of morning, so we pretty much had it to ourselves. Taking a seat on one of the worn couches, I got straight down to business. "Any new developments with Jackson?"

Hyde relaxed back into the couch and crossed one of his feet over his knee while spreading his arms across the top of the couch. His hard eyes held mine in the way someone did when they had something serious to discuss. "That motherfucker needs to die."

"Jackson? I'd recommend not even going down that path, brother. His reach is far and wide. You'd be inviting a whole lotta pain if we did that."

He shook his head. "No, not Jackson. His fuckin' cousin. He's causing *us* a whole lotta fuckin' pain."

Before I could reply, one of the other club members, Kick, joined us. "You ready to kick some ass, brother?" The grin painting his face showed me that *he* was.

"I'm always ready."

"King said you wouldn't let us down. How long you in town for this time?"

"Depends how long King needs me for. I'll only stay as long as that."

"Brisbane need you back?"

"Jesus, Kick, what the fuck is this? Twenty fuckin' questions?"

He remained silent for a moment. "Do you think you'll ever go back to Brisbane?"

"I've just come from there."

Hyde cut in, making my fucking morning. My life was mine, and only mine, to question. I made a point not to get involved in conversations discussing it. "Can we get back to the business at hand, Kick?" Irritation lined his face and I noted the same irritation on Kick's face. Those two often clashed and I could see not much had changed.

"Suits me," I muttered, more than happy to do so.

"Havoc!" King's voice boomed as he entered the room. He strode towards me with purpose and I didn't miss the glint in his eyes. King was unpredictable—who knew what crazy shit he had swimming around his head at any given point.

"King," I greeted him as I stood.

"Has Hyde filled you in on where we're at?"

Hyde joined the conversation. "I was just getting to it."

King took over and gave me an update. "When I called you yesterday, Jackson was threatening to cut off our coke supply. This morning he made good on his threat. We've got a huge order to fill in five days and need our delivery from him. You and I are gonna pay him a visit."

"You got a plan to run with?" I asked. Knowing King, he didn't. I, however, preferred a plan with options for when shit went south.

"Don't need a plan, Havoc. *You're* my plan."

"Jesus," I muttered. "*I'm* not a fuckin' plan."

"Yeah, you are. You're a quick thinker when shit goes down. But I'm not planning to take him on today. We just need to get in and talk to the guy, find out how to fix this with him. If today doesn't eventuate into what we want, *then* we make a plan."

Hopefully Jackson would play nice and restore their orders and then I could get back to more important things.

What the fuck is more important than taking care of club business?

I raked my fingers through my hair not wanting to contemplate the shit filling my mind.

★★★

A couple of hours later, Jackson watched King with a crazy gleam in his eyes— the same gleam that King was renowned for.

It was like a meeting of kindred souls.

Except for the fact neither wanted the other to have their wishes granted.

Jackson didn't appear to want to cave on the drug supply issue. For some reason, the man who was known to only ever look out for himself seemed to have a soft spot for his cousin and was holding tight to it.

"This is business, Jackson," King said. "Family don't come into good business decisions."

Jackson quirked a brow and relaxed back into his seat as if he didn't have a care in the world. "So, you're telling me that if you had a cousin and he'd been fucked with by someone you had business dealings with, you wouldn't let the fact he was family interfere? I struggle to believe that."

If you met Jackson on the street, you'd think he was an ordinary businessman. He wore suits and was well presented. And his mind was usually sharp. Crazy, but sharp. For the life of me, I couldn't figure out why he was backing his cousin to this extent.

Inserting myself into the conversation, I said, "Your cousin owed King twenty grand. We encouraged him to pay, which he did. The debt was settled and we all moved on. Why are you now getting involved?"

Jackson directed his gaze to me. "Havoc, we've known each other for a couple of years and I've always liked you. That is the only reason I agreed to this meeting today and the only reason I'm going to answer your question." He paused for a moment before turning back to King. "Davey, my cousin, is a dickhead who can't help but land himself in trouble. He pisses me off more than he makes he smile, but he's the only family member who has always been there for me. When I was a kid getting my head beat in every afternoon after school, Davey was the one who looked out for me and took the assholes on, even if it meant he also got beaten up. So when *he* gets beaten up now, I have *his* back. I fuck with whoever fucks with him. And when I saw him come home all bruised, at your direction, I figured the best way to fuck with you was to cut your coke supply."

He'd barely gotten his words out when he stood and waved towards the door. "And now I'll ask you both to leave, because as far as I'm concerned, this meeting is over."

This was going to be a lot harder than I'd imagined. I'd never pictured Jackson as the kind to put family over business in that way.

It was clear King had come to that conclusion, also. He stood, his face clear of emotion. I saw the tick in his jaw, though, and that tick meant he was pissed off and plotting his next move.

"As you wish," King said. "This won't be the end of it, though. I can promise you that."

Jackson held King's gaze. "I'd be very careful with whatever you're planning, King. I don't take kindly to threats, if that's what that was."

"I don't issue threats, Jackson. If you knew me at all, you'd know that."

King wasn't lying. He didn't bother with making a threat; he simply went straight ahead and did whatever he would have threatened. The thing he did well was revenge and I wondered what plan his crazy mind was nutting out.

As we walked to our bikes, I asked him that very question.

He turned to me and wild eyes penetrated mine. "It's simple, Havoc. If I don't get what I want in life, I just take it. For too many years, I was denied everything. I vowed never to allow anyone to dictate what I could and couldn't have after that."

It sounded like his plan involved bloodshed and pain.

My soul warmed at the thought.

★★★

"Take the day off, Havoc. I'll call you when I need you," King said as he sunk into the clubhouse couch.

We'd arrived back there half an hour earlier and he'd spent most of that half hour with one of the club whores who he pulled onto his lap as he told me to go home. He appeared to be more relaxed than I thought he would be after the meeting with Jackson. But who the hell knew how King's mind worked. My guess was he needed a release to help clear his mind.

He didn't wait for my reply before burying his face in her breasts, and I had no desire to spend time with any of the other club members in the bar, so I headed out to my bike.

My phone buzzed with a text as I exited the clubhouse and my dick hardened as I watched the video Carla had sent me. She'd done exactly what I'd asked and recorded herself for me. The video was all pussy and fingers and tits.

Swollen, delicious pussy.

Fuck.

I watched it once more before shoving my phone back into my pocket. As much as I wanted to get back to the motel and fuck her, I had some club business I wanted to take care of first.

And club business always came first.

I reached my bike just as my phone rang.

Carla.

"Did you watch it?" she asked.

The breathy tone to her voice hit me right in the gut, coiling desire through me.

"Yeah."

"That's all you've got? Jesus, Havoc, when a woman sends you a text like that, she kinda expects more than 'yeah' for a reaction."

"I'm working here, Carla." Irritation cut across my chest, grating against my desire.

"I know, but I thought it may have warranted a reply at least."

I had to give her credit—she didn't sound pissed off. What I was hearing was more frustration than annoyance.

I blew out a long breath. "Give me about two hours. You'll get your reply, darlin'."

"I'll be ready."

We ended the call and I did my best to ignore the way my stomach knotted.

What the fuck am I doing?

★★★

"Long time, no see, Havoc."

For good reason.

Nikolas Petrova was a man I did my best never to run into. Unless I needed his help with something. He was a thieving, lying asshole who couldn't be trusted, but he had contacts. Sometimes I needed access to those contacts.

Pulling up a seat at his table in the back corner of the small café he owned on Pitt Street, I replied, "I haven't been in town for about five months. How have you been, Nikolas?" I detested small talk, but Nikolas insisted on it.

A slimy grin decorated his face. "Life is good, my friend."

He always did think we were friends.

We weren't.

I didn't have friends.

"Good to hear." I continued the charade simply to keep him on side.

Shifting in his seat, he rested his elbows on the table and narrowed his eyes at me. "What information are you after?"

I'd called ahead to make sure he was in and had mentioned I needed his help. "Do you know Jackson Jones's cousin, Davey?"

He nodded slowly. "Yeah. Why?"

I leant forward. "I need his address and anything you can tell me about him."

"What do I get out of this, Havoc?"

"What do you want?" I had little intention of giving him what he wanted, but it was always a good starting point.

He spent a moment contemplating my question. "A girl."

"What girl?" I shuddered to think what his answer would be. He had a predilection for young girls.

Excitement flared in his eyes and my stomach rolled. "She's this little blonde I've seen—"

I held up my hand as I scowled at him. "I'm not fuckin' finding a girl for you."

Distaste replaced the excitement is his gaze as he clenched his jaw. "Well, I'm not giving you any information then."

The redheaded waitress, who always seemed to be working whenever I visited approached with pen and paper in hand. "Can I get you gentleman anything to eat or drink?"

Nikolas didn't remove his gaze from mine as he shook his head. "No, Havoc was just leaving."

She clearly read the harsh tone he used and slinked away.

"I *will* be leaving soon, but we still have a small matter to discuss that I'd been hoping to avoid," I said before pausing to let that sink in.

Frown lines marred his forehead. "What small matter?"

If I were a grinner, I'd have grinned at that moment because what I had on him was priceless. I wasn't though so my face remained expressionless. "The small matter of you getting Eric Bones's daughter high and then fucking her at a party last month." Eric was one of Sydney's most ruthless men. The kind of guy you went to for a loan only when you were desperate enough or stupid enough to think borrowing money from a man who'd kill you for non-payment was the best option you had.

"His daughter is eighteen, Havoc. You've got nothing."

"That's where it would have paid you to do your research first, Nikolas. Eric is extremely protective of his daughters and if he discovers that not only did you get her high, but that you also screwed her, he'd have more than your balls on a platter."

He stared at me with hate, not saying a word for a few moments. When he blew out a long breath, he stood and spat out, "I know nothing about Davey except for his address. I'll text it to you. And don't ever come here again." With that, he stalked away from me to where his redheaded waitress stood. After muttering something to her, he exited the café.

His text came a minute later.

Nikolas: I thought we were friends.
Me: Friends are overrated. I have none.
Nikolas: Clearly.

As I headed towards where I'd parked my bike, I googled Davey's address. He lived about half an hour from the motel where I was staying so I decided to take a ride out there before making my way to Carla.

My phone rang, interrupting my thoughts. Checking caller ID, I answered, "J. What's up, brother?"

I heard the long exhale of breath before he said, "Fuck, Havoc, what the fuck are you doing with Nash's sister? He's ready to rip your balls from you."

Nash's sister?

What the fuck?

"Back it up, J. Who is Nash's sister?"

Silence sat between us for a moment. "Jesus, you don't know, do you? Carla is Nash's sister."

Fuck.

I raked my fingers through my hair.

Jesus, fuck.

"Had no fuckin' clue, man," I replied, trying to force the anger filling me away. *What the fuck was she thinking?*

"You need to cut her loose, Havoc. Send her home and move the fuck on."

I know.

"Thanks for the call."

"I wouldn't come back to Brisbane in a hurry, either. Or if you do, stay well clear of Nash."

"Gotcha. I've gotta go." I ended the call and sat on my bike, allowing my thoughts to take over.

Two years ago, I'd cleared all connections from my life. I didn't want hassles and I sure as fuck didn't want problems with fellow club members. Allowing Carla into my life may not have been my smartest move.

Though, as much as I wanted to send her home, I knew deep in my bones, I wouldn't.

I couldn't.

She'd stirred something deep inside me. I had no fucking clue how or what. All I knew was that as much as I was fighting it—*fighting her*—my fucking heart had kicked back over and was beginning to rule my head.

Chapter Twelve
Carla

"Why didn't you tell me?"

Havoc stood in front of me, his body tense under the fitted black T-shirt and jeans he wore, and his nostrils flaring. He'd arrived back at the motel just over five minutes ago and had brought a rush of fury with him. I hadn't been expecting him for at least another forty minutes, and he'd caught me by surprise.

His anger caught me by surprise.

Frowning, I replied, "It didn't seem important at the time. This isn't anything but some fun between us. Nash didn't need to know about it, and besides, I don't make a habit of telling my brother the details of my sex life."

"Jesus, Carla, you don't get it, do you?" He rubbed the back of his neck and stared at me, waiting for my answer.

My breathing picked up pace as the weight of his anger crushed over me. I stood my ground. "No, I don't get it, Havoc. I don't get this dumb male shit that Nash has going on. I'm a twenty-three-year-old woman for God's sake. I can run my own life."

"That's between you two. What I'm focused on is the fact I slept with a club member's sister, and he's not happy about it. A problem with a brother is the last fuckin' thing I need in my life."

Steadying my hand on my hip, I threw out, "So, you're saying we should just go our separate ways now?" My blood pumped furiously through my body as annoyance engulfed me.

Why did I come to Sydney with him?

How could I be so stupid?

His body stilled and he blinked, but his anger didn't leave his face. "I'm not leaving you alone in this city," he snapped, confusing me even more.

I threw my arms up in the air. "Well if you don't want anything to do with me, but you won't leave me alone here, I'm not really sure what other options there are."

He paced the small motel room, exhaling a long, harsh breath. Havoc truly was a contradiction. I remained quiet while he paced, unsure of where this conversation would end.

Finally, he stopped pacing and looked at me. "I'll finish what I came here to do and then I'll take you home. And then we're done."

"There is no *we*, remember? So there's nothing to be *done*." I stepped away from him and grabbed my bag and phone. "I'm going to get a decent coffee. Maybe when I get back, you'll have calmed down and got your shit under control."

As I took a step towards the door, his arm flicked out and his hand wrapped around my wrist. He yanked me to him and then shoved his fingers through my hair, gripping me there. His wild eyes bore into mine. "Maybe when you get back, I'll fuck you senseless," he growled.

White hot desire flowed through me at his words.

Angry sex.

The best kind.

His grip on my hair tightened as my arms moved under his so I could place my hands on his shoulders to hold him there. "Maybe you should." My words came out all breathy. "I think it would do wonders for your foul mood."

Another growl rumbled from his chest and he pulled my hair, yanking my head back. We watched each other through lust-filled eyes. There was no denying the attraction we felt for each other.

With one last tightening of his grip on my hair, he rasped, "Go." He let me go as he took a few steps away from me.

The way he'd said that word was as if it was the last thing he wanted me to do, but the one thing he *needed* me to do. Havoc had never frightened me before, but in that moment, he did.

As I walked out of the motel room, I worked to steady my breathing as the concern swept through me.

What the hell has gotten into him?

★★★

"I don't get men sometimes," I complained to Velvet over the phone an hour later. I'd arrived back at the motel room to find Havoc gone. That hadn't surprised me. What *had* surprised me was the note he'd left me on the bed.

I'll be back in a few hours.
Need to blow off some steam.
I'm an asshole.

"What do you think has gotten into him?" Velvet asked.

I settled myself in the centre of the bed with my legs crossed. "I've got no freaking clue. It's like he changed from this guy who asked me to come with him for some fun and sex, to this moody, dark guy who turns angry for no reason."

"Well, I get why he was pissed about the Nash thing. You've gotta admit you were at fault there for not telling him your brother is a member of Storm."

I sighed. "Okay, okay, so I probably should have told him that, but he got shitty at me for wanting to have sex on his bike. He'd agreed to it before we left Brisbane and then when I brought it up, he snapped at me and said he'd send me home if I pushed him about it."

Velvet remained quiet for a moment. "Carla, what are you doing with him?"

I knew from her thoughtful tone what she was getting at, but I didn't want to get into it with her. Hell, I didn't want to get into it with *myself*. "I'm just having some fun. And some good sex. That's all."

"From where I'm standing, it doesn't sound like you're having too much fun with him. And as far as the sex is concerned, you can find that with another guy if that's what you really want."

I moved up the bed so I could lean against the headboard. Pulling my legs up against my chest, I wrapped my free arm around them and groaned. *She's right.* "I don't know anymore," I murmured.

"What do you mean?"

Aargh.

"I don't know what I'm doing with my *life* anymore. I lost my job, my teacher failed me, which puts my plan off track, and I started sleeping with Havoc all at the same time. I never wanted to start liking him. I mean, he's not exactly the kind of guy I see myself settling down with, but I think I've bloody well gone and started liking him."

"So walk away now before it gets complicated, before you start to have real feelings for him. If he's not what you want in a man, don't settle." She was speaking sense and my head was listening, but my heart didn't seem to want to play along.

"I know that's the smart thing to do..." My voice drifted off while my thoughts consumed me. Havoc was as far from my 'perfect' man as he could be, but who knew if my ideal guy even existed.

"Nash told me he's the last guy you want to be hooking up with."

At the mention of Nash's name, irritation prickled my skin and I sat forward, folding my legs together on the bed. "What has Nash said?"

"He doesn't trust Havoc around you. Said something about him being violent, but he didn't give me details. What he did say, though, was enough to convince me that you really should think twice about this." I loved the way Velvet gave me her opinion without lacing it with judgement. I knew she'd be there for me, whichever way I chose to go.

"I know Havoc is violent, but he's never been violent towards me." Images of our last conversation flashed through my mind and I did my best to push it aside. From everything I'd seen of him so far, his mood swing seemed out of character and I was the kind of person who believed in second chances. And as much as I'd felt frightened earlier, I believed he wasn't a man I needed to fear.

"Well, I've never met the guy, and you're the one who has been spending all this time with him, so you would know better. Plus, I also know that men tend to show the women in their lives a different side to what they show the men in their lives. I'm presuming Havoc has an entire part to him that Nash doesn't even know exists. Just promise me you will go slow and be smart where he's concerned."

I sighed. Mainly because she was right. I had a bad track record with men, always choosing the wrong ones. But also because I felt nothing but conflict where Havoc was concerned.

Swinging my legs over the edge of the bed, I stood and made a snap decision. "You are so right. I need to walk away from this as soon as I get back to Brisbane. I need stability in my life and Havoc's a nomad for goodness' sake. There's no stability in being a nomad."

"I've got a guy I want to introduce you to when you get back. I think he might be what you're looking for. He's a vet who owns his own practice. No kids and his family is stable. I've met him and he seems like a good guy."

I should have perked up at the information she was sharing with me.

He's exactly what I want.

A man with a job and stability.

Yet I had that sinking feeling of not wanting any part of something.

I couldn't figure out where that feeling was coming from so I forced enthusiasm. "Where did you meet him?"

"He's the brother of one of my clients and came in to pick her up one day. He's a really friendly guy."

I had to get off the phone so I could try to sort through the mess of thoughts in my mind. "Sounds good, Vi. I'm gonna go and have a bath, but I'll keep in touch with you and let you know when we're on our way home. Can you keep Nash at bay for me?"

A chuckle filtered through the line. "You've gotta be kidding me, right? No one keeps your brother at bay where you're concerned. The only thing stopping him from being in Sydney right this moment is Griff. When he found out Nash was ready to rip Havoc's balls from his body, he laid down the law and told him he had to stay in Brisbane. I think he threatened him with something if he disregarded the order. Then I managed to talk some sense into him, but be warned, when you get back, there's going to be hell to pay. I'd suggest you tell Havoc to drop you off and keep going."

We ended the call and I contemplated what she'd said. Nash was a pain in my ass sometimes, and I hated to give into him, but the last thing I wanted was to cause club problems for him.

You should have thought of this before you agreed to come to Sydney.

I traipsed into the bathroom and flicked on the bath tap. At times when I was mad at myself for rash decisions that led me into trouble, I liked to take a bath, give myself a facial and forget the world.

It was one of those times.

The phone call I received after Velvet's, just as I was about to step into the bath, only proved that further.

Chapter Thirteen
Havoc

Silence greeted me when I returned to the motel room a few hours after I'd lost my shit at Carla.

Fuck, where is she?

I shrugged off my cut and dropped it on the bed before heading into the bathroom to take a shower. I'd call her once I finished in there.

As I stepped through the bathroom doorway, however, I found her. She was in the bath, plugged into her music with her eyes closed and her head resting on the edge of the bath.

I stopped and leaned against the wall with my arms folded across my chest. My gaze travelled the length of her body. Never letting me down, my dick grew hard while I took in her beauty.

"Fuck," I muttered under my breath as I contemplated the wisdom of fucking her again.

I wanted to.

Hell, I fucking *needed* to.

She's a brother's sister for fuck's sake.

I'd spent the last few hours going over and over that fact in my mind. My decision had been to head back to the motel, sleep on the couch and never taste her pussy again.

I hadn't factored in having her naked body on display the minute I returned.

Shit.

"How long are you going to stand there staring at me?" she asked as she cracked an eye open to look at me.

"Until you get out and let me fuck you." Both her eyes had opened and I pinned my gaze to hers, not letting her go.

Her eyebrows lifted. "I thought you were done with me."

"Turns out I'm not."

She stood and reached for her towel before stepping out. Continuing to hold my gaze, she slowly dried herself off.

Teasing the fuck out of my dick.

I fought the desire to reach out and rip the towel from her hands. My carefully constructed self-control was being tested and I knew it wouldn't be long until I caved and took what I wanted.

Finally—*finally*—she finished drying off and closed the distance between us. "What if *I'm* done with you?" I knew she was full of shit by the breathless tone she used and the way her body leaned just that little bit too close to mine. It was as if she was trying to hold herself back, but her body had a mind of its own and couldn't stay away.

I lifted a brow. "Are you?"

"I should be. After the way you've been treating me, I really should be." Still all breathy.

Still in this with me.

I unfolded my arms so I could curl my hand around her neck. Gripping her there, I said, "Yeah, you should be, but you're not."

I feel the same way.

With our faces so close that her breath whispered across my skin, we stared at each other for a long time. The still air in the tiny bathroom consumed our apprehension piece by piece until all that was left was an unrelenting need to satisfy our hunger.

At the first sign of her softening, I tightened my hold on her neck and pulled her mouth to mine. She didn't hesitate and a second later, our bodies pressed together as hard as our mouths did.

The smell of her arousal overwhelmed me and I let her neck go so I could slide my hands around her ass and lift her. Turning, I held her up against the wall and groaned when she wrapped her legs around me. The urge to drive my cock as hard and fast as I could into her sweet cunt threatened to take over as the only thought in my mind, and I took a moment to work through that and get myself under control.

Resting my forehead against hers, I focused on my breathing while I gave myself a talking to.

Focus.

You've got this.

You've fucking done this enough times to know how to control yourself.

But I hadn't.

I'd never fucked a woman like Carla.

Had never been with a woman who stole my control the way she did.

She invaded every fucking sense of mine until I didn't know right from wrong, up from down, red from fucking blue.

"Havoc."

My head snapped up and I found her staring at me.

Unsure.

"Are you okay?" she asked, lines creasing her forehead as she tilted her head, frowning at me.

I stepped back and let her go. "I need to slow this shit down."

She stood naked in front of me with an expression on her face that seemed to be half confusion and half frustration. "What does that mean?"

I wasn't sure I even knew.

"It means I want you sitting cross legged in the middle of the bed waiting for me while I take a minute," I bit out. My head was so damn full I thought it might actually explode.

Too many thoughts.

Too many fucking feelings.

I jerked my chin at her and snapped, "Go."

Her eyes widened a fraction and I pushed my breaths out while waiting for her to submit. When she didn't, I growled, "Carla, I need you to go and sit on the bed. Now."

"I'm giving you five minutes to get your head back in this. I'm all for bossy and shit, but I draw a line at whatever the fuck you call what you've got going on at the moment. Barking orders at me is a whole lot fucking different than dominating me." With that, she stalked out of the bathroom.

Thank fuck.

I dropped down and crouched on the floor. Bringing my hands up, I bent my head and threaded my fingers through my hair, cradling my head with my chin against my chest.

What the fuck are you thinking?

Hello, remember Kelly?

This is just sex.
But, Nash.

My breaths were coming hard and fast while I filed through my mind. The smart thing to do would be to walk out of the motel room and book another. This thing with Carla was not just sex. I wouldn't be losing my shit if it were. I wouldn't be dedicating so many goddamn minutes of my day to thinking about this if it was just about pussy.

I could get pussy anywhere.

I couldn't get Carla anywhere.

What the hell was it about her that had so much pull over me? Because to even think about a club member's sister the way I was contemplating Carla was fucking lethal.

I stood.

Resting my hands on the edge of the vanity, I stared at myself in the mirror. All thirty-one years of my life were etched on my face. Along with a whole lot of turmoil.

And need.

I splashed water on my face.

Just fuck her, and then walk the hell away.

Chapter Fourteen
Carla

"Come here," Havoc demanded.

He'd taken his five minutes—well, six minutes and some seconds, but who was counting—and had finally left the bathroom to stand in front of the bed. Hard eyes stared down at me and I wondered what shit he had sorted in his head to look at me that way. I'd never seen those eyes before and they kinda scared me. Again.

But that voice of his...

It didn't scare me at all. It turned me on in a way I'd never been turned-on and that was enough to make me scoot off the bed and stand in front of him.

His eyes held mine for a good minute before dropping to my throat. I looked down at the same time and saw his hands clench by his side.

Oh, dear Lord.

Yes.

I knew what those hands were capable of and I wanted everything they had to give.

Even if that involved some pain.

After the phone call I'd had from my mother that afternoon, my soul was alive with pain and in my experience, the only thing to dull pain, was more pain. Different pain. And although I'd never had it from him before, I knew Havoc could give that to me.

"Hurt me," I said as his gaze lingered on my throat.

His head jerked up and our eyes met again. "What did you just say?"

"I said, hurt me."

No emotion flashed across his face. He simply continued to look at me through those hard, flat eyes of his. "The last thing you want is for me to even contemplate that."

Even his voice was flat.

Hard.

Cold.

Perfect.

"That's where you'd be wrong, Havoc." I straightened. "It's the only thing I want you to contemplate." It was all *I'd* thought about while he'd been gone that afternoon.

Before this thing with him was over, I wanted a piece of that side of him.

He watched me some more. I could almost hear his brain ticking over.

Right as I was beginning to think he wouldn't do it, he wrapped his hand around my throat. His fingers dug into my skin and his grip threatened to close off the air from my lungs. Flat eyes continued to bore into mine. "How much pain do you want?"

Pain radiated down my neck as his thumb dug in harder, and I gasped for breath. My head began to throb as well, and all I could do was welcome it. "As much as you want to give me." I barely choked out the words because his grip restricted my ability to talk.

Something flickered in his eyes right at the time the vein in his temple twitched. Whatever it was, though, was gone as fast as it appeared. However, the vein twitched again and he clenched his jaw. With one last squeeze of my throat, he let me go. A mutter of, "Fuck," escaped his lips, and then he ripped off his shirt.

As I sucked air back into my lungs, I watched the rapid rise and fall of his chest, taking in the way his muscles were carved into perfection. When his hands moved to the button on his jeans, my gaze willingly followed, and desire pooled in my belly as he revealed his cock to me. I wasn't fussy where cocks were concerned, but after having Havoc's, that could be called into question. He was well endowed and knew how to use it, and I was more than a little concerned that all future men I slept with would not be able to meet the standard he set.

My focus was distracted while thinking about his talents and assets, so he surprised me when he yanked me to him. Our bodies slapped together and his hands grasped me with a roughness that caused more desire to shoot through me.

"I'm not sure where the fuck you got the idea that I'm a man who likes to inflict pain on a woman during sex, so I'm only going to say this once." His eyes were no longer flat. They had a wildness to them that thrilled me. "Never ask me to do that again. I'm more than happy to dominate you during sex, but I will never, *never* hurt you. Have I made myself clear?"

I didn't reply.

I knew he had it in him to give me what I wanted, so I couldn't figure out why he refused.

"Have I made myself clear?" His voice was harder, growlier this time, and it caused me to flinch.

"Why?"

He scowled. Loosening his hold on me he spun me around in his embrace so my back was to his front. His arms tightened around me and his mouth moved to my ear. "I like it rough and I like it dirty, but no fuckin' way am I gonna do what you're asking. Now tell me you understand, because if you push me for this, I'm walking out of this room right fuckin' now and never coming back."

My request had worked him up and my instincts told me to let it go. I was pretty sure Havoc walked a tightrope between good and bad, and as much as I wanted pain from him, I knew deep in my gut that I didn't want him to snap and lose his control.

I nodded. "I understand."

"Good."

He didn't let me go and he didn't move. His arms remained in place around me and his face remained close to mine. I could hear his heavy breaths. They matched mine.

They blared his inner struggle with this.

I hated that I did that to him.

"I'm sorry," I whispered, wishing I'd never brought this up. Somehow, I'd misread him.

His arms loosened a little and I felt him nodding. "Yeah." His voice faded into the air around us and I figured he was still processing whatever thoughts and feelings my request had stirred. Havoc seemed to do more thinking than any man I'd ever known.

"Maybe we should call it quits for the night," I suggested, even though it was the last thing I wanted.

He stilled. "Not fuckin' likely to happen. Not when you've been naked for as long as you have and my dick is as hard as it is." He paused for a moment before adding, "Unless you don't want it."

I expelled a long breath. "Havoc, I'm fairly certain that anytime you're offering your cock, I'll want it."

His body relaxed a little against mine and one of his hands moved to cup my breast. I dropped my face to watch his fingers working my nipple. Havoc's hands were one of my favourite parts of him. They were large and strong. Powerful. But to me, they were also safe. I always felt protected in his hold. It was a feeling I couldn't even begin to understand, having not known him very long, but when his hands touched me, I had this unwavering sensation that no harm would come to me while with him.

I placed a hand over his, running my fingers over the chunky ring he wore to interlock our fingers. He wore two chunky rings, one on each hand, and a leather wrist cuff on his right wrist. He also wore a silver necklace with a yin yang pendant. It surprised me he wore all that jewellery because he was so masculine, but it only showed me further proof there was more to Havoc than met the eye.

As I laced my fingers through his, he sucked in a breath and slid his other hand down my body to run his finger through my heat. Groaning as he discovered my wetness, he pushed his finger deep inside me.

"Oh, God..." I laid my head back and rested it on his shoulder. Closing my eyes, I welcomed every drop of pleasure he gave me.

"You're close, aren't you?" His gravelly voice vibrated along my skin, carrying more bliss with it.

I bit my lip, not wanting to come yet, but knowing it wouldn't be long. "Yes."

"Don't." The command in his tone was clear and I blinked my eyes open.

"I can't stop it, Havoc." Even as I said the words, another pulse of pleasure rippled through my body, bringing me closer to the edge.

He stopped what he was doing and spun me around. "Breathe through it and hold it back." Still so commanding.

My whole body was alive with need and his bossy tone only intensified my desire. Staring at him, I nodded, but didn't say a word. I couldn't. I was too busy focusing on my breathing to get any words out.

He took in my nod and then dropped his eyes to roam my body. When he bent his head so he could take one of my nipples into his mouth while at the same time pulling my body to his, I moaned. His hands gripped my ass and his teeth grazed my breast. I held onto him, digging my fingers into his waist. I wanted to take hold of his cock and pleasure him, but my mind was shutting down as I fought my release. All I could manage in that moment was to hold on tight and breathe.

Havoc's breathing picked up as he sucked and licked and bit my breasts. And his grip on my ass tightened until suddenly, he let my breasts go and he lifted me into his arms. A moment later, he deposited me on the bed before removing the rest of his clothes.

"Lie on your back," he ordered as he moved over me.

Positioning his legs between mine, he slid his hand down my thigh and pulled my leg up to wrap around him. I instinctively did the same with my other leg. He kept that hand on my leg while his other hand was planted firmly on the bed next to me to hold him up. His eyes found mine right before he dipped his head to kiss me.

Rough.

Demanding.

Bliss.

Havoc's kiss tore a whimper from my lips as he took what he needed. His kiss was almost violent, as if he'd wrapped all his fury and frustration into it. I poured all my own confusion and hurt into the kiss, and we matched each other's demand for more.

His lips bruised mine.

My nails clawed at his body.

His powerful frame threatened to crush me.

My legs squeezed his torso.

We kissed and we clung and we raged.

My body begged him to take the pain from my soul.

His body pleaded for me to let him dominate.

Breathless.

Passion.

Anger.

Need.

We gave each other everything we had to give.

And we took everything we could.

From a kiss.

A kiss that broke down our walls.

And crashed through our denials.

A kiss that told me this was so much more than sex.

Fuck.

Havoc knifed up.

Staring down at me through ravaged eyes, he rasped, "Fuck."

He feels it too.

He knelt on the bed between my legs just staring at me, his eyes wild and breathing ragged.

I pushed up so I was sitting in front of him with my legs spread wide. Taking hold of his face, I begged, "Don't stop now. I need you to fuck me."

His gaze traced my face for the longest time while he slowed his breathing down. When he finally found my eyes again, he said, "What the fuck are we doing, Carla?"

I knew exactly what he was asking, but I didn't want to acknowledge it. Not yet. I kept holding onto his face. "That's not a question for tonight." My words were an answer and they were also a plea.

Don't think about this now.

Just think about fucking me.

Eventually, he nodded and moved off the bed. Reaching out to me, he took hold of my hand and pulled me to a standing position. And then he lifted me and carried me into the bathroom.

In one movement, he cleared the vanity of my beauty products into the top drawer, and sat me on the cleared space. "Wait there," he directed before leaving me to go back into the other room. When he returned, he had a condom on and my core clenched at the thought that he was finally going to give me what I craved.

Standing in front of me, he said, "Put your hands around my neck."

His voice was so raw.

Frayed.

Havoc was frayed.

I did as he said and he slowly raised my legs to rest them on his shoulders. I thanked God for all the hours I'd spent doing Pilates, especially when he put his arms around my lower back and pulled me closer to him.

And then he entered me.

Oh. God.

Divine pleasure hit me and my pussy pulsed around his cock.

He entered me slowly that first time.

The second time, he slammed into me hard.

The third, I was sure he was going to break me in half.

I clung to him while he lost himself.

If I'd thought he was frayed before, the act of fucking me only served to unravel him further. He grunted with each thrust, moving faster and faster towards his release. But it never seemed to get any closer.

I came fast, my mind shattering with white light as it drifted away from all thoughts of anything but pleasure. I knew Havoc continued to pound into me, and I still held onto him, but that was the only awareness I had. I hovered in that pleasure state for a long time.

He'd given me pleasure like I'd never experienced and if it was the last time we ever had sex, I wouldn't care because this was everything.

This took the pain away.

I could breathe.

Joy.

The ache of rejection I always carried with me was gone.

Even if just for a short time, it was everything I wanted and needed.

Delivered to me by Havoc.

"Fuck!" He roared as he came.

My eyes flicked open to find a storm of emotion staring back at me. As he caught his breath and allowed the pleasure to ebb from his body, he held my gaze with those stormy eyes. We didn't speak, simply watched.

When he was done, he pulled out of me and helped me down from the vanity before turning and walking out of the bathroom.

I watched him go.

Still no words passed between us, yet a tempest of feelings had been unleashed.

Closing the bathroom door so I could shelter alone in the shower, I closed my eyes briefly.

What the hell have we done?

Chapter Fifteen
Carla

I woke from a fitful sleep at four the next morning. Behind me, Havoc's body pressed hard against mine, and his arms wrapped me in a tight embrace.

As I tried to wiggle out of his hold, he said, "You've been talking in your sleep."

They were the first words he'd said to me since he fucked me on the bathroom vanity. After I'd showered, I'd left the bathroom to find him gone from the room. Hurt had reached for me at his absence, but I'd pushed it aside. I'd shoved it away, not wanting to allow him any more space in my heart. Room I'd never wanted to make for him in the first place.

I'd gone to bed and fallen asleep fast. He'd worn me out both physically and emotionally.

I stilled in his arms. "What have I been saying?" I used to talk in my sleep a lot while growing up, but to my knowledge, I hadn't done it in years.

"Random words mostly, but you've mentioned your father a few times."

My heart rate slowed for a moment before picking up speed.

No.

I broke free of his embrace and sat on the edge of the bed. With my hands planted on the mattress either side of me, I hunched over and worked to get my breathing under control.

This isn't happening.

Havoc shifted on the bed behind me and placed his hand on my lower back. "You kept repeating the word 'no,' over and over, Carla." I heard the concern in his voice and his words inched their way into my heart.

I turned to face him. Although the room was dark, the first hint of sun filtered through the crack where the curtains met, and I could make out his features. "I'm sorry I never told you Nash was my brother. The last thing I want is for you to have club problems."

He frowned. "You're changing the subject."

"No, I'm just continuing a conversation we started yesterday. I want you to know you were right. I should have told you."

He stared at me as if I had two heads. Sitting up in the bed, he raked his fingers through his hair. "Fuck, a woman who can tell me I was right about something."

A smile that didn't reach my eyes spread across my lips. "Yeah, well don't think it will happen too often. Usually men aren't right."

He chuckled, finally losing the serious expression he'd been wearing for far too long. "So I've been told, darlin'." Reaching his arm out, he placed his hand on my forearm. "What's with your father?"

I shook my head. "I don't want to talk about it, Havoc."

"Babe, with the amount of mumbling you've been doing for the past few hours and the thrashing that went along with that mumbling, it seems to me that you *need* to talk about it."

"I've been thrashing in the bed?"

"Why do you think I had you in such a strong hold? Damn near thought you were gonna knock me out at one point."

I took a deep breath.

Shit.

He's right.

"I've never met my father. He left my mother while she was pregnant with me. After they'd already had three other kids. Apparently, Mum got up one day and he'd left during the night."

The concern I heard in his voice before appeared in his eyes as I shared that information. "He never came back?"

"Nope, never." I paused for a moment. "That's why Nash is so protective of me. He and my brother and sister helped raise me. He's been like a father to me all my life, always looking out for me."

"You've never been like this in your sleep the other times I've slept next to you. What's happened to cause it?"

Expelling a long breath, I shared with him what my mother had told me on the phone the day before. "After all these years, my father has just recently contacted my mother. He wants to see us all." My voice cracked as I added, "He wants to meet me."

Havoc's eyes searched mine. "Is your mother going to see him?"

Pain almost swallowed me at the thought of my mother having to deal with this. My father had shredded her once and she'd built herself back up, but on the phone I'd heard her agony. My mother was one of the most resilient women I knew, but after that phone call, I also knew my father had the ability to break her. "My mother only ever loved one man in her life, my father. Him leaving almost killed her from what I've been told by Nash. She's told me she won't see him again, but, fuck, men have this way of fucking women up and making us do things we swore we'd never do. I hope she sticks to her guns."

He nodded and when he spoke, his voice was hoarse. "Yeah, men do have a knack of doing that." It sounded like he was going to say more, but he cut himself off and gulped down some air.

We sat in silence for a while, each lost in our own thoughts, until he asked, "Do you want to see him?"

Torment sliced through me.

No.

Yes.

No.

I shook my head.

Vigorously.

"No, I don't want to fucking see the man who chose to walk away from me before he even met me and who then chose to never have anything to do with me..." My words rushed out in an angry, breathless torrent that I had no control over.

The man who'd scored wounds into my heart that would never heal.

My breaths were coming hard and fast, and hatred wrapped my chest so tightly that I began to struggle for those breaths. Just as a fog of blackness settled over me, strong arms embraced me and pulled me against a warm body.

A body of protection.

I sank against him and let my tears fall as I recovered my breath.

His fingers threaded through my hair and his lips met my forehead.

He held me while I cried, never once easing his grip.

When I finally looked up at him, I found eyes full of compassion staring back at me. "Thank you," I whispered.

He nodded, still not letting me go. Instead, he pulled me with him to a lying position on the bed and curled his body around mine. "You need more sleep."

I closed my eyes and started to drift off.

Although I would have expected it, the last thought that ran through my mind wasn't about my father.

It was about Havoc.

Maybe we can see where this goes.

★★★

"I've gotta head out to take care of some club stuff."

I watched Havoc as he sat on the end of the bed texting someone. He'd woken me up for sex just after seven and after blowing my mind with a hard and fast fuck, I'd joined him in the shower for more.

As he finished with his phone, I straddled him and sat on his lap, looping my hands around his neck. His eyes trailed down my naked body and he groaned. "Jesus, babe, can you put some clothes on?"

I smiled. "That's a strange request coming from you."

"Trust me, if I didn't have shit to do, I'd be taking those clothes and burning them."

Something had shifted between us. I wasn't sure what, but his moody attitude seemed to have disappeared, and he'd softened a little. Not that the words 'soft' and 'Havoc' went together, and not that anyone else would notice, but I did. It was in the way he pressed a kiss to my forehead as he left the bathroom after we'd had sex, and in the way he left the motel room after that to get me coffee from the café across the road because he knew I preferred it to the coffee in the motel. It was also in the way he rubbed his thumb back and forth across my lower back while I straddled him.

I moved off his lap and reached for the robe that lay across my side of the bed. As I tightened it around me, I said, "I'm going to find a supermarket today. Do you want anything?"

He stood and shoved his phone in his pocket. "Some more condoms. We're about to run out."

"How much longer do you think until your work is finished here?"

"You ready to go home?"

"No, but I figured with all this Nash stuff you'd want to sort that out and move on."

He watched me silently for a minute. "Let's play it by ear for now. But in answer to your question, I'm hoping to finish up with my work today."

I bit my lip. "Okay."

His eyes narrowed at me and he opened his mouth to say something, but quickly snapped it shut. The sound of his boots hitting the carpet as he walked towards the motel door was the only sound to be heard.

Looking back at me, he said, "I'll check in with you later."

And then he was gone.

I sat on the bed and wrapped my arms around my body.

God knew how long he'd be working. Chances were I was in for a long day by myself. With many hours to think about my father and our family.

I needed to find something to occupy my time because thinking about that man was the last thing I ever wanted to do.

Chapter Sixteen
Havoc

Christ, am I wasting my time?

I'd been trailing Davey all day, all over town, and had learnt nothing about the guy that would help King. He'd spent the day doing his dry cleaning, having lunch with some woman, shopping for X-Box games, shopping for groceries and was currently at the library.

At the fucking library.

I hadn't heard from King yet, so I figured doing something was better than nothing. I'd trailed him the day before too with no success and was beginning to think the key to helping King didn't lay with Davey.

Maybe I would have to look for dirt on Jackson instead.

Fuck, I wasn't used to being wrong about shit. I'd been sure Davey had to have something deep in his closet.

My phone rang.

Carla.

I answered without hesitation. "You good?"

"One of the things I like about you, Havoc, is your lack of small talk. You just get straight to the point." I could hear the smile in her voice and it settled me. It eased some of my concern over her. She'd been thrashing about in the bed that morning like a fucking maniac and in my experience, the only thing to cause that kind of behaviour was some deep fucking emotions.

"And one of the things I like about you is that you don't bug me incessantly about mindless crap. What's up?"

"Steak or chicken?"

"Huh?" I had no fucking clue what she meant.

"Do you prefer steak or chicken?"

"Steak." I followed Davey out of the library as I answered her. When he turned to walk in the opposite direction to where he'd parked, my attention strayed from the phone call to him.

Where the fuck is he going?

"Okay, steak it is," she said. "I'll see you later."

"Yeah."

We ended the call as Davey entered the park next to the library. I held back and waited to see what he planned to do there. It was only a small park with a few swings and one shaded table to sit at. A few mothers were there with their kids and as I watched Davey walk past them, another guy caught my eye.

I squinted so I could make out what they were doing.

The guy spoke first and then Davey grabbed his shirt and appeared to threaten him because fear crossed the guy's face at that point. A moment later, he produced a package from his jacket and handed it to Davey.

Bingo.

As Davey exited the park with a smug expression, I changed course.

I followed the other guy.

★★★

He works for Jackson?

I'd followed the guy back to Jackson's warehouse and as I killed the engine on my bike, I wondered what the fuck he had going with Davey. I also wondered how long I'd be sitting outside waiting for him.

It was nearing four and my dick ached to get back to Carla. I had plans for her that night that included me getting the fuck back to the motel as fast as possible. Plans that didn't include sitting around waiting for some schmuck while he fucked about inside Jackson's warehouse.

The door to the warehouse opened and the guy walked out.

Well shit, maybe this won't take long after all.

He walked to his car and I followed him as he drove through the streets of Sydney to a small house about fifteen minutes away. After he entered the house, I parked my bike and headed around to the back. As I walked through a well-cared for garden that led to a back yard that had bras and panties hanging on the clothesline, I decided he either lived with a woman or this was a woman's home.

I'd have to be careful.

The back door was unlocked and I easily entered the house. Male and female voices filtered through the hall and I walked in their direction. Startled eyes met mine when I hit the kitchen.

"Who the fuck are you?" The guy advanced towards me, but the woman grabbed his shirt and pulled him back.

I held up my hands. "Easy, man. I've just got a few questions to ask you."

His brows raised. "So you just break into my home to do that? Who the fuck does that?"

I ignored the scared pleas of his woman to leave them alone. My intention wasn't to hurt them, but they didn't need to know that yet. "You work for Jackson Jones, yeah?"

The woman's hand flew to her mouth and she screamed out, "Oh, my God, Paul! You told me he would never find out!"

I watched as she started to lose her shit. Tears streamed down her face and her body shook. She curled into the guy who put his arm around her to try to console her.

Paul's cold eyes met mine. "He knows, doesn't he? Fuck! Davey promised me he wouldn't say anything, but I should have known that good-for-nothing asswipe wouldn't keep his word."

"I don't work for Jackson if that's what you think." I wanted them to keep talking, but I didn't want to give too much away.

His forehead pinched into a frown. "Well who the fuck do you work for, then?"

"That's information I'm not willing to share, but what I do want from you is to know what was in that package you gave Davey today?"

His frown slowly eased and relief crossed his face. "You've got nothing, have you?"

I quirked a brow. "You willing to take a gamble on that?"

The woman wiped the tears from her eyes as she watched me. "Tell him, Paul. Maybe he can help us."

Paul stared at me for a long few moments and I recognised the hopelessness on his face. Whatever the hell was going on with them was clearly eating him up. Eventually, he blew out a breath and muttered, "Fuck." Rubbing the back of his neck, he moved away from the woman and paced in the tiny kitchen. When his eyes found mine again, I knew he was about to give me what I needed. "I'm one of Jackson's right-hand guys. When Davey discovered I was dating Marnie, Jackson's ex, he blackmailed us. He knew that if Jackson found out we were dating, he'd lose his shit over it and God knew what he'd do to Marnie."

He was right. I'd heard of Jackson's inability to let ex's go. Stories of him slicing a guy's dick off over an ex had circulated, and while I wasn't sure whether to believe it, Jackson was psycho enough for it to be true. "Or what he'd do to you."

He nodded. "Right. But I'm more concerned for Marnie."

"How long ago did you break up with Jackson?" I asked her.

"About six months."

"And he's got a new woman?"

She nodded. "He's dated three women since me and has been with the current one for three months now."

I processed that while thinking about the blackmail. "What was in that package, Paul?"

"Cash and drugs."

"Fuck," I muttered. "You're stealing from Jackson to pay Davey?"

He shifted on his feet, looking uncomfortable, but not as uncomfortable as he should have been. Jackson would likely kill him for theft. "It's what Davey asked for. I panicked."

"Please don't tell him," Marnie begged, her eyes wide with fear again.

"Sorry, but that's not an option here. If I were you two, I'd be jumping in my car now and leaving town." Right up until the moment Paul had told me he was stealing from

Jackson, I'd held hope they would escape his wrath. I no longer held that hope. They were screwed, but it was their own doing. People needed to think more about the consequences of their actions.

Paul's anger unleashed itself and he came at me with a punch. I'd been waiting for it, though, and blocked him with ease. The guy wasn't built for fighting.

I pulled him close, twisted him around and settled my arm across his chest to hold him in place. Squeezing him hard, I growled, "There's no time left for you to be fighting, asshole. You've made your bed, now you gotta lie in it. I'll give you the night, but first thing tomorrow morning, I'm taking this information to my boss." I squeezed him hard once more as I asked, "You got that?"

I let him go and pushed him away. As he stumbled back to where Marnie stood, he choked out, "Yeah. Now get the fuck out of my house."

With fucking pleasure.

I've got better things to be doing right now.

Chapter Seventeen
Havoc

It was close to six when I walked through the motel room door that night. Although it had been a long day, a sense of anticipation ran through me that I was beginning to associate with Carla. It had been years since I'd experienced that kind of feeling. I wasn't sure what to do with it, so I tried to ignore it. Trouble was, that was a hard thing to do when your dick was loving the hell out of it.

"Carla?" I called out as I walked through to the bathroom.

She was nowhere to be seen.

I pulled out my phone and sent her a text asking her where she was. A second later, the sound of a text beeped from the bedside table on her side of the bed.

Shit.

Where the fuck is she?

I stalked to the door and yanked it open.

And came face-to-face with her.

I frowned.

"Havoc! Quick, let me in, these are hot!"

I stepped aside to let her through and then closed the door after us. She carried two dinner plates covered in tin foil and quickly dumped them on the table near the television.

Turning to me, she grinned. "You hungry?"

I frowned again, confused about what I was seeing. Jerking my chin at the plates, I asked, "What is that?"

She cocked her head to the side. "Dinner. What else would it be?"

I moved closer to her. "I figured that, but what I can't figure out is where you got them from?" As far as I knew, the motel didn't have a restaurant and I didn't recall one being close enough for her to casually go out to and carry two hot plates back from.

"I cooked them." She answered me as if I'd asked her the stupidest question.

"Darlin', we're staying in a motel with no kitchen and I've never heard of kitchens just being conveniently available for people to cook dinner at, so forgive me if I'm a little confused about *where or how* you cooked our dinner."

Understanding dawned on her face as he made an 'O' with her lips. "Oh, I see what you mean. I thought you might like a home-cooked type dinner so I asked the motel owners if I could use their kitchen. They're this sweet older couple and they said yes."

I thought you might like a home-cooked dinner.

I hadn't had a home-cooked meal in longer than I could remember.

My mind kicked into gear and I remembered our phone call from earlier in the day. "Steak or chicken," I murmured.

She frowned. "Yeah, we went with steak, remember?"

A home-cooked meal.

"Havoc?"

I blinked.

"Steak *was* right, wasn't it?" she asked. "I could swear you said steak."

I nodded. "Yeah, I said steak." My voice was as gruff as my emotions.

She smiled and it lit the fucking room up. "Oh, thank God, because I don't have it in me to go back and cook more shit for you."

I was still trying to gather my thoughts. "You don't like cooking?"

"God no! I might be a waitress, but serving food and cooking it are two different things. And besides, I don't want to be a waitress forever."

"We could have just gone out for dinner, babe."

She paused for a moment. "Yeah, I know, but I figure if you're always on the road, it must be ages since you've had a meal cooked for you. I thought you might like a change from fast food." She gestured towards the two plates. "We need to eat before this goes cold."

For the next ten minutes, we ate and I did my best to keep my emotions in check. Carla prattled on about some shit, but I hardly paid attention. For a woman who didn't enjoy cooking, she sure as shit knew how to cook. The food was delicious. But wrapped up in all that food were thoughts and feelings I didn't want to touch.

My mother.

Kelly.

Devastation and betrayal.

Hope.

"Are you okay tonight? You seem off."

I focused my attention back to Carla who stared at me with open-concern.

Placing my utensils down, I nodded. "Yeah, I've just got some stuff on my mind."

"You wanna talk about it?"

Pushing my chair back, I stood. "No. I'm gonna have a shower."

Before she could say anything else, I headed for the bathroom.

I needed some space.

Closing the door behind me, I pulled my clothes off and turned on the shower.

Silence.

Peace.

"Havoc."

The door pushed open and I found myself staring at Carla as steam filled the tiny room.

"Not now," I rasped, desperate for her to leave me be.

She didn't.

"Yes, now," she snapped. "I cooked you dinner. I went to some trouble for you. And while I don't expect cartwheels and cheers of thanks, a simple acknowledgement would be nice. Just to know you at least enjoyed your dinner would be good."

She rambled and the tangled strands of memories in my mind threatened to suffocate me.

Good.

Bad.

Unfinished business.

I can't do this.

Not again.

"Havoc!"

I snapped.

Closing the distance between us, I pulled at the dress she wore. A moment later, it lay on the floor, along with her panties and bra. As she opened her mouth to speak, I pressed a finger to her lips. "Don't speak."

My voice betrayed the jagged emotions gripping me, and her eyes widened. She gulped back her words and remained silent.

I dragged her into the shower with me and pushed her up against the tiled wall. Lowering my mouth to hers, I tore a kiss from her lips.

Fuck.

Every damn time.

Calm washed over me when she was in my arms. The fury that lived in my soul eased during those moments and brilliant light flashed through my mind. The kind of light that gave a man hope.

Hope that I didn't want to feel, but that I could no longer deny.

Because it burst through me every single fucking time I was with her.

She began stroking my cock while I kissed her, and I groaned.

How can one woman make me feel so fucking good?

How the fuck can she come into my life and break my resolve so easily?

I deepened our kiss as my hands moved over her body. Unable to decide which part of her I wanted to touch the most, I chose to touch her everywhere.

Our mouths never left the others.

Our hands worked frantically to give each other pleasure.

And our souls joined to bring each other solace.

She was my refuge as well as my bliss and in that moment, I embraced it all.

When I entered her, she clung to me and moaned my name. The sound of my name on her lips jolted me to my senses. "Fuck, we need a condom," I muttered, pulling out of her.

"We're both clean." Her words were almost a plea, as if she couldn't wait the minute or so it would take me to get a condom.

My need matched hers. "You want me to keep going?"

She nodded and I didn't hesitate. I thrust back in and fucked her how I knew she loved it.

When we came, it was together.

Fingers digging into flesh.

Teeth on skin.

Bodies slamming together.

Resolutions broken.

Chapter Eighteen
Carla

Havoc's arms circled me from behind as I stood in front of the bathroom mirror. His body moulded to mine. A smile touched his lips, causing my tummy to flutter.

"That was the best damn dinner I've had in years," he said, only heightening the warm fluttery feeling in my stomach.

"Did it take sex for you to figure that out?"

"Smart ass," he muttered.

When I'd gone into the bathroom to give him a piece of my mind about not acknowledging dinner, I hadn't expected the reaction from him that I'd received. The minute his eyes had met mine, I'd known he was struggling with something. When he'd told me not to speak, I'd realised he was close to breaking point with whatever it was. And something *had* broken in him. I was convinced of it, because the way he watched me since wasn't at all the way he'd ever looked at me.

As much as I wanted to know what was troubling him, Havoc wasn't a man to be pushed. I figured he might open up at some point; I just had to be patient. Instead of bringing it up, I asked, "What are your thoughts on Gloria Pritchett?"

"Who the fuck is Gloria Pritchett?"

I grinned. "Oh, you are gonna love her. Let me introduce you."

Confusion flashed in his eyes and I tried not to giggle. I was sure Havoc wasn't a Gloria type of man, but I needed my *Modern Family* fix so I wasn't going to let a thing such as the truth get in the way. "Is she in Sydney?" he asked and I bit my lip to stop the laugh bubbling up.

"No, she's a character on a TV show." I dragged him out to the television and switched it on while indicating for him to sit on the bed.

He gave me an amused look—that I loved on him—but didn't argue. I grabbed the television remote and scooted up the bed to sit next to him. When his arm slid across my shoulders a moment later and he pulled me close, I couldn't contain the smile his gesture caused. We'd never done anything so domestic as this before and I decided I liked it.

The episode hadn't started yet. While we sat through some ads, Havoc said, "Nash left a message on my phone today. Have you heard from him?"

"He's left me a few messages, but I haven't called him back." I was avoiding him as best I could.

"I'm not going to call him back, but I will go see him when we get back to Brisbane."

I shifted so I could look up at him. "Really? Maybe you should just drop me off and keep going." The words hurt as they came out, but if Nash was hell-bent on keeping me away from Havoc, I didn't want to cause problems for him or for the club.

He listened to what I said but didn't reply straight away. "A man doesn't walk away from his problems, Carla. I'll hash it out with him. I don't need this to cause shit between the club and me. Not dealing with it would only do that."

Gloria's voice blared from the television at that moment, distracting him from the conversation. She had to have one of the most distinct voices I'd ever heard and while it drove some people crazy, it didn't bother me. A couple of moments later, he turned back to me. "Jesus," he muttered.

I tried not to laugh. "Keep watching. I promise you this is one of the funniest shows on TV. You'll get used to her voice."

The way he raised his brows told me he wasn't convinced, but he did as I said and gave the show his attention. He even laughed once during the episode.

When it finished, I crawled onto his lap and straddled him. "Thank you."

His hands moved to cup my ass. "What for?"

"For letting me watch that. It's one of my favourite shows."

Frown lines scored his forehead. "Babe, you don't need me to *let* you do anything. You wanna do something, you go right ahead."

I smiled. "I've dated some dickheads and trust me when I tell you that most of them tried to dictate what I could and couldn't do."

"Carla, you don't strike me as the kind of woman to put up with shit from any man. You're not seriously telling me that you let those guys control you, are you?"

Sighing, I replied, "No, but there have been times when a guy I've been with has made it clear he's not interested in doing something I wanted to do, and I let him have his way. And it's not that I expect a guy to want to do everything I want to do... I think what I should have said was thank you for watching it with me."

He pressed a kiss to my lips. "You had me intrigued with the Gloria thing."

"What did you think of her?"

"She's got a hot ass and tits, but no way could I listen to that voice for longer than about five minutes."

I loved his honesty. Cocking my head to the side, I asked, "What kinds of shows do you like? I'm picking you for a *Game of Thrones* or *The Walking Dead* kinda man."

His lips twitched with a smile. "I do like those shows. Or any real-life serial killer documentary. The more violent the better."

I narrowed my eyes at him. "You're fucking with me, aren't you?"

He laughed and fuck, when Havoc laughed, it was a beautiful thing. "Yeah, I'm fucking with you, darlin'. I don't watch a lot of TV. I do like most movies or shows about spies though. Thrillers more than actions."

"I should have picked that about you."

"Why?"

"Because I'm pretty sure you're a deep thinker, so I can see the appeal of a good thriller over an action for you."

He sat forward and in one motion, had me on my back while he positioned himself on his knees between my legs with his hands planted on either side of me. Staring down at me through eyes that held too much thunder, he growled, "You're getting in my fuckin' head, babe. It's not a good place to go searching."

The Havoc who had laughed with me a moment ago was gone, and in his place was the intense Havoc I knew well. The one who held me at arm's-length. I reached for his face and held it with both hands. "Are you scared of what I'll find there?" My breaths were choppy and my heart rate had picked up.

His eyes searched mine. "You won't like what you find there, Carla."

I held my breath. "Maybe you should let me decide that for myself."

He continued to watch me and I wished I knew him enough to have an inkling of what thoughts were running through his mind. Instead, it was as if we were suspended in a space where I didn't know which way to jump, and so I was left hanging, waiting for him to give me something.

Anything.

Up until that point, I had never really pushed him for much.

Maybe it's time to push.

I tightened my hold on his face. "Tell me the one thing I wouldn't like if I dug deep in your mind."

I held my breath again.

Waiting.

Hoping.

His body tensed and his jaw clenched.

He forced a long breath out.

"I killed my own grandfather. With my bare hands. And I wouldn't hesitate to do it again." His words came out in a grunt. Feral almost.

We stared at each other while his words smothered us with darkness.

"Why?"

He grunted and moved to straddle me. "Why did I kill him or why would I do it again?"

"Why to all of that. *Tell me.* I know there's so much more to you that you don't show." I wiggled out from under him and kneeled in front of him. Placing my hand on his chest, over his heart, I begged, "Tell me who you are. Show me what's in here."

Something I said caused him to shut down and he pushed up off the bed and stalked outside. The slam of the door sent a jolt through me.

Oh no you don't.

I scrambled off the bed and followed him outside where I found him staring at the road, his hands gripping the railing tightly. His dark eyes met mine, but he didn't speak.

"Why won't you let me in?" I demanded as the noise of the cars rushing past the motel filled the night air.

"Why the fuck do you want in?"

"God, Havoc, isn't it human nature to want a connection? For fuck's sake, our bodies have connected in ways most people only dream of. Why can't the rest of us connect?"

"I don't want connection, Carla. I just want to fuck you." His mouth was saying those words, but I didn't believe them for a minute.

"You are so full of bullshit. Can you even be honest with yourself for one minute?"

His chest pumped up and down as his breaths came hard and fast. "All right, you want honesty? I'll fuckin' give you honesty and you decide what to do with it." He tore his gaze from mine to stare back out into the inky night for a few moments. When he finally turned back to look at me again, he gave me what I had asked for. "My mum's father was a member of Storm. I remember growing up and worshipping the ground he walked on. I loved bikes, I loved him and I loved Storm. I always knew I'd join the club. On my eighteenth birthday he helped me do that. And then he took me down a dark path where my violent streak was celebrated and encouraged."

He stopped talking and turned away. I waited a few moments, not sure what to do, and then thought to hell with it. When I laid my hand on his back, I hit a wall of rock.

He flinched and I heard his sharp intake of breath. "I can't even tell you how many men I've hurt in the name of club business. You asked me where I got the name Havoc... I've caused a lot of it along the way. My real name's Callum, but the club named me Havoc after one particularly violent night," he continued, not giving me his eyes. "And I make no apologies for it, Carla. It is who I am now."

"I'm not asking you to change anything about yourself. I'm not asking you to even tell me about that stuff. All I'm asking is for you to open yourself up to me."

Silence hung between us and I wondered if it was actually possible to crack through his walls. I knew he'd had at least one relationship with a woman in his life—the blonde who'd gone to his house one morning when I'd been there—but I didn't know the depth of that relationship.

Maybe he's closed off and unable to give me more than he has.

"My grandfather was not a good man." He gave me his eyes and the pain I saw there stole my breath. "I was too young and dumb to understand shit at first, but the older I got, the more I realised he wasn't who I thought he was. The day I caught him double-crossing Storm in an effort to make some quick cash was the day I finally acknowledged his true colours. And the day I found my mother half beaten to death by him, *by her own father,* because she begged him to stop what he was doing so that it wouldn't have any impact on me, was the day I crossed that line of no return." He paused to take a breath. "My mother died a day later from that beating and I didn't hesitate to take his life in return."

As his words spilled from his lips, his body sagged a little. His eyes never left mine and I kept my gaze on him, wanting to let him know I wasn't going anywhere. I didn't have any knowledge about how Storm operated, but my own personal beliefs and values were such that I believed in loyalty and family and looking out for those you loved. I also believed in an eye-for-an-eye. If you fucked with me or those I loved, be ready for me to fuck back.

I didn't usually struggle for words, but I had none. What did you say to someone who'd been through what Havoc had? Instead, I decided to give him the one thing that he seemed to crave the most: touch.

Reaching my hand up, I curled it around his neck and pulled his mouth to mine. When our lips met, he opened his mouth and let me in. His pain flowed between us and I held him tighter. I could never take that pain from him, but I could try to make the weight less of a burden.

I could give him love.

God knew he needed it.

Ending the kiss, he rested his forehead against mine. "I've never told anyone outside of the club or my family that before."

"What about your ex? You never told her?"

He lifted his head and I saw the scowl on his face. "That bitch walked away from me just before it happened."

"And she never came back to make sure you were okay?"

He shook his head. "No. I lost my business and all my money, and Kelly decided I wasn't good enough for her anymore. She walked away without a backwards glance and shacked up with some other guy who had more cash than me. Five years of history and I never heard from her again. Not until I returned to Brisbane just recently and that was two years after she left."

Anger filled me that a woman could do that to a man. And my heart broke that he'd lost his partner, his business, his wealth, his mother and his grandfather all around the same time. No wonder his walls were up.

"You know... come to think of it, I *did* think you were being rude to her that morning she dropped by your house. Makes sense now."

My statement caused a shift in his mood. When he spoke, his words were lighter, with a tinge of sarcasm. "You think?"

A slow smile spread across my lips. "Well, at the time I just thought you were being your usual assholey don't-fuck-with-me self, but now I see it differently."

He shook his head as he gave me the beginning of a smile. "Fuck, how do you do that?"

"Do what?"

He gripped my waist and pulled me to him. "That thing you do where you manage to crash through my anger or whatever shitty mood I'm in and drag a smile out. That thing that makes me feel shit I haven't felt in years."

I beamed. "I'm a woman of many talents. You should know that by now."

He nodded slowly. "Yeah, I'm starting to realise that, darlin'."

"Thank you for telling me all that stuff." My voice was soft, but it held the emotion I was feeling. He'd shared a part of himself with me that he hadn't shared with many other people.

He trailed a finger across my lips.

His touch held none of the Havoc I knew.

This was a new kind of touch.

Soft.

Gentle.

Affectionate.

It was all he was going to give me in response to what I'd said, but it was enough for me. I was slowly learning that Havoc rarely spoke of his feelings; he expressed them through touch.

Kissing me slowly, he pulled back and said, "Thank you for still being here."

I wouldn't be anywhere else.

His lips returned to mine and he pulled me back into the motel room.

To our sanctuary.

To the place where we'd begun to strip back our layers of hurt and rejection and damage.

The place where we'd finally shown each other our need for love and acceptance.

Chapter Nineteen
Havoc

"F_{uck!}"

I eyed Jackson as he processed the information King and I had just shared with him. Discovering the cousin you'd always supported and looked out for was robbing you couldn't be easy.

He slammed his hand down onto the office desk in between us. "I'll fucking kill both of them!"

"So where does Storm stand now with that delivery?" King asked.

Jackson's furious gaze landed on him. "That's the last thing on my mind!"

King snarled. "Well, you need to move that up on your list of priorities. I need that delivery and I need it fucking fast."

"I couldn't give a shit about your delivery."

King's carefully controlled anger erupted and he finally lost his shit. I'd been waiting for it and had been surprised as hell when he'd treaded with care over this problem with Jackson. But I figured he had his reasons. King always did.

With one swift movement, he cleared Jackson's table of all its contents before jumping up onto the desk. Bending, he reached for Jackson's throat and wrapped his hand around it, squeezing tight until Jackson's face was red and he was struggling for breath.

As Jackson desperately fought King off, King bellowed, "I've been playing nice with you, motherfucker, trying to keep peace on the street, but I've come to the end of my patience. You *will* make that delivery to us this week or else I will make you regret that decision deeply." He squeezed Jackson's throat again. "And when I say deeply, I mean from deep in the fucking ground." He let Jackson go and planted his boot against his chest so he could shove him backwards onto the floor. Jumping off the desk, he squatted next to him. "And if you think I don't have the ability to take you on, you'd be seriously underestimating me."

Jackson glared at King before finally nodding. "I'll make the delivery," he spat out. "Now get the fuck off my property."

King's lips spread out into an evil grin that matched his crazy eyes. Standing, he said, "It'd be my fucking pleasure." With that, he turned and jerked his chin at me. "Looks like today's gonna be a good fucking day after all, Havoc."

As I followed him out to our bikes, I said, "Not really sure why you bothered asking for my help. Seems to me you've got a handle on things without me."

He turned to me with another grin. "Never can be sure when I'll need help. Besides, you were the one who worked out Davey was stealing from him. That was what saved us, brother."

I shook my head. "You didn't need that information, King. Although I'm still not sure why you held back from taking Jackson on yourself. That bullshit about keeping peace on the streets doesn't even sound like something you'd say."

"Yeah well, let's just say that Storm doesn't need any complications at the moment. Lotta shit going down and we need to keep as many people on our side as possible. You coming back to the clubhouse or are you heading out of Sydney now this shit is dealt with?"

I grinned. "I'll see you next time I'm in town. I've got shit to do now."

He returned my grin. "You've got a woman? That's the kind of look a man gets on his face when he's thinking about pussy."

Reaching my bike, I replied, "Let's just say that if you call me today, don't expect an answer."

He raised his chin at me. "Go and eat, my friend. I'll see you next time we need you."

Five minutes later, I was on my way back to the motel. I planned to shut the world out for the next twenty-four hours and have Carla every fucking way possible.

★★★

I stared down at the text that had just hit my phone.

Yvette: Dad's not doing well. You need to come home ASAP.
Me: Has he had another heart attack?
Yvette: The doctors aren't sure yet. Come home, Havoc.
Me: I'll be there.

"Is everything okay?" Carla asked, dragging my attention back to her.

I'd arrived back at the motel three hours ago and my focus had been on her ever since. She'd wanted coffee so I'd headed out to the café to get some and had just returned when the text arrived.

"We've gotta go home, darlin'. My dad's not well."

She moved off the bed, her beautiful face lined with worry. "What's wrong with him?"

I passed her the coffee. "It's his heart. He's had problems with it for years and may have just had another heart attack."

"I can be ready in ten minutes if that's okay. I'll just have a quick shower and throw my stuff in my bag."

Her concern and readiness to leave at the drop of a hat warmed my cold heart. Pulling her to me, I murmured, "Ten minutes, huh?"

She placed her hands against my chest, gently pushing me away. "What? You don't think I can get ready that fast?" I loved the look of indignation that crossed her face. She could be feisty as fuck and that shit turned me on.

"Well, for a woman who can take forever in the bathroom—"

She cut me off as she moved out of my hold. "I wouldn't continue that sentence. Not if you want my body again."

I snagged her around the waist and yanked her back to me. "Babe, if you think I can't find a way to have what I want, you are underestimating my abilities."

"And if you think *your* abilities are any match for mine, *you* are fooling yourself."

Christ, my dick was hard as hell. Groaning, I let her go and muttered, "Go. You've got ten minutes."

She stepped close again and ran her hand over my crotch. "I think we'd better take care of this first. No way in hell can you ride for as long as we have to with a hard-on."

A woman after my own heart.

I wasn't sure what I'd ever done to deserve an angel. She'd been right when she'd said we all needed connection. I'd just forgotten that somewhere along the way. Who knew where this would all end up, but I was gonna take everything she wanted to give me.

Chapter Twenty
Carla

I stepped through the front door to my home with some disappointment. The last few days away with Havoc had been an escape from my life. Being back home meant I had to begin dealing with the fallout of my job loss and subject failure. It also signalled another fork in my journey with Havoc. He'd just begun opening up to me. Coming back to Brisbane and going our separate ways could mean the end of that.

"Carla!" My mother greeted me when I entered the kitchen.

Havoc was right behind me, his hand on the small of my back, and I saw my mother's gaze move swiftly from me to him. As she hugged me, she murmured, "So this is the man causing Nash to go off the deep end."

I pulled out of her hold and stepped back into Havoc's space. When his hand slid around my waist, I smiled. I loved his need for touch. I had that same need. Placing my hand over his, I replied, "Mum, this is Havoc. Havoc, my mother, Linda."

He reached his free hand out to Mum and she shook it. "Good to meet you, Linda."

Although my mother was a woman who treated everyone equally, I wasn't sure how she'd react to Havoc considering he'd stirred Nash's anger. However, I needn't have worried. A brilliant smile touched her lips. "Come in, sit down. You must be so tired after that long trip."

"Mum, Havoc probably just wants to get home to his f—"

His hand tightened around my waist as he cut me off, "I'm not in a rush. Yvette has everything under control at the moment."

Well, shit.

I hadn't expected that.

Mum made coffee while we sat at the kitchen table. Havoc appeared calm, while I sat bouncing my leg, more nervous than I'd ever been when Mum met a guy I was seeing.

"So Nash tells me you're a club member," she said as she placed mugs in front of us.

He nodded. "Thank you, and yes. I grew up around the club and have been a member for thirteen years."

"But you don't stick to the Brisbane club?"

"Two years ago I chose to become a nomad. I tend to go wherever I'm needed now."

Frown lines wrinkled her forehead. I loved that she was trying to get to know him and understand how the club worked. "So you travel all over Australia? What do you do to help?"

I almost choked on my drink.

In true Havoc form, her questions didn't ruffle him. "Yeah, all over the country. The clubs call on me to help sort out membership issues or supplier issues for their businesses. Things like that mostly."

Catching his eye, I attempted to cover my smirk.

He ignored me.

"Oh, okay, so you must be good at your job then, if they call on you from all over," Mum said.

I coughed. Needing to change the subject, I said, "Have you heard any more from Dad?"

Sadness clouded her eyes. "Not since he dropped by the other day."

What?

"He dropped by? I thought he phoned you."

"No, he came here to talk to me. I told you that on the phone."

Anger bubbled up and I was helpless to control it. "No! He can't come here! I hope you told him to never come back."

She reached across the table to place her hand gently on my arm. "I did. I told him we would contact him if and when we were ready."

Havoc's hand landed on my knee under the table and he squeezed my leg. I turned and found him watching me with eyes full of concern. Taking a deep breath, I took hold of his hand on my leg and squeezed it back. His support calmed me.

Looking back at mum, I nodded. "Good. And for the record, I will never be ready to contact him."

Mum nodded her understanding. "I know, baby. But if you ever change your mind, I want you to know I will support you fully and be there for you however you need."

The front door slammed, jolting our attention from the conversation.

"Havoc!" Nash's voice boomed through the house as he made his way to the kitchen.

His furious eyes met mine a moment later, only holding my gaze briefly before turning his full attention to Havoc.

"Nash," Havoc said as he stood to meet my brother. His always-on-alert body tensed more than it usually did and the vein in his neck pulsed.

Oh, shit.

"What the fuck are you doing sitting in my mother's kitchen drinking coffee?" Nash demanded.

Mum interrupted. "Nash—" but he cut her off.

"No!" he bellowed. "He has no right to be in this house."

I stood. "Jesus, Nash, what century do you live in? I'm a grown woman who makes her own decisions and Havoc has every right to be in this house because he's with me and this is *my* home."

Nash's eyes widened. "What the hell do you mean he's with you? Last you told me, this was just some fun. I didn't think you two were actually together."

Havoc's deep voice crashed over all of ours. "Nash, let's take this outside. This is between you and me."

I swung my angry gaze to him. "No, this is between all three of us, Havoc!"

His dark eyes met mine and he shook his head. "Yeah, it is, but for now, Nash and I need to get some shit sorted. Alone." He used the tone he took when what he was saying was final. I knew better than to argue so I let them go.

And I prayed they both walked away from this unharmed.

Chapter Twenty-One
Havoc

We barely made it out the front door before Nash's fist landed on my cheek. I gave him that one, but it would be the last one he'd have.

"I don't want you anywhere near Carla!" he thundered, veins bulging and fists clenched ready to attack again.

I'd seen Nash in fight mode and he was lethal. I didn't get my name for nothing though, and he should have remembered that. However, there were two things holding me back—the brotherhood of the club and Carla.

"It's too late, Nash. And besides, she's right when she says she's old enough to make up her own mind." I focused on my breathing and keeping my natural fight instincts under control.

"I don't fuckin' need *you* coming into my family and telling me how it should be run." His eyes held the wild look I'd seen many times in him and I knew his first punch was only a warm-up. Nash was just getting started.

"I'm just trying to be honest with you here. And what I'm saying is that I thought this thing between me and Carla would be done by now, but it's not. It's far from done. Do whatever you feel you need to do, but if I were you, I would take into account your sister's feelings on this. Fighting her will only push her away."

He threw another punch, but I blocked him and punched him in the stomach. As he recovered from that, I moved so I could grab him in a headlock. He was quick though, and knifed his elbow back into my gut. Winded, I stumbled back, attempting to work out my next move.

Nash didn't ease up. He came at me, fists flying. I avoided each one, ducking and weaving, until finally I managed to punch him hard in the face, dropping him to the ground. He didn't stay down though. Within a couple of moments, he was back on his feet ready to keep going.

Any other fight and I'd be all in and loving the fuck out of it. Nash was a worthy opponent. But I didn't want to fight him. He, on the other hand, was intent on making his point.

He kept coming at me with punch after punch. Some, he got in and some, I managed to block. We must have kept going for a good ten minutes until we found ourselves sweaty, bloody and battered. But neither was backing down.

And then my phone rang. It was Yvette's ring tone and it distracted me for long enough to allow Nash to land one final punch, almost knocking me out completely. As I lay sprawled out on the grass with a bloody nose and pain radiating through my body, he glared down at me. "Leave my sister the fuck alone or else you and I are gonna have problems you don't want."

I sat up and watched him leave. As he stalked through the front door of his mother's house, Carla attempted to exit.

"You're not fuckin' going out there," Nash bossed her.

"Move out of my goddamn way, Nash! You can't stop me from doing what I want." They had a standoff for a few moments before she eventually pushed past him. I couldn't see his face, but I could hear his grunts of disapproval before he continued on inside.

Carla came to me with a look of horror. "Fuck, your face is a mess. I'm gonna go back inside and get some tissues or something for your nosebleed."

I reached out and grabbed her wrist. Shaking my head, I said, "No, I'll just use my shirt." Before she could argue, I stood and ripped my shirt off so I could use it to stop blood going everywhere.

"Did you let him win?"

I chuckled. "No. My phone distracted me. Probably a good thing, otherwise I reckon we'd still be here going at it." I grabbed my phone from my pocket and listened to the voice message Yvette had left.

Carla frowned. "Is everything okay?"

"Yeah, I don't think she meant to call me. There was all this garbled talking and I don't think it was directed at me."

"Why do you look so weird about it?"

With my one free hand, I pulled her to me. "When your sister is on the end of the phone talking about pussy she wants to eat, it's kinda weird."

Her eyes sparkled with mischievousness and she laughed. "Must be a Caldwell thing, this love of pussy."

My body was in a world of hurt. Blood ran from my nose and I could feel parts of my face beginning to swell. I had a sick father to get to, but in that moment all I saw and heard was Carla. Once again, I was struck by the realisation that she lit up my fucking world when it had been grey for so long.

I almost forgot about my problems with Nash and the club.

Almost.

★★★

"You took your time," Yvette muttered when I joined her in Dad's kitchen a little while later. "And what the hell happened to your face?"

The bleeding had stopped but I knew I had dried blood on my face. I probably had bruising as well, to go with the swelling. "A difference of opinion."

"Jesus. What kind of opinion is worth that kind of fight?" As the words came out of her mouth, understanding dawned on her face and she added, "Shit, was this about a woman?"

Wanting to avoid this conversation, because my sister could be a pain in my ass, I moved to the fridge and grabbed ice out of the freezer. I then wrapped the ice in a towel and placed it against my cheek.

"Holy shit, it is!" she carried on. "Please tell me this woman lives in Brisbane and you're going to stick around."

I raised my hand and shook my head to indicate she should stop. "Can we just talk about Dad? How is he?"

She narrowed her eyes at me. "Don't think this is the last about that. Dad's been having a lot of chest pain and his blood pressure has been scary. I'm really worried, but he just seems so blasé about it all."

"In what way?"

"He's refusing to go to the doctor and get checked. Keeps grumbling that he's spent enough time in hospital to last a lifetime. I need you to talk some sense into him or failing that, put him in the damn car and take him because he won't listen to me."

I was contemplating what she said when there was a knock at the front door followed by, "Yvette, you said you'd be like ten minutes max, babe" as the woman who owned the voice walked down the hallway and into the kitchen. When her eyes met mine, they widened. "Oh sorry, I didn't realise you had company."

I settled my ass against the kitchen counter and crossed one ankle over the other. "Knock yourself out. I can wait," I said as I eyed her. She was a gorgeous woman with long brunette hair, killer curves, pouty lips and a feminine air that I would never have picked my sister to be attracted to. However, if the way they were looking at each other was any indication, they were hooking up. Yvette had embraced her sexuality at a young age and was a loud and proud lesbian who didn't scream femininity. She had packed muscle onto her frame and her hair was cut short and spiky. Her favourite things to do were work on her car and try any kind of extreme sport out there. The woman who'd just barged into the house wore a flowy red dress and looked like she'd just stepped out of a fashion magazine with her makeup and hair. Definitely not Yvette's type, but the thing I'd learnt was sometimes our 'type' was not at all what we thought.

She blasted me with a smile, which was another key difference between her and Yvette. My sister smiled at no one most of the time. Reaching for my hand, she said, "Hi, I'm Gillian."

I shook her hand, liking her instantly. She was a breath of fresh air for Yvette and maybe she'd soften her rough edges. "Havoc."

If I thought she'd hit me with a smile before, her face lit up more at the mention of my name. "Yvette's brother!" she exclaimed. "I've been wanting to meet you for ages."

"How long have you two been going at it?"

Yvette scowled. "Havoc," she chastised. "Watch your mouth."

Well, fuck me, Gillian had already changed her. She'd never had a problem with my mouth before. My sister's mouth was as dirty as mine most days.

Gillian ignored her. "We've been seeing each other for about a month now. We met at a race."

"A race?" I couldn't picture the woman standing in front of me at any kind of race.

"V8s, Havoc," Yvette answered me in her short voice. Her eyes had the look in them that told me she wanted no arguments from me when she said, "Can you give us a minute?"

I pushed off from where I stood. "It would seem I'm not the only one who likes privacy when it comes to women," I muttered as I left them to head into the bathroom and clean up. As I was about to round the corner into the hallway, I turned and threw back, "You should be careful who you butt dial, sis. I got an earful of something about pussies earlier and as much as I love pussy, I don't love hearing about you eating someone out."

Gillian slapped a hand over her mouth to stifle a giggle while Yvette glared at me. She mouthed *ass* at me and I shrugged. In this family you had to give as good as you got, and I copped a lot from her. It was only fair I took a shot when I could.

★★★

"Why won't you go to the doctor, Dad?" I asked my father after I showered and cleaned up my face. Nash had gotten some decent punches in and one of my eyes was black and swollen. Dad was used to seeing me with black eyes so he didn't flinch or question me about it.

I'd found him sitting in his armchair in the lounge room watching television. The blank expression on his face jolted fear through me. I wasn't scared of much, but Dad checking out was one of them. As much as we irritated the other, we had always been close. He'd shared his love of bikes with me. He might not have been a biker, but he'd been a mechanic and had loved restoring old bikes. Dad had taught me everything I knew about bikes, and my love for them had led me to set up my own bike restoration business. I had good memories of him dropping by my work and spending hours with me.

"I don't need a doctor, Havoc." His blank expression remained and he didn't give me his attention for long. Instead, he turned back to the television and resumed watching the crime show he had on.

Frustrated, I moved to the television and switched it off. "Yvette seems to think differently so I want to know why you don't want to go."

He scowled, but answered me. "I've got my spray for any chest pain I have and as far as the blood pressure is concerned, it's been high for awhile now. I'm on medication for it. Nothing else they can do for me, son."

"If the medication isn't working, I'd say there probably *is* something else they can do for you. Humour me—let me take you to see Dr Bennett this afternoon."

"No."

Fuck.

"Dad—"

He cut me off as he stood, "I said no. You need to respect my decision."

I pulled out my phone as he left the room. If he refused to go to the doctor, I'd bring the damn doctor to him.

Chapter Twenty-Two
Carla

"So things are serious between you and Havoc?"

I traced the words written on the mug that sat in front of me, while I considered my mum's question. After Havoc left, Nash and I had a huge argument that ended with him storming out of the house. I'd broken down in tears and mum was the one to console me. I hated fighting with Nash. He was my rock in this crazy life and I didn't want to push him away, but we had gotten to the point in my life where I needed the space to either succeed on my own terms or fail by my own hand. Nash desperately wanted to stop me from screwing shit up, and I understood that, but he had to let me go.

"I like him, Mum. Like, *really* like him, and I never saw that coming. He's not the kind of man I ever saw myself falling for, but I'm pretty sure I've fallen. But whether or not it will go anywhere, I'm not sure."

"Why isn't he the kind of man you thought you'd fall for?"

I sighed. "I just want someone stable. Someone who won't let me down. And I always assumed I'd find a man who was educated and who had a good, well-paying job. Havoc is a nomad who goes from city to city. I don't see that as stable."

"Your father was educated and had a good job," she said softly and I didn't miss her point.

"I know."

"Are they the only things important to you in a man, honey? Education and income?" There was no judgement in her tone. It was simply a question. Mum was one of the best people to go to when you had a dilemma because she had this way of talking you through the problem to come up with a good solution.

"No, and I've realised that now." *Now that I see Havoc's good qualities.* "I want a man who will put me first and who won't try to change me. Someone who will always protect me. Honesty is important too, and I want a man who I can trust."

She smiled. "All good qualities to look for."

"Yeah, and I think that those things might actually come before education and income."

Nodding, she agreed. "Absolutely. Do you think Havoc can give you those things?"

"Yes." My heart rate picked up as I contemplated a relationship with him. I could see it except for the fact he didn't live in Brisbane. He didn't live anywhere really. That would be a huge problem.

Oh, God.

Why did shit have to be complicated?

Which reminded me... "What are you going to do about Dad? I mean, are you going to let him back into your life?" I dreaded that she might say yes, but I had to know.

The look that flashed in her eyes revealed her inner conflict. Mum had always had a bleeding heart and a tendency to forgive too easily. "I think he's sick."

"So?" He'd never cared when we'd been sick. He'd never come back to check on us so why should him being sick make any difference to her decision.

"Carla, I let your father go in my mind many years ago. He'll never own a place there again, but I worry for you kids. I want you all to make peace with the hurt he inflicted. Closing yourself off from that pain and not allowing it to wash out of you will only eat you up for the rest of your life."

My chest tightened at the thought of what she was suggesting. "Are you saying we should forgive him?"

"Forgiveness is for you, not him." Her eyes and her voice pleaded with me to agree, but I never would.

Pushing my chair back, I said, "I don't need to forgive him. What I need is for him to go away and never come back." I fumed as I headed for my bedroom.

Not at my mother but at my father.

No fucking way would I ever meet him.

★★★

An hour later, I gave up trying to get some sleep. I was exhausted after the long ride home, but my mind wouldn't switch off.

And I missed Havoc.

I pulled out my phone.

Me: I miss your cock.

He came straight back.

Havoc: It misses you.
Me: I think we should give him what he wants.
Havoc: I'm tied up for the next few hours but after that he's all yours.
Me: Is your dad okay?
Havoc: Not sure yet. Doctor is coming over soon.
Me: I hope it's good news. I'll talk to you after.
Havoc: I'll call you later, babe.

Damn. Now I was horny as hell.

With no promise of sleep and hours before Havoc would be free, I decided to see if Velvet could fit me in for a facial. I'd never been to her work before, but she'd given me facials at home and they always relaxed me.

I phoned her and was lucky—she'd had a cancellation and could squeeze me in.

Perfect.

Girl time was just what I needed.

★★★

"You've fallen for him, haven't you?" Velvet said after I'd answered all her questions about my trip away with Havoc. She'd finished my facial and we were passing the time until her next appointment. The salon where she worked wasn't busy that day so we had plenty of time to catch up.

"Yes. And Nash is ready to kill him, I think."

"There should be no *I think* in that sentence. He *is* ready to kill him. But only because he's convinced Havoc is dangerous."

"Velvet, he's not dangerous to me. He's got a side to him that I don't think he shows many people. I just wish Nash would trust me on this."

"It's not you he doesn't trust, Carla. How do you know he wouldn't be violent towards you? From everything Nash has said, Havoc could just snap and lose it."

I leant forward so I could drop my voice. "I don't want to go into detail, but I kinda asked him to do stuff when we were having sex and he refused. He told me he'd never do anything like that to a woman. He's a good man, Vi."

"Jesus, what kind of stuff?"

"I asked him to hurt me. Pain gets me off sometimes, but he wanted nothing to do with it."

While she was processing what I'd said, the front door to the salon opened and Madison entered. I'd met her a few times through Nash and liked her. She was married to Jason Reilly, one of the Storm men and was the daughter of the club president. She saw us and smiled before talking with Roxie, the hairdresser who owned the place. A moment later, they both joined us.

"Hey, Carla, how's things?" Madison greeted me as she dumped her huge handbag on the floor and sat down in the chair next to mine.

"I'm doing okay. How are you?"

Roxie cut in, "Ask her about her biker dude." She'd listened to everything Velvet and I had been discussing about Havoc and had a few things to say. Seemed she wasn't a huge fan of the Storm men and their bossy ways.

Madison's eyes widened. "Which biker are we talking about? Tell me everything."

I threw Roxie a glare. I really liked her, but I could have done without this conversation. God knew what Madison thought of Havoc and I really didn't want to hear it.

"Havoc Caldwell," I replied.

She whistled. "Wow, is he back in town? I haven't seen Havoc for years. He'd left town by the time I came back. I was sad to hear about his mum dying and also about all the shit that went down with his ex."

"I met him about a month or so ago and he's back here for his dad who isn't well."

Madison frowned. "He's not dying, is he? That would be a blow to Havoc, to lose both parents so close."

"I don't know. He's got the doctor seeing his dad today."

Velvet joined in. "Do you know him very well, Madison?"

She rested her chin on her fist as she contemplated the question. "J and Havoc used to be close so I did spend some time with him. I really liked him. He had a good business doing up old bikes and at the time, I thought he had a good life. He'd been in a steady relationship with Kelly and we all thought they were going to get married, have kids and live happily ever after. But apparently something happened to his business and I think he had to declare bankruptcy. After that, Kelly left him. And then his mum died. J said he lost his shit. Just went off the rails. He shut everyone out and ended up leaving town. I always wondered what happened to his business because up until that point, it had been so successful. Havoc had it all."

"Wow," Velvet said. "Maybe Nash has it all wrong about him."

Madison frowned. "What do you mean?"

"My bloody brother thinks that Havoc is dangerous and doesn't want me to have anything to do with him," I answered.

"Well, I can't really say. I do know that he had a reputation for handling club issues and I did see him in action once and it was pretty scary, but you know what? I've seen J and Nash in action, too... actually, Scott as well, and they're pretty scary themselves, so for Nash to say that is a little hypocritical."

"That's a very good point," Roxie said.

"Nash is just scared to let Carla make what he thinks could be a mistake," Velvet said.

Madison nodded. "I get it, but he needs to let that go."

"A-fucking-men," I said. I was so glad I'd run into Madison. She'd shared some useful information with us and I was hoping Velvet would take it back to Nash and try to talk sense to him again.

Chapter Twenty-Three
Havoc

At what point do you give up in life?

I'd turned that thought over and over in my mind a lot during the last two years. I hadn't come to a final thought on it yet. Watching my father with the doctor, I wondered what the catalyst had been for him. He'd given up. I was sure of that, but why?

Was it losing Mum?

Was it two years of being on his own and he was done?

Was it his deteriorating health?

Or something else?

The doctor came to me. "I want to admit him and keep an eye on him. Probably just overnight, just so we can keep track of his vitals. This constant chest pain has me concerned."

"And the blood pressure?"

"We'll need to tweak his medication. Hospital is the best option all round. I'll call an ambulance to come get him now."

"I can drive him."

"I know, but with this pain, I want him monitored."

Dad shot me a filthy look. "I don't want to go to bloody hospital."

My patience with him snapped. He'd been arguing with me most of the afternoon while we waited for the doctor and I was way past the point of caring what he wanted. "You're going," I yelled as I pointed at him. "I'm not arguing about this again." With that, I strode into his bedroom, yanked his overnight bag out of his closet and threw some clothes and toiletries in there for him. I then took the bag and dumped it at the front door, ready for the ambulance.

"Havoc," Yvette said in a tone that told me she thought I was being too harsh. "When I said I wanted you to get him looked at, I didn't mean for you to spend all afternoon fighting with him."

I stared at her in disbelief. "Well, what the fuck did you think was gonna happen? The old man's as stubborn as hell, no way were we getting him there without an argument or two."

"I just think you could go a little easier on him, that's all."

"Trust me when I tell you that I've been going easy all afternoon." I took a deep breath. "He's given up and I don't fuckin' like it."

She frowned. "Given up on what?"

"Life." Anger at that thought gripped me and I jabbed my finger at her. "I'm not letting him give up. I don't care if I have to spend every minute of every fuckin' day arguing with him, he's not checking out."

Without waiting for her reply, I headed back to where Dad sat in his armchair. He glared at me as I entered the room, but I ignored him. Taking a seat in the armchair next to his—Mum's armchair—I solidified that declaration in my mind.

I would make sure my father got through whatever it was he was going through.

I refused to lose another parent before their time.

★★★

Yawning, I rubbed the back of my neck. It was just after nine that night and I was about to leave the hospital. Dad was fast asleep and the nurses assured me they would look after him.

I hadn't heard from Carla, which surprised me. However, I loved the fact she gave me the space I needed.

I settled myself on my bike and sent her a text.

Me: You awake?
Carla: Yeah. How's your dad?
Me: They admitted him to hospital, but he's ok.
Carla: Glad to hear it.
Me: I want to see you.
Carla: Is your dick still missing me?
Me: Something like that.

Her text didn't come straight back so I rang her.

"Havoc," she murmured into the phone.
"You sound sleepy."
"I'm tired. You must be so tired."
"I'm way past tired. I need you in my bed tonight."
She didn't speak and I wondered if she was still on the line.
"Carla?"
"I'm here. I was just trying to figure out if I could remember you ever telling me you needed me. I liked the sound of that." Her sleepy voice had turned into her sexy voice, one I couldn't get enough of.
"I'm gonna come pick you up."

"You're one persistent man. As much as I want what your dick wants, I'm not sure I have the energy for sex so maybe we should just catch up tomorrow."

I gripped my phone harder. "I'm not asking for sex tonight, angel."

Silence again, and then, "Come get me."

Thank fuck.

★★★

I pulled Carla tighter against me in the bed. Her back was to my front and my arm had her securely in my hold. Burying my face in her hair for a moment, I said, "Whatever the fuck you washed your hair with tonight, you need to always wash it with."

Her body shook gently with laughter. "So damn bossy," she murmured, almost asleep.

My hand cupped her tit. "You fuckin' love that about me."

She wiggled against me. "No sex, Havoc. I'm too tired."

"Babe, I can keep my dick in my pants, but I need to hold you, so the boob stays in my hand."

Her hand moved over mine and she kept it there. "I do love that about you."

"Go to sleep. You need all the rest you can get because tomorrow morning, I'm going to wear you the fuck out."

I fell asleep faster than I ever had.

★★★

Fuck.

I groaned as I regained consciousness.

"What time is it, darlin'?" I asked Carla as she worked my dick with her hand. It was dark as hell in the bedroom. I figured it couldn't be any more than three in the morning.

She bent and whispered against my ear, "I don't know. All I know is sleeping next to you makes me horny as hell and I need to get this dick inside me faster than you can say please."

"Fuck," I muttered, moving my hand to scoop her body up and over so she was on top of me.

She wasted no time. As she sank her pussy down onto my cock, she placed her hands on my chest and moaned her pleasure.

"Christ, did you wake up that wet or did you get yourself there?"

"Baby, I woke up that wet, but it's all thanks to you."

I let her ride me up until the point where I knew she was getting close and then I flipped her onto her back and went down on her. No fucking way could I not get my fill before I pumped my orgasm into her.

Her fingers threaded their way through my hair and she gripped me hard while I tongued her. Jesus, no pussy had ever tasted so good. I'd been a starved man before I met her and I hadn't even known.

I lifted her legs up and over to rest on my shoulders as I pushed my mouth hard against her. She writhed under my touch, her reaction making me harder. Needing to watch her, I pulled my lips from her pussy and finger fucked her.

She was fucking glorious.

My eyes had adjusted to the light and I took in every inch of her while she came.

Her fingers clawing at the sheets.

The arch of her back as the pleasure ran through her body.

The way she faced to the side with her cheek flat to the bed with her face tilted up, exposing her neck to me.

She was so damn wet. My hand and face was coated in her.

When she finished coming, she opened her eyes and smiled a long, sexy smile at me. Crooking a finger, she whispered, "Come here."

I positioned myself over her with my hands planted either side, and bent my face so our lips almost touched. "You taste so good. You wanna taste?"

She licked her lips and pulled my mouth down. Our tongues tangled and she moaned as she tasted herself. That shit turned me on. As we kissed, I ran my dick along her pussy and entered her. Not all the way, though.

"Havoc," she grumbled as she wrapped her legs around me. "I want you all the way in."

I grinned. Fuck, I couldn't help myself. I loved the way she always wanted more from me. Pushing all the way in, I said, "Happy?"

"I am now," she replied as her muscles contracted around me.

Her sass pushed all my buttons and I grabbed her wrists and spread her arms out across the bed, pinning her down. Pulling out of her, I then thrust in hard. As she cried out, I demanded, "You want it harder?"

"Yes." Her answer was more of a plea.

I pulled out and slammed into her again, over and over until she squeezed her eyes shut and clung to me.

Our bodies moved as one while I fucked her.

Hard and rough.

When we came, it was together and it was fucking beautiful.

I finally sank into the awareness that sex with Carla was a whole new experience.

It wasn't just pleasure.

It was so much more than that.

Chapter Twenty-Four
Carla

I eyed the woman exiting her car outside Havoc's house. It was his ex. She was making her way up the path to the front door and he was in the kitchen on the phone to the hospital.

When she knocked on the door, I took great delight in answering it. Her wide eyes and surprise were enough to make my day. Hell, they made my fucking month. "It's you again," she said with scorn. Her eyes darted to try to see into the house.

"Yep, me again. Sorry, I've forgotten your name."

I hadn't.

She didn't need to know that.

"Kelly," she retorted, trying to push past me.

I pushed back.

No way was she getting inside this house.

"Havoc's busy," I said before adding, "He's actually just setting up our new sex swing. Can I pass on a message? No, scratch that. Havoc made it pretty clear to me that he never wanted to see you again." I waved at her before shutting the door in her face.

"That was impressive." Havoc's voice sounded from behind me and I turned to find him with his arms crossed over his chest while he watched me with amusement.

I grinned. "That was kinda fun. It serves her right for interfering with us last time."

He raised his brows. "A sex swing?"

Before I could reply to that, Kelly banged on the door. "Havoc! I know you're in there. Let me in."

Irritation flashed across his face and he took the few steps to the door. Pulling it open, he said, "I'm in here for everyone but you. Now fuck off."

I loved the way he didn't mince his words. I also loved that he stood his ground with the woman who'd ripped his heart out. He hadn't told me a lot yet, but I knew enough to know that.

"Are you seriously choosing her over me? She's not even your type." Her words were mean and I wondered what she meant about his type.

"How the fuck do you know what my type is? It's been two years since we broke up. A lot's changed in that time." His fury surrounded him and I was glad I wasn't on the receiving end of it.

"Types don't change," she said. Geez, she never fucking gave up.

"You know what I realised, Kelly? I fuckin' realised *just this week* that the reason I didn't have a woman was because my compass was all out of fuckin' whack. It was leading me to the wrong *type*. Thank Christ I made a pit stop one night in a bar I made a habit of never visiting. I found my type all right and she's a fuckin' angel. Now step the fuck back so I can close this goddamn door and go and show my woman how fuckin' thankful I am that you're a greedy bitch who decided I wasn't good enough for her."

He slammed the door in her face and turned to me, his face a mask of intent. My heart raced in my chest at his words. About me. Warmth flooded my body and I smiled at him.

I was lost for words after his declaration. I went with the first thing that came to mind. "That was a lot of fucks in those sentences."

His eyes watched me with an intensity that caused my lady bits to start dancing with joy. "You good with those fucks?"

"I'm good with those fucks."

"And with everything else I just said?"

I stepped into his space so our bodies were touching. "Oh, I am more than good with everything you just said. I'm particularly good with that part about showing me how thankful you are that—"

His lips crashed down onto mine and he did more than show me how thankful he was.

He brought heaven to my goddamn door.

Again.

★★★

Havoc dropped me off at home on his way to the hospital. I had to start thinking about my studies and a new job. My life plan had been altered in more ways than one and I wanted to spend some time alone working through it all in my mind. Havoc planned to spend the day with his father. He promised to call me later.

"That you, Carla?" my mum called out as I opened the front door.

"Yeah."

I found her in the kitchen filling the slow cooker.

"A young man dropped by earlier to see you. He said he knew you from school and wanted to discuss a business idea with you." She passed me a piece of paper with his name and number.

"Wow," I mumbled as I read the name on the paper. Looking back up at her, I said, "This guy was a year ahead of me and started his own design business when he finished. It's doing well. *Really* well. I wonder if he wants to offer me a job?" This could be the answer to at least one of my problems.

"Nash dropped by to see you this morning also."

"Shit. Did you tell him where I was?"

"I'm not going to lie for you, Carla. I told him the truth."

"Fair enough. I'm going to go see him today. Try to get him to see my point of view."

"That's a good idea. Invite him over for dinner if you want. I'm making enough."

"Is there enough for Havoc if he can come?"

She nodded. "Absolutely."

I gave her a kiss and swiped my car keys off the table. "I'll let you know who's coming later today," I promised as I headed outside to my car.

Hope swirled through me. Maybe I could convince Nash to give Havoc a go. We didn't need his blessing to carry on with seeing each other, but it would make life easier for everyone.

★★★

"Hey Carla," J greeted me when I arrived at the Storm clubhouse. He was on his way inside when I pulled into the car park. He stopped and waited for me.

"Hi, J."

"You looking for Nash?"

I nodded as I eyed the building. It was rare that I visited the place. "Yeah, can you see if he's in for me? I'll just wait out here."

He gestured for me to come in. "You don't have to wait out here."

I shook my head. "I want to have a conversation with him and I think it's best to do it in private."

"No worries. I'll go find him."

A few minutes later, Nash walked towards me with a grim look on his face.

"Hey, you," I greeted him, trying to keep a friendly tone in my voice.

"Mum tell you I called over to see you this morning?" Yeah, he was pissed.

"She did. I was gonna come see you anyway. We need to talk."

"You know where I stand on this, Carla."

My hope faltered.

This was going to be harder than I thought.

I dropped my gaze and stared at the ground while trying to get my thoughts together. This had to come out right because I was sure I only had one shot at changing his mind.

He reached for my chin and lifted my face. For the first time since this had all started, I saw care there. "Talk to me." His voice had softened and while I briefly wondered where that had come from, I didn't want to ponder it for too long. God only knew how long it would last.

"Dad leaving and never wanting anything to do with me caused a shitload of insecurities for me, Nash. I'm sure you realise that, but I'm not sure you realise just how deep they run. I promised myself a long time ago that I'd never end up with a man like our father. I wanted a nice guy, a steady man who would never let me down. The trouble was I never believed myself worthy of that, so I kept choosing the wrong men. When I met Havoc, it honestly was only supposed to be a quick fling. A biker wasn't in my life plan, no offence."

Listening intently, he nodded at that.

"I know you've said Havoc is violent and dangerous for me, and for sure, I've seen his temper. But he's never once shown me any violence. In fact, he's gone out of his way to give me the opposite. He also gives me honesty in a way that no other man ever has. He respects me and doesn't tell me I have to change who I am. And he's super protective of me." I paused, waiting for him to say something, but he didn't, so I continued, "Nash, you've seen me with other guys. You know that I'm a mess most of the time if I'm dating someone. Do I look like a mess at the moment? Do I seem unhappy and insecure?"

I watched him closely to gauge his reaction and I could have sworn I saw conflict work its way across his face. But in the end he said, "Carla, you haven't known Havoc as long as I have and you haven't seen the shit I've seen. I know you think you know him, but you don't. And he might be giving you all those things now, but we all know relationships start off with best behaviour. It won't last."

My mouth fell open. I'd stood there and been honest with him and all he could give me in return was that? "You're not willing to even stop and consider what I've said?"

His jaw clenched. "I did, but it doesn't change anything."

"Oh, my God, you frustrate me, Nash! You always think you know best. Let me tell you, you don't know best on this."

He stiffened. "You're not going to stop seeing him, are you?"

I shook my head. "No."

"Fuck, Carla. You never fuckin' learn when it comes to men. I just don't want to see you get hurt again."

"I've heard you loud and clear. If he hurts me, I'll own that. But can you at least give us the chance to see where this goes without harassing him?"

He stood there fuming and I thought for sure he was going to continue arguing with me. In the end, though, he jabbed his finger at me and declared, "If he so much as causes you one tear, he's fuckin' dead."

With that, he turned and left. I stayed rooted to the spot, stunned at what he'd said. Just before he disappeared inside, I yelled out, "Dinner tonight at Mum's. You and Velvet are invited."

He didn't turn back or stop, but rather nodded and said, "We'll be there."

I failed to mention that Havoc was invited.

Tonight would either be an epic failure or a new beginning for all of us.

Chapter Twenty-Five
Havoc

"Thank you for coming tonight. Your dad's going to be all right without you, isn't he?" Carla said as we entered her mum's house for dinner.

"Yeah, Yvette's with him at the hospital tonight. I spent most of day with him before visiting the clubhouse. He's had enough of me for today." The doctors were busy tweaking his medication, so until they were happy with that, they weren't letting him go home. Dad was still pissed at me for his hospital stay.

"Uh, I need to confess something to you," she said as she halted our progress down the hallway. Voices filtered from the kitchen and I was fairly sure of what she was about to tell me.

I raised my brows. "Keep going."

Biting her lip and looking anything but confident, she said, "Nash is here. I didn't want to tell you in case you said no to coming. I think tonight might give you guys an opportunity to move past where you're at." Her words rushed out in a nervous mess and I fought not to smile at them. What she didn't realise was that I'd say yes to almost anything if it involved being in the same room as her. I could try to deny it, but I was fucking done for where she was concerned.

"Don't hold your breath, darlin'. Nash can be a stubborn asshole when he wants to be. But I'll be on my best behaviour."

She reached up and gently touched the lingering bruise near my eye. "God, I'll bloody punch him myself if he does this again."

I grinned. "I don't doubt it."

Grabbing my hand, she said, "Okay let's do this."

I squeezed her hand and followed her into the kitchen where everyone was. When we entered the room, the talking died down as all eyes came to us.

"Carla. Havoc." Carla's mother gave us both a smile and motioned for us to sit with them. Nash's eyes met mine and I jerked my chin, but the only response I received was his continuing glare.

"Nash," Carla said in a low voice and I figured that was her warning to him. He simply threw a glare her way also.

I greeted Linda who then introduced Nash's girlfriend, Velvet.

And then we attempted to play happy fucking families.

★★★

"Did you contact that young man who came over looking for you?" Linda asked Carla as she served dinner. She'd cooked roast beef and vegetables and it looked like it might be the highlight of my day. The other highlight was the fact that Carla's mother was easy to get along with.

"Yes!" Carla exclaimed and I took in her excitement. We hadn't had much time to talk during the day so I had no clue what this was about. "He offered me a job."

"Doing what, darlin'?" I asked.

"Jack and I attended the same college and he loves the designs I did for various projects. He wants me to come on board as a designer in a new company he's building. It's an online business. He's ready to go now so I'll start working on designs tomorrow. The best thing is that I can work from home."

"That's great, Carla," Velvet said, throwing her a smile. Nash's woman had impressed me so far. She'd welcomed me without any bitching and had tried to pull

Nash into line when he'd started to grumble some shit at me.

"What about your studies?" Nash asked.

Carla's smile seeped from her face. "I'm going to do that subject again next semester, but I'm not looking forward to it because I'll probably have the same teacher."

My skin crawled with anger at the mention of that asshole. I'd asked her for his information a few times and she'd fobbed me off and told me Nash would help her. I was sure she hadn't given the info to Nash either, though. "If you get that same teacher, he and I *will* be having words."

"I'm with Havoc on that," Nash said, surprising the fuck out of me. "And while we're on that subject, you need to be giving me his name regardless. I'd like to give him a piece of my mind."

The smile returned to Carla's face. "Wow, something you guys have in common. Who would have thought, huh, Nash?"

He scowled but didn't respond.

"Right, eat up before it goes cold," Linda instructed as I made a mental note to force that information from Carla.

Linda was a hell of a cook. The roast was one of the best I'd ever had and that was saying something because my mother had been a great cook.

My enjoyment of her food was cut short when a loud bang sounded from outside, as if there was someone in the yard.

Nash and I pushed our chairs back and stood in unison. I ignored the glare he gave me and followed him outside through the back door.

"Stay there and don't come outside," he ordered the girls over his shoulder.

There was no light in the back yard but plenty of noise. "Definitely someone out here," I said.

"I've got this, Havoc. You can go back inside and keep an eye on the girls."

"Don't be a dick, Nash," I muttered, tired of his carry on.

He abruptly stopped and I almost ran into him as he turned to face me. "I don't know what the fuck you thought you were doing coming here tonight. And *this*"— he swung his arms out to the side to indicate he was talking about our search—"I sure as shit can look out for my women on my own. Been doing it my whole life and I'm gonna continue to do it. *Especially* when you screw my sister over." He thumped his hand on his chest. "*I'm* the one who's always there to pick up the fuckin' pieces for her. And I'm warning you now, you fuck her up and I'll fuck *you* up."

I couldn't be angry with him when I'd be saying the exact same thing if it were my sister. "*If* I fuck her up, come at me. Because I'll deserve everything you do to me.

Carla means something to me, Nash, and I'm gonna work hard not to screw that up."

"She means *something* to you? She should mean the fuckin' world to you, and if you can't see that happening in the near future, you need to get the hell out of this relationship before it even gets off the ground." His unhappiness rolled off him, even in the dark.

"I can see it happening."

My words took him by surprise and he blinked and snapped his mouth shut.

I decided to explain myself—something I did for no one, but I felt Nash needed it if he was ever going to think about backing off from me and Carla. "You know my history with Kelly, which means you know that before she fucked me over, I gave her everything in that relationship. Anything she needed to be happy, I found a way to get her. Back then, I wasn't the asshole I am now. I let life and the shit it threw my way sidetrack me, and I let it turn my heart cold. Getting to know Carla has changed me and opened my eyes. I want more in life again. And I want it with Carla."

Something I said must have hit home for him. His permanent scowl disappeared. "You've got one shot. You screw it up, I'm not going back for seconds. Carla might, but I won't give you that."

I blew out a long breath and nodded. "I'll take it."

A rustling noise down the side of the house distracted us and Nash took off in that direction with me following close. I hoped we caught whoever it was. I figured we could both do with the opportunity to take our frustrations out on them.

As we rounded the corner of the house into the front yard, the front door light illuminated the area and horror engulfed me as I came face-to-face with Paul, the guy who'd been stealing off Jackson Jones. He had Carla by the throat with a knife and pure evil blazed in his eyes.

"Fuck!" Nash bellowed and as he took a step forward to go to them, I reached out and pulled him back. This was my shit and I would deal with it.

"Hey, asshole," Paul yelled at me. "How does it feel? Having someone you care about threatened? Because that's what you did to me! You took my fucking life and trashed it."

I held up my hands as I slowly advanced towards him. "She means nothing to me. Do whatever the fuck you want with her."

Carla's eyes widened in fear.

The words grated on their way out of my mouth. I could only imagine how they sounded to her, but I figured Paul was out to hurt me and if he thought she meant nothing, I hoped he would let her go.

His brows lifted as he drew a tiny amount of blood from her neck.

Fuck.

As she winced, pain sliced through my heart.

No fucking way was he going to hurt her.

"Don't you fuckin' hurt her!" Nash thundered, shoving past me.

Linda and Velvet screamed from the doorway and a moment later, Velvet ran down the front steps. Nash's attention was diverted for a moment as he tried to hold her back. I ran towards Paul, desperate to move Carla out of the way.

"Motherfucker!" Paul screamed, clinging to Carla while he slashed the knife in the air. This made it impossible for me to get to her.

She fought him, trying to unlock his arm from around her neck, but his grip was strong. In the background, I heard Nash and Velvet arguing.

Everything happened so fast.

Paul and Carla struggling.

Nash moving towards us.

Linda screaming.

Finally, Nash managed to get behind him while I had his attention in the front. Nash punched him hard enough for his hold on Carla to loosen, which allowed me to shove her to the side. She fell to the ground and I shifted my gaze to her for only a moment, to make sure she was okay, before turning back to Paul.

He'd dropped the knife so I punched him as hard as I could in the gut.

"Fuck!" he roared as he stumbled backwards into Nash.

Nash's hands curled around his biceps and he held him in place while I moved closer. "What the fuck made you think it was a good idea to come here?" I demanded.

Paul's upper lip raised in a snarl. "Marnie's lying dead in a hospital morgue. *That's* what made me come here. When I saw you at that biker clubhouse today, I was fucking ecstatic. I'd been waiting for you, wondering how long it would take for you to show up there."

I jabbed my finger at his chest. "That shit is on you, not me. You stole from Jackson and you chose to date his ex knowing how he felt about that kind of thing."

Paul struggled in Nash's hold. "Settle the fuck down!" Nash thundered, tightening his grip.

Paul didn't settle down, though, and continued to fight against Nash. The anger pushing at the inside of my skull intensified.

He'd come here and threatened Carla.

No fucking way would he walk away from this.

My fists clenched.

Red blurred my vision.

Heat exploded through me as my anger burned.

My fist connected with his face. The crack of his bone rang through the night air. His head lolled to the side and blood oozed down his cheek.

Nash let go and pushed him to the ground. His angry eyes found mine. "What the fuck was all that about?"

I was more concerned with ensuring Paul was unable to hurt Carla. Ignoring Nash, I kicked Paul, rolling him onto his back. His eyes fluttered open and he groaned, but no words left his mouth. I watched as his eyes closed again and was confident I'd knocked him out enough to move him to another location. Away from Carla's house so I could deal with him once and for all.

"Are you gonna fuckin' tell me what that was about?" Nash roared, every muscle in his body tense with fury.

"That was tied to a job I did for King. Can you settle the fuck down so we can deal with this?" I snapped.

He shoved his fingers through his hair. "Jesus!" Jabbing his finger in Paul's direction, he said, "That shit should never have made its way to my house."

Carla inserted herself between us. "This is not *your* house, Nash. And give Havoc a break, it's not like he could control that asshole." She glared at Nash as her breaths came hard and fast.

I loved her determination, but I didn't want her fighting my battles.

"I agree, Nash, and I'll take care of him so he never has another opportunity like this again. Now, are you gonna help me or are you gonna continue with your bullshit?" As I said this, I attempted to move Carla from between us but she refused to budge.

Shrugging out of my hold, her angry gaze met Nash's.

"This is why I don't want you with Havoc!" he yelled at her. "He's mixed up with a lot of shit and it could blow back on you, like this has."

"Oh, for fuck's sake, can you hear yourself? You are so hypocritical! Havoc is involved with the same stuff you are," she argued back.

I reached for her arm and turned her to face me. "Babe—" I started, but Carla's eyes widened as she looked past me.

Her hand flew to her mouth and she screamed, "Havoc! No!"

I spun around to see what had caught her eye and came face-to-face with Paul again. He'd regained consciousness while we'd been arguing and held the knife in his hand. He had the same look of evil in his eye as before.

"Fuck you." He snarled as he stabbed the knife at me.

Hot, piercing pain radiated from just below my chest.

Heat I never imagined ever feeling.

"Oh, my God, Havoc!" Carla's cry penetrated my subconscious, but I couldn't respond.

The last thing I remembered seeing was Paul going down after Nash punched him.

Chapter Twenty-Six
Carla

"That was a huge knife, Nash, and there was so much blood! And why the fuck is it taking so long for the doctor to come out and tell us what's happening?" My skin itched and my chest felt like it would explode from the onslaught of emotions raging through me. Fear, anger, frustration, hatred. I wanted to kill the man who had done this to Havoc.

Nash's strong arms circled me and he pulled me close. "Havoc's a fighter, babe. I've seen him survive fights I didn't think he'd pull through on. And he's in the best possible place."

"Nash is right," Velvet agreed. "And the doctors are busy working on him. You don't want to drag them away from what they're doing."

I stared at them. "It's been hours!" All my fears collided and I could no longer hold back my tears.

I can't lose him.

Nash held me until my tears stopped. "Like Velvet said, the doctors are looking after him and they'll be out when they have news. And I'm sure it'll be good news." His words surprised me. He'd been so angry with Havoc when Paul threatened me. The gentle tone he'd just used was a vast change.

When I pulled out of his embrace, I whispered, "Thank you."

He nodded and let me go. "I need coffee. You want one?"

"Yes, please."

He pointed at the seats. "Take a load off and don't go anywhere." He took drink orders from Mum and Velvet and then left us.

I watched him leave before taking a seat next to Mum. She slid her arm over my shoulders and pulled me close. "Havoc means a lot to you, doesn't he?"

Nodding, I replied, "Yes. More than I realised."

"I think he's good for you, baby. I've never seen you so happy with a man before."

I rested my head on her shoulder and closed my eyes. It had been a long night and exhaustion embraced me. I wanted to stay awake for Havoc but the act of resting my head caused my body to relax.

Mum murmured something but her words floated past without me deciphering them.

Havoc has to survive this.

I need him.

"Carla Walker?"

My eyes snapped open and I lifted my head.

When I saw a doctor approaching, I jumped out of my seat. "Yes."

My breathing slowed when I took in the grim expression on his face, but I fought to remain calm. Who knew, maybe he always looked like that?

"I wanted to give you an update on your partner," he said. I had to tell them Havoc was my partner for them to give me any information. "He's had a significant liver laceration that has resulted in massive internal bleeding. The severe blood loss caused his blood pressure to drop dangerously low. We've given him a blood transfusion to replace the lost blood volume and prevent his body from going into shock."

Internal bleeding.

Blood transfusions.

Going into shock.

The room spun while my brain processed all that.

This can't be happening.

"Miss, are you okay?" The doctor took hold of my elbow and encouraged me to sit again.

"Carla." My mother's voice dragged me from my haze and I blinked as she came into focus. "Take a deep breath, baby."

I sucked in as much air as I could.

I can't breathe.

The doctor gently touched my arm. "We'll let you know when we have new information."

As soon as I nodded, he left.

Just like that.

I didn't know what I was looking for from him, but it wasn't any of that.

Havoc was stabbed.

Stabbed!

People die from that.

What else were you expecting?

The room spun and the darkness engulfed me.

★★★

"Carla."

Nash.

"Carla, can you hear me?"

A hand rested against my cheek and I flinched awake. Nash's face hovered above mine and I took in the deep frown settled on it. "I can hear you," I mumbled as I tried to get my bearings.

He moved his face and slid his arms under my armpits. Lifting me off the floor, he settled me on a seat and crouched in front of me. "You fainted and fell off the chair. Luckily, Mum kinda caught you so that your head didn't hit the floor. How are you feeling?"

I touched my head. "I'm fine." My fear for Havoc crept back to me. It was funny how someone could come into your life so unexpectedly and then be such an important part of it so fast. I had that deep-in-my-bones feeling that I would be heartbroken if something happened to Havoc.

Nash's eyes searched mine before he stood. Passing me a bottle of water, he said, "I've gotta go and deal with some club shit. Will you be okay for awhile without me?"

"Has something happened?"

A look crossed his face as if he was carefully weighing his next words. "Let's just say that once we're done, Havoc won't have to worry about being stabbed again."

I knew what he was saying. I was sure it should have caused some sort of emotion in me, disbelief perhaps, but the only emotion it triggered was relief. And it felt like justice.

"I'll be good. Don't worry about me. You just go and take care of what you need to." I reached for his hand and added, "Thank you."

He spoke with Velvet for a few moments before kissing her goodbye and leaving the three of us alone. Nash had left a message with Havoc's sister, but so far, we hadn't heard from her. I knew his dad was in hospital, but I didn't know which one. I hoped his sister would arrive soon because his father needed to know what had happened.

Mum, Velvet and I sat waiting for the doctor for what felt like an eternity, but in reality was just over two more hours. Two hours were a long time when you were waiting for the kind of news we were waiting for.

As the doctor approached, I bolted out of my seat.

Same doctor.

Same grim look on his face.

My heart sped up.

"Tell me it's good news." The words gushed out of my mouth.

He nodded, but the grim expression he wore didn't change. "He's out of surgery and will be moved to intensive care where we'll monitor his vitals. His condition is serious, but for now he is stable."

"So he's going to be okay?" *Please say yes.*

"It's too soon to say for sure, but he's stable for now. We need to keep an eye on his liver enzymes and make sure his blood pressure stabilises."

Oh, God.

He's not saying yes.

I stared at him, willing him to say something else, something good, but in the end, all he said was, "If you want, you can head up to ICU now and wait for him. It will still be some time before you'll be able to see him, but if you let the nurses know when you get there, they'll notify you as soon as you can go in."

My words were captive in my throat, so Mum thanked the doctor. My heart crumbled as he left.

Dizziness circled my head and my legs threatened to give out on me.

He's going to be okay.

He will pull through.

He has to.

My chest tightened with fear.

What if he doesn't?

Chapter Twenty-Seven
Carla

"Here, I got you coffee," Nash said as he sat next to me and handed me a takeaway coffee.

"Thanks."

After I took a sip, I stretched my back. The clock on the waiting room wall told me it was just after 5 a.m. We'd been at the hospital for about nine hours and I could hardly keep my eyes open. I didn't want to sleep, though. I wanted to be awake when the nurse came to tell us he was conscious.

They'd allowed us in briefly once they had him settled in the ICU, but he'd been connected to tubes and had been sedated. He hadn't looked like the strong, dominating man I knew, and it had thrown me. I'd visited loved ones in hospital before but seeing Havoc lying on that bed unconscious with all those tubes was too much. The knowledge he could die had slapped me in the face.

I wanted to rip those tubes out and shake him back to life.

I wanted to take back the invitation to dinner at my mum's. If he hadn't been there he would never have been stabbed.

I would have given anything to have him bossing me around again.

I'd been talking to God for the last few hours, promising all sorts of things if Havoc pulled through this. Hell, I'd even promised not to argue with everyone as much—something I knew I'd struggle with because arguing and me went together.

"You should think about heading home and getting some rest," Nash said. He'd returned an hour earlier and had sent Velvet and Mum home to get some sleep. We still hadn't heard from Havoc's sister, which continued to concern me.

"No. I want to be here when he wakes up."

"I know, but I can call you when he does and you can come straight back."

I held his gaze. "I'm not leaving, Nash, so don't keep on me about this, okay?"

He gave me the almost-scowl that he gave me when he was frustrated and nodded. "He better fuckin' appreciate your concern for him."

"A bit like yours, right?" He'd impressed me with the way he'd been at the hospital and taking care of club shit for Havoc. But I knew from the tone he'd just taken that he was still in denial about how he felt.

His almost-scowl morphed into a full scowl. "I'm here for you, not him."

I was tired and over his issues. Sighing, I said, "Nash, you guys are club brothers. You've known him for years and had each other's backs for as long. I don't understand why you can't get past this bullshit."

"I don't think you will ever understand the level of responsibility I feel for you, Carla. As far as I'm concerned, I'm gonna be looking out for you till the day I die. Any man who wants to be with you will have to jump through fuckin' hoops to get my approval, because over my dead body will I allow another man to harm you the way our father has."

His eyes held a depth of emotion I rarely saw from him and I reached for his hand. "One of these days you're going to realise you get more with honey than vinegar, Nash Walker. I love you for looking out for me, and I know we will never stop pissing each other off, but I need to tell you that if you were to share your heart more like you just did rather than getting all bossy and assholey, we'd get along so much better."

His eyes softened. "Assholey fits me better, babe."

I swatted him. "Ask Velvet what *she* thinks. I'm sure she'll agree with me."

He grinned the trademark Nash grin. "I'm sure I could persuade her not to."

I shook my head. My brother always had a way of making me smile and forgive his annoying ways.

He put his arm around my shoulders and pulled me close. "If you won't go home, I want you to put your head on my shoulder, close your eyes and get some sleep." His eyes met mine and his grin was gone. "No arguments."

"God, always so assholey," I muttered, but I did as he said.

Weariness had claimed me and I knew I *needed* sleep, even if I didn't want it.

"That's because you're always so damn argumentative. I bet Havoc would agree with me on that."

I smiled.

He was softening; it would just take him some time to admit it.

★★★

Voices pulled me from a deep sleep and I blinked as I straightened.

"I'm Havoc's sister, Yvette."

I squinted. The sun streamed through the window of the waiting area straight into my eyes, obstructing my view of the woman speaking.

Nash removed his arm from my shoulders and stood. Extending his hand to her, he said, "Nash. We were wondering where you were."

Yvette grimaced. "My phone battery died and I wasn't at home to charge it. Worst timing." She looked in the direction of the ICU before turning back to us. "Is he awake? And what the hell happened? I couldn't really make out too much in your message except for the fact he was here."

I could see Havoc in her. And not only in her facial features, but also in her cut-to-the-chase manner. She also looked like the kind of woman who could take care of herself. Her body was packed with muscle that looked like it took hours in the gym to build. Just like Havoc. And she appeared to be a no-fuss woman. Her clothes were not feminine at all, jeans and a T-shirt, and her hair was cut in a short style that wouldn't require much effort in the morning.

Nash relayed what had happened while I stretched and drank some water. I watched while he explained it all to her and while concern shone in her eyes, she didn't appear to be surprised. I wondered how often Havoc had gotten himself into trouble over the years.

After Nash filled her in, she turned to me. "You must be Havoc's new woman."

"He's told you about me?" I was surprised.

She shook her head. "No, my brother doesn't share shit easily, but I picked it."

Something about what she'd said caused my tummy to flutter. I loved that his sister could sense that he had a woman.

I extended my hand. "I'm Carla. Nash's sister."

As she shook my hand, she said, "Good to meet you. Promise me you'll pull my brother into line."

I raised a brow. "I'm not sure he's the kind of man to be pulled into line."

"You might be surprised. I know he's a force of nature, but something tells me you might just have a shot."

If he survives.

A wave of worry hit me all over again.

"Carla."

I spun around at the sound of my name.

A nurse looked at me with kind eyes and I shot another prayer up to God that those eyes were kind because she had good news and not because she had to tell me something bad.

"Is he awake?"

Please say yes.

I'll do anything, God.

Anything.

She smiled. "Yes, he's awake. He's still a little groggy, but he asked for you."

Oh, my God.

Relief coursed through my body and I felt a little lightheaded. I reached for Nash to hold onto. "So I can come in now?"

She continued to smile. "Yes, but only for a quick visit. Follow me." She eyed Nash and Yvette. "I can only take two in."

Nash indicated for Yvette to go with me and we followed the nurse. My legs were shaky and my breathing had picked up.

He's awake.

He's okay.

Thank you, God.

The nurse led us through the ICU and as we approached Havoc's bed, I took a deep breath at the sight of him. Even in his wounded, groggy state, his eyes tracked me and he had that intense aura that was all Havoc.

"Carla," he said, his voice raspy.

I moved to the bed and placed my hand on his arm. "I was so worried." As my words came out, my tears fell. I couldn't hold them back.

"Angel," he murmured as he gripped my arm. His face contorted in pain, but he didn't let me go. "I'm not going anywhere."

Tears flowed down my cheeks and I nodded. Burying my face in his neck, I clung to him until I stopped crying. When I let him go, I took in his expression. He'd never looked at me that way before. It was a softer Havoc, and while he'd given me soft once or twice, it had nothing on this.

This soft told me he wanted me.

It cleared up any doubt I had.

"Thank fuck you're not going anywhere. I want to see this woman pull you into line," Yvette said.

Havoc's lips twitched. "I see you've met my sister," he said to me. "Don't mind her, she's a smartass."

"I take after my brother," she quipped.

Their banter reminded me of my family. I loved listening to them because although they were sparring, it was clear they felt deeply for each other.

He'd been groggy and in pain when we'd come in and it looked to me like he was struggling to continue the conversation. But Havoc being Havoc pushed through. Always the fighter.

When they finished talking, I touched his cheek. "You should go back to sleep."

"I'm good," he said.

I shook my head. "No, you're not. You need your rest."

He started to argue with me, but Yvette stepped in. "Sleep. We'll be outside when you wake." Bossy like her brother. I loved that.

I pressed a kiss to his lips and promised, "I'll see you when you wake up."

He nodded and closed his eyes.

A minute later, he was asleep.

I battled conflicting emotions—happiness that he was okay and worry that he was still fighting for his health.

★★★

"You didn't call me to say he'd woken up," I accused Nash later that day. I'd gone home just after I'd seen Havoc and slept. Nash had promised to call me when he had news. When I'd woken at five, I'd been pissed off that he hadn't called.

He shook his head. "He hasn't woken up again, Carla. So I let you sleep."

"What do you mean he hasn't woken up again?" I demanded.

"Exactly that. He's slept all day."

Alarm spiked through me. "Are the doctors doing something? Why is he still asleep? What did they say?"

He placed his hands on my shoulders. "Calm down, babe. They're saying he's sedated and still stable. And they've run his bloods a few times to check his levels. I'm sure if there was something to worry about, they would have told us."

I took a deep breath. "Okay." Looking around the waiting room, I asked, "Where's Yvette?"

"She's with their father, but will be back here later." His gaze shifted to look past me. Jerking his chin, he said, "Scott."

I turned to find Scott Cole approaching. I'd met him a few times over the years and he'd always struck me as a moody guy, but Nash was pretty close to him so I figured he couldn't be too bad.

"Nash," he returned the greeting before eyeing me. "Hi, Carla. How's Havoc?"

"He's stable."

But not awake.

"Good." He turned his attention to Nash. "You got a minute, brother?"

"You okay here?" Nash asked me and I nodded.

"Thanks," Scott said. "J will be by later to check on him."

As they walked out into the corridor, I sat. Thankful the waiting room was empty, I allowed my tears to fall. I wasn't the kind of woman to cry often. Usually when shit wasn't going my way I fought back. But this situation didn't give me that opportunity.

I couldn't fix this.

Instead, I'd have to dig deep and get myself together.

Havoc needed me to be strong for him when he couldn't be strong for himself.

★★★

Havoc drifted in and out of consciousness that night and the next day. The doctors kept drawing blood to check his levels and they kept telling us he was stable.

Stable.

I fucking hated that word by the end of the second day.

Why couldn't they give us something more?

All I wanted to hear was that he was going to be okay, but whenever I asked that question, they gave me their standard answer.

Stable.

Fucking stable.

I refused to go home again. I'd hated leaving him that first day. I wasn't doing it again. I put work on hold and took up residence at the hospital. This meant Nash and I bickered constantly. He came and went a few times, and whenever he visited, he tried to boss me into leaving. In the end, Mum got sick of it and told him to leave if he was going to keep arguing with me.

So by the end of the second day, he and I sat next to each other, arms folded over our chests, both of us with a scowl on our faces.

"Fuck, hospitals suck," I declared, blowing out a harsh breath.

"Won't argue with you there, babe," Nash agreed.

It was nearing 9 p.m. and we were alone after Mum and Velvet had gone home for the night, and Yvette had left us to grab some dinner.

"Do you believe in heaven?" I asked.

"Yeah."

"And hell?"

"Yep."

"So you believe in God and the Devil and all that?" We'd never had this conversation and besides killing time, I was interested to know his beliefs.

"Yes. I have to."

I turned to him. "Because of Aaron?" His son who had died.

"I believe Aaron is in heaven and I believe it's a better place than Earth. It's the only thing that got me through some bad days." I heard the raw emotion in his voice.

I placed my hand over his. "He's definitely in a better place, Nash. And you're going to see him again one day."

His jaw clenched and I knew this had turned into a hard conversation for him. I loved him all the more for continuing it. "Yeah."

The doors to the ICU opened at that moment and a nurse walked our way. "Carla?" she asked.

"Is he awake?"

She nodded and I almost sagged in relief. "Yes, you can come through and see him."

Nash gripped my hand and pulled me up. We followed her in and a couple of minutes later, I was looking at the man who had taken up a lot of space in my heart.

"Darlin'."

It was one word, but it meant the world to me.

He looked better and sounded better.

And I felt it in my bones.

He's going to make it.

Chapter Twenty-Eight
Havoc

"So they're letting you out today?" Scott said as he settled himself on the end of my hospital bed. He, J and Nash had arrived five minutes earlier and they'd all made themselves at home in the tiny room I'd called home for far too many days.

"Yeah, thank fuck," I muttered. If I'd had to spend one more night in the hospital I would have gone crazy. Being cooped up in one place for any length of time tended to do that to me.

"I'm gonna drop in on your Dad this afternoon," J said. "Make sure he's doing okay."

I had to give them credit, Storm had really come through for me and my family since I'd been in hospital. They'd checked up on not only me each day, but also Dad, and they'd gotten him home yesterday. Yvette had been called out of town for work so J had helped out.

"Thanks, brother," I replied.

"Nothing you wouldn't do for me," he said. I wasn't sure of that though. A few years ago I would have agreed, but I'd changed since then. Maybe not for the better.

I eyed Nash who stood at the end of the bed scowling. He hadn't said a word since arriving. Hell, he'd hardly spoken to me since I'd regained consciousness days ago except to express his anger again over the fact I'd put Carla in danger.

"I heard from King this morning," Scott said, dragging my attention from Nash. "He said to tell you to get better fast, he's got more work coming up for you soon."

Nash rested his hands on the bed and bent forward. "You planning on sticking around or are you gonna do what you do best and walk away from everything and everyone?" His hard voice vibrated around the room as he glared at me waiting for my answer.

I shifted in the bed and winced at the pain that shot through my body. "Do I look like I'm able to leave anytime soon?" I threw back, my voice just as harsh as his.

"I'm thinking long-term and I'm wondering just how long you plan on letting Carla think you're gonna stay."

"And I'm just thinking about getting through my recovery," I snapped. My chest tightened at the same time my pulse quickened.

I don't want to think about this.

"Let's just take one thing at a time," Scott suggested, his forehead creasing in a frown as he looked at Nash.

Nash pushed off from the end of the bed and took a step back, still glaring at me. "You need to get your shit figured out, Havoc, and fast because Carla's investing herself in you now. She's been at this fuckin' hospital day in and day out, and she's put her new job on hold all that time." He raked his fingers through his hair before adding, "I knew this would fuckin' happen!"

"Nothing has happened, Nash," J said.

Nash threw his hand out in the air, gesturing at me while staring wildly at J. "Did you not see the way he wouldn't commit to staying? That tells you every-fuckin-thing."

"Coffee anyone?" We all turned to find Madison standing in the doorway holding four coffees.

"Thank fuck," Scott muttered as he stalked to her.

Nash didn't move. He remained at the end of the bed, his glare never leaving mine. No more words were exchanged but it was clear where we both stood.

The step forward we'd taken before I was stabbed had been erased and a step back had replaced it.

As much as he pissed me off, I knew he was right.

Carla was invested.

And I had to figure out my next move.

I wanted her in my life.

I just had to find out a way to make that work for both of us.

★★★

"Sit there and don't move!"

I quirked a brow at Carla. "Bossy is fuckin' hot on you, darlin', but don't get too used to it. Give me a week and I'll be back to full strength."

She placed her hand on her hip and hit me with a look that screamed her doubt. "Oh, really, Mr I've-Got-No-Fucking-Idea? The doctor said it will be around four weeks before you can even contemplate getting back on your bike, maybe longer. So I'm not sure how you think you'll be back to your normal self in one week."

I'd come home from hospital two days ago, a day after my father had also come home. Yvette had to go away for a week for work, so Carla had taken it upon herself to move in for the week to help Dad and me while we recovered. I hadn't argued. The thought of having her with me twenty-four seven made me happy.

We were battling over my desire to help her cook dinner. I didn't want her doing everything around the house, but that was exactly what she'd been doing for the past forty-eight hours.

I slid my hand around her waist and tried to pull her to me. Pain shot through my body and I did my best not to show it. When she moved closer, I said, "Do you really think it's gonna take me that long to recover? Not fuckin' likely."

She placed her hands on my chest, being careful not to touch my wound and to only touch me very gently.

Fuck, she's treating me with fucking kid gloves.

I hated that.

"Havoc, you're not invincible. You have to let me help you for awhile." Her voice was soft and reminded me that she was going through this too. I might have suffered the pain and would be the one to do the physical recovery, but she'd suffered the mental and emotional turmoil that went with it.

I dropped a kiss onto her lips. "Okay."

Her eyes widened. "Why was that so easy?"

I chuckled. "Fuck knows."

Dad entered the kitchen. "Is he giving you shit, sweetheart?"

Carla grinned. She and Dad hit it off the minute they met. They'd bonded over their mutual goal of making my life hell during my recovery. "He's always giving me shit, Al."

Dad nodded as he reached into the fridge for some juice. "Sounds like my son."

I sat at the table where she'd told me to. "Pass me the potatoes. I'll peel and chop them."

"I've got this," Carla said, clearly exasperated with me. "You just sit there and rest."

I decided to give her that even though it went against every one of my instincts.

Dad sat with me because she'd made it clear to both of us that she didn't want our help around the house while we recovered. The doctors had sent him home with instructions to improve his eating and exercise. He'd stopped caring about either of those things over the past couple of months. A psychologist had spent some time with him while in hospital. She confirmed my fears that he'd given up on life. I'd expected him to come home in a cranky mood, and he had, but it hadn't lasted long. Carla had snapped him out of it pretty fast while I'd sat in awe of her skills.

"Heard that bed creakin' last night," he said. "Pretty sure the doc wouldn't be too happy about that." The old man always tried to stir shit up.

Carla threw me a wink and replied, "Al, for an old man you've got good hearing, but I can assure you Havoc wasn't doing any of the work."

"There was no fuckin' work going on, darlin', and that was the only problem about last night," I grumbled. The doctor had given me strict instructions for no sex until at least my next appointment, which was in five days. They'd discuss it then and see how I was. I'd tried to talk Carla into a little action, but she was strictly following his orders.

"She's just like your mother, son. No way would she go near my dick if the doctor told her not to. Bloody women."

Carla laughed while I shook my head. "Dad, I'm all for sex and shit, but hearing about you and mum and your dick isn't on my list of things I ever need to know."

He shrugged. "Carla doesn't seem to mind."

"Nope, you talk about whatever you want, Al. I'm actually a bit surprised at your son. For a man who has the dirtiest mouth I've ever heard and all the right moves, you'd think he could talk about dicks till the cows come home."

Dad grinned at me. Jerking his thumb at her, he said, "She's a keeper, boy. You need a woman like her to keep you in line."

I watched the smile spread across her face while Dad sat in front of me with a grin on his. For the first time in fuck knew how long, a sense of peace settled over me.

This was what happiness looked like.

I'd forgotten that somewhere along the way.

★★★

"Havoc!" Carla pushed my hands away. "No sex!"

I groaned. "You got any idea how hard my dick has been for days?" It had been four days since I'd come home and she'd pushed me away every fucking night. My cock had been permanently hard the whole time. I'd whacked off in the shower that morning after she'd refused me again.

We were lying in bed and at my question, she sat and faced me. She eyed the bandages over my wound before giving me her gaze. "I'm lucky to even have the possibility of your dick, Havoc. You nearly died on me and that was one of the scariest things I've ever lived through. And up until that point, I hadn't realised how much I wanted you in my life. You're a closed-off, moody, bossy man who doesn't fit into any life plan I've ever made for myself, but fuck, I realised I want to throw all those plans out the window and make *you* my new plan. And as for your complaints about no sex, I don't care how much you grumble. I'm not going anywhere near your dick until the doctor tells you it's completely safe for me to do so."

I soaked her words in.

Hell, she was fucking spectacular. And as much as I grumbled and carried on during my recovery at her tendency to fight me at every turn, I loved the shit out of the way she stood up to me.

A piece of her hair had fallen across her face so I pushed it behind her ear. "Who fuckin' knew I'd love a bossy woman? I'm not down with a permanent hard-on that you won't touch, but I love everything else you just said."

A smile slowly worked its way across her face and she bit her lip. A moment ago, she'd passionately stood up to me and now she looked at me with a vulnerability that made me want her more than I already did.

"You do?"

Fuck, her doubt slayed me.

I ignored the pain it caused and moved to a sitting position. Jerking my chin, I indicated for her to straddle my lap, which she did, with reluctance. Running my finger down her cheek, I said, "I do. I know I can be a pain in the ass most days, but I want to be in any life plan you make. I'm figuring my shit out as we go but I want to be the man you need by your side while you're out there kicking ass. I never saw this thing between us coming, but I'm sure as shit gonna do everything I can to keep it."

She took hold of my hand that was near her cheek. "Me too," she whispered.

I brushed a kiss across her lips. Her mouth opened and let me in. God, this had to be one of the best places in the world to be. Kissing Carla was almost as good for me as burying my dick in her. I loved the connection I felt when our lips joined.

She pulled away, breathless. "We need to stop or else neither of us are going to be able to."

I grinned. "That was kinda my intention, angel."

"I know."

"Next time I'll make sure my injury doesn't prevent me from fucking you."

Her body shook with laughter. "I'm pretty sure you think about your cock for about twenty-three hours of a day."

"I'm pretty sure my cock is all *you* think about for those twenty-three hours too."

"And why are you so sure about that? What proof do you have?"

I threaded my fingers through her hair. "I'm sure about that because you have the dirtiest mouth and mind of any woman I've ever met. It's like you were made for me and if that's the case, then I know the shit that runs through your mind."

Her eyes searched mine. "Soul mates," she whispered.

I'd never believed in soul mates, but I figured if there was ever a woman who'd been made as mine, it had to be her.

★★★

I pulled Carla close to lay a kiss on her before she left for the day. Cupping her pussy, I growled, "Tonight, angel. This is mine." Fuck, it couldn't come fast enough. I had my post-op ten-day follow up that day and the doctor would be giving her the permission she'd been holding out for.

Her eyes glazed over with the same desire I felt. "Havoc, he might say no."

"I don't give a flying fuck what he says. Tonight, I *will* be fucking my woman."

She didn't argue with me. Instead, she gave me another kiss and said, "I'll be back by three to take you to your appointment. Don't kill your father in the meantime."

"Smartass." I smacked her butt on her way out and then headed into the kitchen to see how Dad was going with his breakfast.

He looked up as I entered. "Carla gone?"

I nodded. "Yeah. What plans have you got for the day?"

"Nothing planned, son."

I nodded towards his bowl of cereal that Carla had gotten him. "You gonna eat that?" His eating habits had improved but he still didn't eat enough as far as I was concerned.

"I'm not hungry." He pushed the bowl away.

I pushed it back towards him. "Dad, you need to eat."

He scowled. "I'll eat later."

Frustration caused me to lose my shit. I slammed my hand down on the kitchen table. "Why have you given up?"

He didn't even flinch. He just stared at me through sad eyes. Silence filled the room for a few minutes while we sat and watched each other. Eventually he said, "I miss her, Havoc." *Mum.*

Fuck.

His words were honest and raw and I couldn't fault him for his feelings.

I nodded. "I know. I miss her, too. But Yvette and I are still here and we need you."

"No you don't. You left and made a new life. Yvette's got her woman and is making a life with her. You don't need me."

I rubbed the back of my neck. "Jesus, Dad, that's not true."

"Isn't it? You left, Havoc. Without a backwards glance. That's true."

The resentment his words carried hit me in the gut. I'd never stopped to think about anyone when I left. My pain had been too great. "There was so much going on back then. Losing my business because my best friend screwed me over and stole from me was a kick in the guts I never thought I'd recover from, especially when I had to file for bankruptcy. I thought I had Kelly to fall back on, but then she walked away. That shit fucked with my mind, Dad. When Mum died, it killed me. I wanted to die. I wanted to give up, just like you are, but that's not in me to do, so I gave up in every other way. I'm sorry I didn't come to you and ask for the help I needed to get through that."

"I offered you the money to pull your business out of the shit it was in. You should have taken it," he said and I felt his pain that I hadn't allowed him to do that for me.

"I couldn't, Dad. I couldn't be the one responsible for anything happening to you if I never paid you back."

"That's what parents do for their kids, son. We'd go to the ends of the Earth if we had to, even if it meant we had to walk over hot coals and swim with fucking sharks. I hated seeing you drowning. *That* killed me, maybe more than losing your mother."

Fuck.

I'd fucked up.

But that was the thing about life: sometimes shit didn't go the way you planned and you dealt with it the best you could at the time. Learning to live with our decisions was the key. Because if we looked back all the time and regretted shit, we'd just end up living with a whole lot of bitterness and disappointment.

I reached for his hand. "We can't go back. We can only go forward. I'm here now and I'm not going anywhere anytime soon. I'm here for you and I'm here for Yvette. And watching you give up isn't something I'm willing to do."

He took that in and spent a few minutes thinking it over. "You're a stubborn ass, just like your mother."

I pushed his bowl of cereal closer to him.

He scowled but he picked up the spoon and took a mouthful.

Yeah, I was a stubborn ass.

But it was one of my best traits.

Chapter Twenty-Nine
Carla

I stared in disbelief at the letter from my college.

They didn't have a spare place for me in the subject I needed to repeat.

This fucked with my life plan.

What fucking life plan?

You threw that out the window.

"Fuck!" I threw the letter down on the table. "Now what the hell am I going to do?" I yelled.

Havoc entered the kitchen. Frowning, he asked, "What's wrong?"

I snapped my head up to look at him. "I didn't get into the class I needed. My plan is ruined!" Panic began to set in. What the hell was I going to do?

He closed the distance between us. "I know you've had your heart set on this for a long time, but just because you didn't get in this time doesn't mean you won't get in next time. You can reapply, right?"

I nodded. But he didn't understand. "It's not as simple as that. This had to happen so the next step in the plan could happen."

He took hold of my shoulders. "I get it, babe, trust me, I get it. I had a plan once, too. And I worked that fucking plan like it was the only thing that mattered in life. In the end, none of it mattered."

"Do you mean with your business?"

"Yeah."

"What happened there? You never told me how you lost the business."

His jaw clenched as he let go of me. "My best friend did my books for the business. He fudged my tax returns for years without me knowing and pocketed the cash that should have been paid in taxes. When the tax office clued on, I got hit with a huge tax bill which wiped me out."

"God, what a shitty friend." The magnitude of what he'd been through during that time in his life hit me, and suddenly, my fucked-up life plan didn't seem so bad.

"Yeah. Needless to say, we're not friends any longer."

I slid my arms around his waist. "Thank you for that. It was what I needed to hear."

"What? That my best friend fucked me over?" His hands moved over my ass as he hit me with his sarcasm.

"No. I needed to be reminded that in the scheme of things, my setback is minor. I've still got those I love close. I can still pay my bills and I still have opportunities. Screw my plan. I'm getting a new one."

"Or you could fly by the seat of your pants for awhile and see where that takes you."

God, the thought freaked me the fuck out. "I'm not sure I could do that."

"I don't mean have no plans, but you could try having loose ones that allow for flexibility."

"I'll think about it." I wasn't sure how that would go, but I could try.

"And besides, you've got a job doing what you love, without needing that piece of paper to say you know your shit."

"I know but I wanted that piece of paper. It's what I've been working towards for so long. And education is what we're told we need to succeed these days. I just have to change my thinking a little, that's all."

"We make our success in life by our own hand, darlin'. Don't listen to anyone who tells you otherwise. You can kick ass however you choose. Now, talking of plans, what do you have on today? Are you working?"

I'd been spending most days working on dress designs, but I was taking the day off. "Nope, not working today. You wanna do something?"

Heat flared in his gaze. "I was thinking we could take care of this." He guided my hand to his erection.

It had been two weeks since the doctor had told him we could have sex if he felt up to it. Of course, Havoc always felt up to it. The doctor had been strict in his instructions—I had to do most of the work and Havoc was definitely not to lift or hold me up. My man liked to push himself, though. He wasn't good with being told what to do.

"Have you been getting yourself ready or something?" I asked as I moved my hand over his jeans.

His hand moved to the button of my shorts and undid it. "What do you think?"

I grinned.

He was always ready.

"Let's move this to the bedroom so your dad isn't subjected to us again."

He chuckled. His dad had walked in on us in the lounge room once. I'd been horrified, but they'd just carried on like it was an everyday occurrence.

"Okay, angel, start walking then," he ordered as he turned me to face in the direction I had to move.

We'd almost reached our destination when his phone rang. He groaned as he reached into his jeans for it. I listened to his conversation and realised we wouldn't be taking care of his erection anytime soon.

"Fuck," he muttered as he ended the call. "That was Yvette. She needs my help with some stuff."

I frowned. "You can't really do anything while you're recovering."

"It's not physical stuff. She's going through Dad's shares and tax stuff and needs some help with it. Today's the only day she has to do it. She's on her way over here now, so we'll need to take a raincheck."

"I'll hold you to that."

Who was I kidding, though? Havoc was not the kind of man who needed to be reminded of promises of sex.

★★★

"Sorry I took up so much of Havoc's time," Yvette said to me four hours later. They'd just finished going through everything. Havoc had left us so he could take a call from J outside.

"No worries. I did some work and got some awesome ideas so it was good that you guys took all that time."

She smiled. It was the first time I'd ever seen her smile. "I love that Havoc has deviated from his usual type with you. I think you're good for him."

"What's his usual type?" Kelly had mentioned this too and I'd been wondering about it ever since.

"He used to always go for blondes with big boobs and hips. You know the type, shallow with no brain cells to speak of. Most of them disliked me and gave him hell for spending time with me. You're so easy going and encourage him to be with his family. It's a nice change."

I suddenly felt inadequate. I had no hips or curves to speak of and my boobs were tiny. And he liked blondes?

I twirled my hair as my throat turned dry.

Why did he even look twice at me?

All my insecurities rushed to the front of my mind. Havoc had never said or done anything to make me question his attraction, but I had confidence issues around being rejected that stemmed from feeling unwanted by my father and being cheated on repeatedly. I'd had counselling sessions over this so I knew where the insecurity came from. As much as I'd tried, though, I'd never been able to permanently kick it to the kerb.

It was all well and good to tell myself to get the fuck over shit, but my mind could be a neurotic bitch over some things and this was one of them. Which sucked, because mostly I was tough as nails. I hated that I struggled with this.

Havoc joined us while I turned all this new information over in my mind. He reached for me and pulled me close with his arm around my waist. "You good?"

"Yes. Why?" I wasn't good, but he didn't need to know that. I needed some time to think.

He frowned. "You don't look okay. You look like you've just found out someone died or something bad like that."

I forced a smile. "No, really, I'm okay."

His gaze didn't move from me for a good few moments.

In the end, Yvette interrupted, "I'm out of here, people. I've got a hot date and I can't be late. She's promised me se—"

Havoc cut her off. "We get the picture, sis."

She turned to me. "He's such a prude when it comes to lesbian sex."

He scowled. "Fuck. If it concerns my sister, I don't need to know. Other than that, I'm all about women all over each other."

Yvette muttered something about him being a prude again and then she left us.

And I was left with a whole lot of questions and insecurities.

Chapter Thirty
Havoc

I stared at my bike, savouring the rush I'd felt for the first time in four weeks. The doctor had finally given me clearance to take the bike out and it had felt fucking good to be back on it. Life was finally starting to get back to normal.

Well, as normal as possible considering everything had changed in the last month. I was still living with Dad, helping him get his shit together. He was doing well and I was finally convinced he'd turned a corner. Carla was back living at her mother's house. We saw each other every day. I couldn't go a day without having her and I'd spent many hours thinking about our future together. Her life was in Brisbane and as much as I tried to talk myself into putting down roots again, I hadn't been able to come to a final decision. The open road called; my heart lived there. Trouble was, it also lived with Carla and I knew that when we finally had this conversation, I'd choose her over the open road if need be. I just hoped our relationship could survive that choice.

I headed inside and jumped straight in the shower. Carla was on her way over and we were going out for drinks at the clubhouse.

As I turned the shower off, I heard Carla's voice. She was talking with Dad, so I wrapped a towel around me and made my way out to the lounge room. I was reaching for the handle of my bedroom door when it turned and she opened it.

When she came into view, I halted and tried to process what I was seeing.

Blonde hair.

Boobs pushed up and out in a tight black dress.

Her staring at me waiting for my response.

"You dyed your hair." It was fucking obvious so I wasn't sure why I stated it, but I was at a loss for words.

"Yeah, do you like it?" The tone in her voice told me she desperately wanted me to like it. The vulnerability blazing from her eyes confirmed that. This wasn't the Carla I knew, the one who would kick your ass for looking at her the wrong way.

I had to tread carefully here. "Darlin', you could walk in here bald and I'd like it."

Lines creased her forehead as she frowned. "You don't like it?"

Fuck.

"I do like it." In fact, I loved it, but I'd always loved blondes so it was a given. I just wasn't sure what was happening here. Carla was off. Something was wrong.

"You're lying." Her voice wobbled.

"Angel, what's going on? You seem upset."

Her eyes widened. "I wasn't upset, but I'm getting there fast. I just want you to be honest with me and tell me if you like me as a blonde."

I tried to take a step closer to her, but she placed her hand against my bare chest and stopped me. "I just told you that I did."

She stared at me for a long few moments before exhaling a long breath. "Fuck, Havoc! I try to do something for you and you don't like it. I thought you loved blondes with big boobs."

"Jesus, you changed for me?"

"Yes, well, sort of, for you and me."

"Why?"

"Because that's your type. And I've always wanted to try being a blonde. I figured I could kill two birds with one stone."

"The only *type* I have is you. And I never want you to change anything about yourself for me."

"But you used to like blondes with big tits. Why did you even sleep with me that first night? And why did you keep seeing me if I didn't fit what you liked?"

Her hand was still against my chest, holding me back. I forcefully removed it, scooped her around the waist and pulled her to me. "Number one, I slept with you that first night because you turned me the fuck on. Number two, I kept seeing you because you kept turning me the fuck on. Number three, I will admit I used to love big tits, but now the only tits I want in my hands and in my mouth are yours, and I don't give a fuck if they are an A cup or a fuckin' F cup. Number four, I will also admit I like blonde hair. But again, the only hair I want to be pulling or getting lost in is your hair. Blonde, brunette, red, purple, what-the-fuck-ever colour you want, I'll happily get lost in it. Number five, never, *ever*, change yourself for anyone. Not for me, not for anyone. You are perfect the way you are. Sure, you might argue too much with me, and you might talk my fuckin' ear off most of the time, and you might not suck my cock as often as I'd like, but I wouldn't have you any other way. You got all that or do I need to repeat myself? Because I'm happy to repeat myself over and fuckin' over until that sinks in. I love you, for you."

She stared at me with wide eyes while I made my declaration. And then she said, "You want me to suck your cock more than I already do? Fuck, Havoc, I've got that thing in my mouth daily. Sometimes twice a day."

I raised a brow. "*That's* what you took from that?"

Her smartass attitude that I loved returned. "Well, it seems pretty important. I don't think I can suck it any more than I already am."

"Carla, I just fuckin' told you that I love you and you wanna stand here and argue about blow jobs?"

"For the record, you don't go down on me often enough. I'd like more of that."

I raked my fingers through my hair. "Are you fuckin' with me here or what?"

Her lips curled into a grin and she threw her arms around my neck. "I love you, too, Mr Bossy Pants." She kissed me before pulling away and adding, "I do stand by my last request though. There should always be more of that."

"Duly noted." I dropped my gaze to her body. "Babe, this dress is too short. We need to take it off and find you a new one."

"Good try, but all my dresses are at my place, so you'll have to live with this one tonight. And besides, there's no way I'm fucking you before we go out, which I know is what would happen if this dress came off. It took me forever to get my hair to look this good. I'm not wrecking it with sex."

I smirked. "I promise not to wreck it while you suck."

She smacked me. "Suck your own damn dick. I'm going to wait outside for you because I can't trust you at the moment."

"Why can't you trust me?"

"Because you have ways of convincing me that sex is always a good idea."

"It fuckin' is."

She pointed towards the lounge room. "I'll be waiting out there." She paused for a moment and the vulnerability returned to her eyes. "Thank you for loving me the way I am," she said softly. "I've never had a man do that, well, except for my brothers, but that's different. As much as it probably doesn't seem like it, I struggle a little with believing in myself so you accepting me means more than you'll ever realise."

"You put on a good show, darlin', but I can see that your father leaving screwed you over. For the record, I like the blonde on you, but I like what's in here," I placed my hand over her heart, "more than your hair. Don't ever forget that."

Her lips curled up in a smile. "You've got all the right words today. Keep that shit up and I might just be the one to bring heaven to *your* door."

I pressed a kiss to her lips. "You already did, angel," I murmured, not wanting to leave this room for the night.

She held my gaze for a few moments, her eyes glazing over with desire, before turning and leaving.

I tracked her ass as she exited my room.

I loved that ass.

Almost as much as I loved her.

★★★

"You're looking better than the last time I saw you," Velvet remarked when she and Nash caught up with us at the clubhouse later that night.

I chuckled before taking a mouthful of beer. "I hope so." I hadn't seen her since a couple of days after I left the hospital when she dropped over with a casserole she'd cooked.

"He's feeling better too, Vi. Never lets up about wanting me to suck his c—"

I cut Carla off as I took in the scowl that flashed across Nash's face. I pressed my lips to hers in an effort to shut her up. When I pulled away, I muttered, "Fuck, woman, are you trying to cause the shit to hit the fuckin' fan?"

She grinned and whispered, "Just keeping you on your toes."

I shook my head and promised on a whisper-hiss, "I'm gonna take that out on your ass later."

"Havoc!" someone yelled out, interrupting us.

I turned at the familiar voice.

King.

He grinned as he approached. "Good to see you up and about, brother. I've got shit for you to do in Sydney. When do you think you can get back down there?" His gaze landed on Carla and his grin grew. "You must be the woman I've been hearing about. I'm King."

She cocked her head. "What exactly have you been hearing?"

"Only good things, I promise. But I've gotta say, I've never seen Havoc look as fucking relaxed as he does right now. He's usually wound so tight that even I would hesitate to take him on. Whatever you're doing, keep it up."

"I'm glad to hear that but I'm fucking exhausted by his demands, King. Maybe you could take him off my hands for a little while," she quipped. The sexy smile I loved lit her face as she spoke. "I'm Carla by the way, nice to meet you."

King laughed before raising his brows at me. "I see why you look so damn relaxed." Giving his gaze back to Carla, he said, "I'll leave him with you for awhile longer, but I'll need him in a couple of weeks."

I eyed Nash while King spoke with Carla. He watched her with a look I couldn't place. The scowl had disappeared and in its place sat a pensive stare. I had no clue what his thoughts were except he still held his grudge towards our relationship. He'd made that clear over the last month.

King slapped me on the back. "I've gotta go see Marcus, but I'll catch up with you later for a drink."

After he left, Velvet and Carla took over the conversation, discussing a girls' night out they had coming up. J entered the room and I excused myself to go talk with him.

"Hey, brother," he greeted me with a jerk of the chin.

"Madison not coming tonight?"

"Yeah, she got stuck talking with some of the girls. She'll be in soon. How are you doing? Did the doc clear you to ride?"

I nodded. "He did. I headed out for a couple of hours today, down to the Coast. It's been too fuckin' long."

He reached for the beer Harlow passed him on her way through the crowd and thanked her before turning back to me. "So are you thinking of sticking around or are you itching to get back on the road?"

"Not sure yet."

He watched me thoughtfully. "Would you be more sure if Carla wasn't around?"

I looked over at where she stood laughing with Velvet and Nash. "Yeah." Shifting my gaze back to J, I shared the thoughts I'd been keeping to myself for weeks. "I want to make a life with her but I'm not sure how to do that. She's just getting started in a new job and it's going well. I won't ruin that for her by asking her to come on the road with me."

"So what, you'll do the long distance thing with her and just see her every couple of weeks?"

I raked my fingers through my hair. "Fuck, I don't know. I'm still figuring shit out. I've also got Dad to consider in all this. He's doing better but I want to keep an eye on him for awhile longer."

He took a swig of his beer. "Life's never fucking easy, is it?"

I eyed Kelly on the other side of the room.

Fuck.

No, life was far from fucking easy some days.

She was the last person I needed to run into. I hadn't heard from her since the day I'd slammed the door in her face and I didn't want to hear from her again.

J followed my gaze. "Shit, she still harassing you?"

"Haven't spoken with her in weeks. I'm hoping that run of good luck continues."

Her eyes met mine and she froze for a moment. My night was made when she blinked and kept going without acknowledging me or heading my way. And when she latched onto another club member and he pulled her close for a kiss, as if they were together, I breathed a sigh of relief. Kelly had always had a thing for bikers and it looked like she'd finally found another one.

"Lady luck's playing nice tonight," J said with a slap on my back. "I'm gonna go find my woman. Catch you later, man."

He met Carla as he walked away and after they exchanged some words he kept going and she came to me. Snagging her around the waist, I pulled her close and laid a kiss on her lips. "This dress is causing me some pain, angel," I murmured into her ear.

She placed her hand on my chest. "The night is only young, romeo. I suggest you pop a painkiller and man up because you've got hours ahead of you before you're gonna get any relief."

The way Carla used her words turned me on more than any dress she would ever wear. "You keep talking like that and I'll make damn sure I get some relief a lot fuckin' sooner," I rasped in her ear.

Her breathing picked up and heat flared in her eyes. Scanning the room, she asked, "How soon do you think we could get out of here?"

"I'd say less than a minute."

She frowned. "Don't you want to stay for a bit and hang out with everyone?"

I grabbed her hand. "Fuck no. The only thing I want to do right now is get inside you. It's been too long and I'm hard as hell."

"It's only been about nine hours," she said as I led her out of the room.

"That's nine hours too long, darlin'."

I fucking loved that she was counting the hours in between having me.

As I led her out to my bike, I recalled my conversation with J and realised a long distance relationship would blow. I wasn't sure I could do it.

Chapter Thirty-One
Carla

I laid out my new designs on the kitchen table and smiled as I assessed them. Jack, my boss, had seen some of them but I had five new ones for him and was working on a sixth. There had only been two he wasn't fussed on and I had reworked them. I was confident he would love the changes. Our working relationship was easy so far and I hoped that would continue. I had never felt so happy in my work. To be able to spend my days doing the one job I'd always dreamed of had to be the best thing in the world. The high it gave me cancelled out the stress I felt over not completing my course. Havoc might have been on to something when he suggested I fly by the seat of my pants for a while. I'd been doing that for weeks and had never felt more at peace.

My phone rang and I grinned when I saw it was Jack.

"Hey, Jack, I was just going to call you."

"What's doing?" His casual attitude made me love working with him even more. It made work fun, which in turn inspired a rush of ideas.

"I'm just going over the new designs and can't wait to show them to you."

"Can we meet tomorrow? I've got some other things I want to go over with you as well."

"Tomorrow would be perfect."

"Your place?"

"Sounds good. Have you got a minute now to talk about something I want to run by you?"

A knock on the front door interrupted my thoughts and I traipsed down the hall to answer it.

"Sure. Shoot," Jack said as I opened the door to Velvet.

I ushered her into the kitchen and mouthed, "I won't be a minute."

She nodded and took a seat at the table, eyeing my designs.

"I wanted to discuss my working arrangements. As in, where I work. Would you be okay if I didn't always work from home in Brisbane?" I bit my lip waiting for his response, hoping he would give me the go-ahead to work from wherever I chose.

He was silent for a moment and I held my breath.

Please say yes.

"Are you thinking of travelling?" he asked.

"Maybe, but only if you are okay with it. Work is my number one priority, always, so I don't want you to think it isn't."

"I don't see why you can't work from wherever you go. I'd need to see you every now and then, so as long as you make yourself available when that is, everything should be good."

"Awesome. I'll keep you updated with my plans. I don't have anything organised yet because I wanted to run it by you first."

"Carla, I just want to create a business that people love to work with so if you're happy, I'm happy. And if you keep creating designs like the ones you have been, I'm bloody ecstatic."

I wasn't used to praise like his when it came to work. Waitressing had always been a hard slog and I'd often completed eight-hour shifts feeling exhausted and unappreciated. Working with Jack was a whole new experience.

"Thank you, Jack, that means a lot." If he could see the grin on my face, he would have understood just how much.

"Okay, I've gotta go, but I'll see you early tomorrow, say nine?"

"Absolutely," I agreed and we ended the call.

I placed my phone on the kitchen table and turned to face Velvet. "My boss loves me," I blurted out, still grinning. My body buzzed with excitement at not only his praise, but also at his permission for me to work from anywhere.

Velvet smiled. "I kinda got that impression. What was that all about? Are you thinking about leaving town?"

I took a deep breath. "I'm not sure, Vi, but I want to be with Havoc and his life is on the road. I figured I should work out what my options are."

Her brows lifted. "Wow, I'm surprised."

I shrugged. "Well, he might not even want me on the road with him, so it may never eventuate. And I wouldn't even consider it if Jack wasn't good with it. Work is my top priority."

Her mouth spread out into a smile. "I didn't mean I was surprised in a bad way. I'm happy for you that things are falling into place. And I'm really happy that you're okay with your plans being altered. The way you're rolling with the changes and making new plans without losing your cool is awesome. Even Nash mentioned it."

"Really?" Nash and I hadn't spent a lot of time together since Havoc left the hospital. All I knew was that he was still against our relationship.

She nodded. "Yeah, he watched you guys together at the clubhouse the other night and mentioned that you seemed really happy. Well, after I prodded him to admit it, that is."

I sighed. "Of course he would need you to drag it out of him. I wish he would just get over himself and accept this for what it is."

"Your brother is a stubborn man, you know that." She paused and her gaze shifted to my hair. "I love the blonde on you. When did you do that?"

"I saw Roxie a few days ago, on your day off." I twirled a few strands of my hair. "So you think it suits me? I'm still getting used to it."

"It really does. When I saw you the other night, I did a double-take because I hardly recognised you."

"Thanks, Vi. I've often thought of trying it and when Havoc's sister told me he loved blondes, I figured it was a good time to do it."

She narrowed her eyes at me. "You didn't do this for him, did you?"

"I did it for me. I mean, the fact he loves blondes spurred me on, but I'd never change something about myself solely to keep him happy. I will admit that I was really nervous about his reaction, though." I paused for a moment as my insecurities heated my face. "I hate feeling anxious about what my man thinks. It's something I've struggled with whenever I've dated a guy I really liked and thought could be the one."

Her face creased in a frown. "Does Havoc make you feel that way?"

"Not at all and that's what I love about him. Honestly, up until this point I hadn't felt any of my usual insecurities. His sister threw me off when she told me he had a type and I didn't fit it. I know it's stupid, but—"

She cut me off. "But it's what us women do, right? We second-guess ourselves and we shouldn't."

"Well, I'm working on not doing it anymore."

"So this whole idea to travel with him isn't just to fit in with what he might want?"

I smiled. "I love how you worry about me. No, it's about compromise. He doesn't want me to change for him and I don't want him to change for me. If he loves the nomad life, I'm willing to make some adjustments to my life for him. But like I said, who knows what he wants because we've yet to discuss it."

She nodded. "Looks like that's something you guys need to talk about."

It was absolutely something we needed to talk about and it would be the topic of our conversation when he took me on a date that night.

★★★

I sat cross-legged on my bed and watched as Havoc lifted his T-shirt over his head. "Thank you for dinner," I said, a little distracted by his muscles.

He dropped his shirt and reached for his belt buckle. With a frown, he said, "You didn't eat much, darlin'. Are you not feeling well?"

His movements continued to distract me as he removed the rest of his clothes. I had to force myself to drag my gaze back to his. "I feel fine, I just wasn't very hungry because I ate a huge lunch."

A moment later, he positioned himself on the bed next to me and pulled me onto his lap so I straddled him. His gaze dipped and he trailed a finger along my collarbone. "Why are you wearing clothes?" When we'd arrived home after our date, I'd changed into my favourite piece of clothing to wear to bed—one of his shirts.

I grabbed his finger and halted his progress. "Do you have any idea what your voice does to me when it sounds like that?"

His eyes met mine. "Sounds like what?"

"All gravelly. I'm surprised you don't have more women lining up at your door with that voice."

Those eyes of his flashed heat causing my belly to do somersaults. *God, this man.* He only had to look at me like that and talk to me in his I-wanna-do-bad-things-to-you voice and I would let him have his way, *any way*, with me. "I don't want other women, angel. I only want you."

I let his finger go. "That's a good answer, romeo." Our lips met and I pressed my body hard against his. My fingers threaded through his hair and I moaned as our tongues found each other.

I will never taste him enough.
Or have him enough.

He slid his hands down my sides and around to grip my ass. Pulling his mouth from mine, he rasped, "These clothes really need to come off." As he said this, he hooked his fingers over my panties and forced them down.

I moved so he could remove them and then sat back down, loving the feel of his hands cradling my ass and his thumbs stroking my skin. "We need to talk," I whispered.

Raising his brows, he said, "Really? I'm kinda in the middle of something here."

"You've only just started."

"Like fuck I have. You wore that tight-as-hell dress to dinner. This started then, sweetheart."

I grinned. "I'm surprised you managed to wait this long."

"That makes two of us."

"So you can wait a bit longer then. This is important."

He moved his hands from under me and glided one up to hold my waist while the other rested on my thigh. "What's up?"

"I've been thinking about us and about the fact you move around a lot. And I've been wondering what your plans are for that?"

His lips pressed together before he replied. "Settling back in Brisbane was never on the cards for me but everything's changed since meeting you. Now I wanna be where you are. Problem is, I love being on the road so I'm not sure where that leaves us." I loved his honesty and the way it bled into his voice. Havoc had gone from being closed off to me and anything a relationship between us could offer, to being willing to lay his feelings down and open himself up.

I ran my fingers along his arm. "Would you take me on the road with you?"

His brows pulled together. "That would be hard when your work is here."

"What if my work could be done from anywhere?"

After taking a moment to process that, he said, "If you're telling me you've figured out a way to be on the road with me, I'll be packing you a bag and sitting that beautiful ass of yours on the back of my bike as soon as I can."

I looped my arms around his neck. "Looks like you're gonna have to pack me a bag. I only see one problem."

"And what's that?" His hands landed on my ass again. One of my favourite places for them to be.

I pressed my mouth close to his ear. "You told me once that putting me on the back of your bike wasn't your best move so I'm concerned that your cock will be in permanent pain."

He laughed and found my gaze again. "Looks like I'll just have to pop a painkiller and man the fuck up."

"Good to see you listen to me sometimes," I said as I savoured the sound of him laughing. Laughter looked good on Havoc and I loved that I'd caused him happiness.

His hands left my ass so he could grip my waist. In one swift movement he had me repositioned with my back to the bed. He hovered over me, his eyes dark with desire and his hands wrapped around my wrists, planted to the bed either side of me. "Now, can I get back to where I was?" he demanded and I quivered at his tone.

Yes.

I nodded but didn't say a word. I simply waited in anticipation for what was to come.

He pressed my arms into the bed before letting go of my wrists, and ordering, "Don't move."

My pulse spiked.

Bossy Havoc could order me around any day.

He removed my shirt before bending to lick one of my nipples and then the other. I almost whimpered at the loss of his mouth when he moved to press kisses down my stomach. Shifting on the bed, he settled in between my legs, drawing them up to rest on his shoulders.

His eyes found mine.

He stilled.

The air vibrated with electricity as we watched each other.

This man was the one for me.

My passion.

My protector.

My love.

I would never want a man as much as I wanted Havoc.

"Fuck." The word tore from his lips, bruising the air with its intensity.

I forgot his order to not move my arms. Placing my hand on his cheek, I whispered, "I know."

"Do you?" He forced his demand out on a heavy breath.

I swung my legs off his shoulders and sat. Moving my face close to his, I nodded. "It's this feeling of being overwhelmed, of being so thankful for this and yet being unsure of where it will end up and hoping it won't ever end, but knowing if it does, that you'll have done everything you could to try and force a different outcome. It's a rush of need, feeling like you can't ever have enough or be close enough, and wanting it all right now in case you miss out on it later. It's happiness that shit went down in life because it led us here, to each other, and for being so fucking glad that plans got fucked up even though at the time it sucked." I paused to take a deep breath. "And it's relief to have found my person, the one who accepts me in all my screwed-up glory and loves me in spite of it. My soul mate."

I searched his eyes, waiting.

My words lingered in the room as his eyes searched mine too.

He gripped my neck and crushed a kiss to my lips.

Powerful and demanding, he consumed me. I lost my bearings as he revealed his need for me.

He pushed me for more and I gave it all to him.

He could have everything.

Anything he wanted.

So long as I had him.

As he thrust inside me, he gripped my hair and stilled for a moment. "It's every-fuckin'-thing you said. Except I know how this is gonna play out and there's no chance it's ever gonna end. You're mine now, Carla."

I am.

And I'd fight like hell to make sure I always was.

★★★

Havoc's hand glided down my stomach to my pussy where it settled. His groan next to my ear was the kind of sound any woman loved to wake up to. And the erection he pressed against my ass resulted in me reaching my hand up to wrap around his neck. As I pulled his face down, he growled, "I want to wake up next to you every morning for the rest of my life."

I parted my legs to give him access to what he craved. A moment later, I moaned when his finger entered me. "I want you to wake up next to me every morning and do that." My words came out in a pant. I'd woken up wet for him and if he continued his finger action, I'd come fast.

"Roll onto your back, darlin', I want those tits in my mouth."

Obeying his direction, I stared up into his brown eyes for a beat.

I love those eyes.

Havoc's eyes told me everything I needed to know. Turned on, happy, frustrated, pissed off, avoiding me—it was all there and I had learned how to read him much better. That morning they told me how much he wanted me. And how much he loved my boobs.

After he dedicated some serious time to my breasts, he gave me back his eyes. The need I saw there shot heat straight to my core. "Fuck, you could make me come from that look alone," I said as I writhed under his gaze.

A knock on the front door distracted him. "You need to get that?"

I took hold of his face. "No, just ignore it and finish me off." My reply came out more as a beg than a request and he chuckled.

When the knocking on the door grew insistent, I grumbled, "Fuck, they need to go away."

He moved off the bed and pulled his jeans on. "I'll take care of it."

I watched him leave, annoyed at whoever had dragged him away. When I heard his voice raise a couple of minutes later, I figured I should see who had caused his mood swing.

After throwing some clothes on, I joined him at the front door. An older man, probably in his sixties, stood talking to Havoc. His facial features reminded me of Nash and when he uttered the word daughter, the room spun.

His eyes met mine. "Carla," he murmured.

Havoc's arm snaked around my waist and he pulled me close. "Angel, you don't have to do this. I can take care of it for you." Love and protection wrapped itself around me as he spoke.

I gave him a smile to let him know I was okay. "Thank you," I whispered, "but I need to do this." My arm wrapped around him to let him know I wanted him to stay. Havoc's support would get me through this; there was no way I was letting him go.

Turning back to my father, I said, "You shouldn't have come. I don't want to see you." Ice coated my words as years of rejection and hurt slammed into my heart.

"I had to come," he started before stumbling over his words. "I'm sick and I don't know how much time I have left."

Anger bubbled up and out of me. "You're kidding, right? I've been here for over twenty years waiting for you. We had all the fucking time in the world!" I shook my head in a frantic motion. "You don't get to come here now that you're dying and tell me we don't have much time."

As my emotions engulfed me and I yelled at him, I couldn't help but take in every inch of him.

My father.

The man who helped give me life.

The man I'd dreamt of since I was a little girl and whom I'd have given anything to know.

The man who should have taught me all the things Nash did and protected me in all the ways Nash had.

It killed me that I wanted to commit him to my memory. But the heart wants what it wants and she could be a hypocritical bitch at times.

Regret blazed from his eyes. *Green eyes like mine.* "You've gotta understand, your mother and I weren't in a good place when I left. I wanted to come back to see you kids, but I couldn't. I had to fix myself before I did that. The trouble was, I never fixed myself."

My eyes widened. "That would have to be the worst excuse I've ever heard. And a load of absolute bullshit. No one's perfect." I took a deep breath and added, "No, wait, there *is* such a thing as a perfect father, he's the father that *does* stick around. Because even in his imperfect ways, he's doing the one thing a man who has a child should do—he raises that child up and is there for it every step of the way regardless of the doubts he has." I clung to Havoc as I tried to catch my breath and silently willed my father to leave.

"Carla—" he began but Havoc cut him off.

"She's made her point and it's pretty fuckin' clear where she stands," he snapped.

"Just go," I said. "I'm never changing my mind."

My father stood on the doorstep silently for a few moments, almost as if he still held hope I'd take everything back and welcome him inside. In the end, though, he shoved a piece of paper at me and left.

His phone number.

I crumpled the paper up.

But being the bitch she was, my heart didn't allow me to throw it away.

★★★

"These are exactly what I was hoping for, Carla," Jack said a few hours later as I showed him the dress designs I'd been working on. Havoc had gone home after dedicating more time to my boobs and I started work soon after. Thoughts of my father had consumed me and I'd been relieved when Jack arrived.

"Oh, thank God," I said. "I mean, I love them but I had no idea if they would be what you'd love."

"They're fresh and I think they're exactly what our market is looking for. Something new, you know?"

He'd asked me to design dresses that I'd love and thought the market wasn't catering to. His praise gave me the confidence to show him some other designs I'd been playing around with.

"Can you give me a minute? I've got some more in my room that I want to show you."

He nodded. "Sure, I'd love to see them."

"I'll be right back."

It took me longer to retrieve the designs than I thought because Havoc had moved them the previous night and I couldn't locate them. When I returned to the kitchen where Jack waited, I found him talking to Nash.

"Hey you," I greeted Nash with a smile.

He gave me a chin lift. "Hey." Jerking his thumb towards the designs I'd already shown Jack, he said, "These are good."

Nash had always supported me in my studies and while he knew next to nothing about fashion, he'd watched as my skills improved over the years. He'd been there for me when frustration had set in while trying to master my talent. He knew what my work meant to me. We may have had countless arguments over the years, but he always had my back.

"Thank you," I said as a smile spread across my face. "So you two have met?"

Jack nodded. "Yeah, Nash was just telling me how you used to put on fashion shows here and make your family sit through them." He grinned as he recalled their conversation.

"Oh God, I'd forgotten about that." My gaze met Nash's and I found him watching me with that same thoughtful look he'd given me at the clubhouse recently.

Jack checked his watch. "I've got about five minutes until I have to leave for another meeting. Do you have those other designs?"

I handed them over. "These are a little different to what's on the market at the moment so I'll totally understand if you don't love them or if you think they won't sell—"

"Fuck, these are stunning," he said, cutting me off. "The ones you showed me before were great, but these are just wow." He looked up at me. "I'd love you to work on more of this line."

My breathing slowed at his compliment and a giddy sensation spread through my body. Taking the designs back as he passed them to me, I said, "Okay, great, I'll get onto that."

He nodded and scooped his keys up off the table. "I'll check in with you in a couple of days. Message me if you need anything in the meantime."

After he left and the door had definitely closed behind him, I turned to Nash, threw my arms up in the air and squealed. "Holy fuck! He loves my shit!" This high would last for days.

Nash chuckled. "Yeah, I got that impression too."

I took a moment and recovered my breathing. I then cocked my head to the side and asked, "How come you're here?"

"I haven't seen much of you over the last few weeks and I've got the morning off so I figured I'd drop in and see how you're going."

His voice held none of the anger or tension it had since he'd discovered I was seeing Havoc. The combination of that and my high caused my frustrations with him to subside. "I've missed you," I said. It was the truth. Feeling disconnected from him had been hard, but my stubbornness had prevented me from reaching out.

He rubbed the back of his neck, a pained look settling on his face. "Fuck, this has all gotten out of hand. I was just trying to look out for you."

I reached for his hand and squeezed it. "I know. And I just wanted to do something in my life without you going all dad on me. Between us we had no chance. We're both so damn stubborn."

"That's the fuckin' truth."

I let his hand go. "So where are you at with Havoc?"

He blew out a long breath. "I'm reserving judgement for now, but I'm not gonna give you hell over it anymore."

"What made you change your mind?"

"I saw the way you were at the clubhouse the other night and now here today. You're different, more confident, and I think Havoc has helped with that. He's not the guy I'd choose for you, but even I can see what being with him has done for you."

A smile tugged at my lips. "How hard was that for you to admit?"

I'd expected him to scowl or to tell me where to go. Instead, he surprised me again. "Let's just say I won't be having this same conversation with Havoc."

"What do you mean? You're not going to talk to him at all?"

"Oh we'll be talking. I'll be making it clear what will happen if he fucks you over."

"I love you, Nash. Thank you for looking out for me." Where annoyance would have once sat, gratitude pushed its way in. I wasn't exactly sure how that had happened, but somewhere along the way I'd changed. And thank God because it was a hell of a lot easier not to argue with him.

He nodded. "Always, babe. Anytime you need me, I'm here for you."

I dropped my gaze for a moment, thinking about our father's visit that morning. When I found his eyes again, I said, "Dad came to see me this morning."

He clenched his jaw. "What did he say?"

"Just that he's sick and can't I understand why he never came back."

"Did you let him in?"

"Fuck no. His excuses are weak. *He's* weak. I've gotten this far in my life without him and I sure as hell don't need him now."

He pulled me close and wrapped me in a hug. His lips brushed across my forehead as he held me.

No more words were exchanged but we didn't need them.

All I needed was his assurance he would always be there for me.

Love is a verb.

And although his actions were sometimes not what I would have preferred, Nash's love for me couldn't be denied.

Chapter Thirty-Two
Havoc

"Pass me a beer," J said as I searched the fridge in the clubhouse for a drink.

"Summer's coming," I said as I handed him the beer. The heat had ratcheted up that morning and the air conditioning in the clubhouse struggled to keep us cool. I'd arrived about an hour ago and my shirt clung to me in places.

J took a swig of his drink. "Gonna be hot out there on your bike. Maybe you should think about sticking around town instead."

My gaze met his. "I considered it, but I'm itching to get back on the road."

"What does Carla think about you leaving?"

A week had passed since she and I discussed our plans to travel together and since then we'd made a loose plan for where we would head first.

"She's coming with me."

He raised his brows. "Nash know about this yet?"

I downed some beer. "I'm gonna catch up with him about it today. We haven't spoken for awhile."

"Good luck, brother. He's a stubborn asshole sometimes."

"Who's a stubborn asshole?" Nash asked, joining us.

J chuckled. "You." He drank some more beer before adding, "I'm outta here. Like I said, good luck."

After he left, Nash eyed me. "Carla tell you I spoke with her last week?"

"Yeah. I thought I would have heard from you after that."

"I've been busy with shit." He reached into the fridge and retrieved a beer.

I decided now was as good a time as any to break our news to him. "I'm leaving town in a couple of weeks and Carla's coming with me."

He didn't react the way I thought he would. There was no instant anger that Nash was known for, but rather an acceptance of sorts. "Figured that was on the cards. Doesn't mean I love the idea but I'm done fighting you two. Carla's a grown woman now and far as I can tell, she's happy with you. So long as she stays happy, I won't step in again. But mark my fuckin' words, Havoc, the minute I discover you've done something that hurts her, *you'll* be in a world of hurt."

I nodded. I could respect that. "It's not gonna happen. Carla means the fuckin' world to me."

I'd used the words he said to me once and the look of recognition on his face told me he remembered. "Good," he muttered before taking a long swig of beer. After one last look at me, he left the room.

At the same time, Scott stuck his head in. "Footy's on, brother. You gonna watch it?"

I lifted my chin at him. "Be there in a minute."

"Bring more beer with you, yeah?"

He left me alone with my thoughts while I grabbed drinks from the fridge.

Who knew where my friendship with Nash would end up? Fuck, who knew where anything in life would end up? My life hadn't panned out the way I once thought it would and every day seemed to alter my path lately. But the road I'd chosen to travel was one that gave me hope.

Being with Carla and building my Storm ties again gave me something that had been missing in my life since I'd walked away from it all.

Faith.

I'd never lost belief in my family, but I'd sure as hell lost faith in everyone else. Carla had broken down my walls and proved that a woman could want me for more than what I was worth. And that regardless of my financial status or my behaviour or my past, she would be there, right by my side giving me every piece of her heart.

I trusted that she'd never let me down or walk away when shit got real.

And that trust was all I needed to know that Carla was my future.

★★★

I entered Dad's house later that afternoon to the sounds of him, Yvette and Carla laughing. The fact she spent time with my family made me more than happy. Carla's eyes met mine with a smile when I found them sitting around the kitchen counter. "Who won the footy?"

Scooping her around the waist and pulling her close for a kiss, I said, "Who do you think?"

"Oh God, don't tell me it was the Broncos?"

"Of course it was the Broncos. The Cowboys have lost it this year, babe."

She smacked my chest. "Pfft, they're gonna win. You'll see."

I grinned. This argument would never grow old so long as I was having it with her.

When I didn't say a word but simply kept grinning, she pressed hard against my chest trying to escape my embrace. "Oh I see how this is gonna go, Mr I'm-So-

Sure-Of-Myself. I'm gonna have to spend the next couple of months listening to you go on about how good your team is. But you can bite me. My team is gonna whoop your team's ass."

Tightening my hold on her, I bent to her ear. "I'll happily bite you any time you want, darlin'."

She smacked my chest again and I smirked as she said, "You better watch your words. There might be no biting in your near future."

Fuck, this was what had been missing in my life for far too long.

I let her go. "We both know that's never gonna happen."

Yvette cut into our conversation. "Carla, it's your turn."

Eyeing the Monopoly board they sat around, I asked, "Who's winning?"

"You're not playing, Havoc," Yvette muttered as she sent me a dirty look. "No one ever has a chance when you play.

Carla raised her brows. "Really?"

I moved to the fridge to grab some cold water. "Yeah, really."

"Challenge accepted," she threw out, a determined glint to her eyes.

Yvette groaned. "No, he can cook dinner while we finish up this game. You two can get your own game on later."

Carla grinned, not taking her gaze off me. "It's a date. You, me and Monopoly tonight."

"I didn't realise you had this competitive streak, angel," I said as I pulled some steak from the freezer.

She rolled the dice to take her move. "I've had it from way back. But it's gonna be so fun playing with you. Winner takes all, and I'm not talking money."

Dad chuckled. "Gonna be some more creakin' in that bedroom tonight, is there?"

"When is the bed *not* creaking, Al?" Carla shot straight back.

Dad's chuckle turned into a full belly laugh. "That's pretty spot on, little lady. I taught my son well."

Yvette rolled her eyes. "God help me."

Dad turned to Yvette. "I taught you well, too, Vettie. Never knew I'd raise a daughter to love women as much as I do, but I'm mighty proud of that achievement. And don't think I never heard your bed creakin' when you lived here. My hearing always was good."

Yvette shook her head. "Jesus, Dad, is there no end to your dirty mouth?"

Carla laughed at Yvette and Dad as they had words. When she caught my gaze she pointed at me and then at herself while mouthing, "You, me, tonight."

I nodded and closed the distance between us. "You're on, darlin', but be prepared because you're going down."

She smirked. "I think you've got that around the wrong way, romeo. It'll be *you* going down."

"Fuck, I love the way your mind works," I said before brushing a kiss across her lips.

As I ended the kiss, she turned her head towards the television that was on behind us. "*Modern Family*!" she exclaimed.

"God fuckin' help us," I muttered under my breath. She loved that show and that woman on there—the one with the screeching voice I'd pay good money to shut up.

She whipped back around to glare at me.

Dad aimed the television remote at the TV and raised the volume. "There you go, sweetheart. Just tell Havoc to pop a painkiller and man the hell up."

"Jesus fuck, do you hear every-fuckin'-thing?" I asked with a scowl at the old man.

Carla burst out laughing. "Thank you, Al." She pointed at me and added, "There's asprin in the cupboard."

Yvette chimed in. "I've clearly missed something here, but I love this show, so everyone *shush*."

I shook my head as they all shifted their attention to the television. But as much as I appeared to be bothered by it all, that was as far from the truth as it could be.

My family getting on with my woman was one of the best things in the world to watch.

★★★

"I'm taking the lead."

I scowled at Nash. "No, I am."

He returned my scowl. "She's my sister. I should be the one who gets to fuck this asshole up."

"She's my woman. I fuck anyone up who fucks with her."

He blew out a long breath. "For fuck's sake. You take the lead, but I'm getting a punch in."

I didn't wait for him to possibly change his mind. Stalking down the front path of Carla's ex-teacher's house, I clenched my fists. I'd been waiting a long time for this.

A couple of minutes after I knocked on his front door, the asshole yanked it open and barked out, "What?"

I placed my boot inside his house and pushed his door open as I stepped inside.

"What the fuck, man?" he yelled, but I shut him up with a fist to his stomach. When he doubled over in pain, yelling obscenities, Nash and I pushed our way in and slammed the door shut.

"We've heard that you like to bully female students into sleeping with you in exchange for passing them in a subject," I said.

Fear blared from his eyes. "They sleep with me willingly, dude. I don't rape them."

My anger erupted and I fought to keep it in check. Gripping his shirt, I thundered, "That's not what I've been told, asshole."

Nash took hold of his hair and yanked his head back. "You wanna know what we do to people who do shit we don't like?"

Sweat pooled on the guy's forehead and he gulped for breath. "I won't do it again. I swear!"

Nash yanked his head again, causing as much pain as he could. "I fuckin' know you won't do it again. Not after we're finished with you."

I shoved him hard against the wall and punched him again. When my fist connected with his cheek, satisfaction coursed through me. It was about time this guy got what he deserved.

"We're gonna keep a close eye on you from now on. Whenever you leave your house, know that we'll be watching. You won't be able to take a shit without us knowing. You got that?" I smacked the side of his head.

He nodded with a desperation my violent side loved and I had to push that need down. I wanted nothing more than to cause him more pain, *a lot of fucking pain*, for what he'd done to Carla, but I had to control that urge. I took a few deep breaths, concentrating on them instead.

Nash punched him hard in the gut causing him to scream out in agony as he clutched his stomach. "If you ever force a woman to sleep with you again, this will be like a walk in the fuckin' park."

My chest tightened and my head pounded with the need to make him hurt as I watched Nash punch the guy.

It was all I could think about.

Red blinding light flashed through my mind and it threatened to consume me.

"You good?" Nash asked when he turned to face me.

I had to find a way to control the urges.

Carla.

I was there for Carla.

The red light receded.

My need for pain subsided.

I blew out a few quick breaths.

"I'm good," I finally told Nash.

"Thank fuck. For a minute there, I thought we had another death on our hands."

His words caused the teacher to panic. "Don't kill me! I won't do it again!"

Needing to remove myself from this guy's presence, I walked towards the front door.

"Where you going?" Nash yelled after me.

"I'm done. If he fucks up again, I won't hold back, but for now I've had enough. Do what you want with him," I replied before heading outside.

I'd come close to losing it in there.

The only thing that had saved him had been Carla. She calmed me in a way no one else ever had. In that moment, I knew what I needed to do.

★★★

"Carla!" I bellowed through the house when I arrived home forty minutes later. She was working from Dad's house that day while he was at the hospital for a check up that Yvette took him to.

I searched high and low, but couldn't find her. Pulling out my phone, I called her.

She answered on the third ring. "Hey, baby. What's up?"

"Where are you?"

"At your house. Why?"

"Angel, I'm at home and you're not here."

She laughed and it sounded like one of her embarrassed laughs. "I'm out in your shed."

"Why?"

"Just come find me. I'll tell you then."

I hung up and headed out to the shed. I'd set it up years ago so I could restore bikes out there. It was also an area where the boys could come over and kick back. I had a couch and a television and bar set up, but I hadn't used it much since leaving town. Carla had cleaned it up when she stayed with Dad and me during our recovery time.

I found her sitting on the couch with designs spread out in front of her on the coffee table. She looked up as I entered. "Hey."

"Are you designing out here?" I couldn't understand why she'd choose to work in my shed. Especially in the warm weather when we had air conditioning inside.

She stood and came to me. Tugging gently on my shirt, she said, "Being out here makes me feel close to you and I find that makes my designs flow better. I know it sounds strange bu—"

I cut her off by placing my fingers against her lips.

It didn't sound strange.

I got it completely.

Because she did the same for me.

She centred me and gave me purpose in life again.

"I love that," I admitted.

Her face lit up. "Oh, thank God. I thought it was kinda silly."

"Babe, whatever you feel isn't silly and you never need to make excuses or hide shit from me. I love you for all that you are."

"Thank you," she said.

The way she looked at me with vulnerability shining in her eyes caused a rush of desire straight to my dick. I picked her up and threw her over my shoulder.

"Havoc! What are you doing?" she squealed.

I stalked into the garage part of the shed. The area that housed the very first bike I'd ever ridden.

When I arrived at the bike, I placed her on the ground. Cupping the back of her neck, I kissed her while my other hand moved to the hem of her short skirt. It didn't take me long to find what I was looking for, and my dick grew harder as I slid my fingers through her wetness.

Her body arched into me and she moaned as I fucked her with my fingers. Dragging her mouth from mine, she said, "Fuck, you should come home in this mood ever day."

I let her neck go and, using both hands, ripped her panties off. At her wild-eyed expression, I growled, "You wanted me to fuck you on my bike so that's what you're gonna get."

The wild-eyed expression she held changed to one of excitement. "It's about time, romeo," she said as her hands moved to the bottom of her top. In one quick movement, she had it and her bra off. I yanked her skirt down and stilled for a moment so I could take in her beauty.

"Fuck," I said, reaching for my belt while my gaze roamed her body.

My movements slowed and she smacked my hands away from my belt so she could take over. I'd never grow tired of her impatience for my dick.

When we finally stood in front of each other naked, she moved close and threaded her fingers through my hair. With her gaze firmly on mine, she asked, "Why now? Like, you seemed to have avoided this for so long... What changed your mind?"

I traced her lips.

God how I loved those lips.

They were capable of giving me so much.

Words of comfort.

Sass that made my day.

Hours of pure bliss.

"Every time I thought about fucking you on my bike it brought back memories of Kelly. She always wanted me to screw her on it. I didn't want those memories because if I thought about that, I also thought about all the other shit that went down with her and my business. Between all that and my mother dying, it was the worst time in my life and I just wanted to shove it to the back of my mind and forget it." I stopped tracing her lip so I could cup her cheek. Rubbing my thumb across her skin, I continued, "I realised today that being with you lets me live with that pain without being consumed by it. You calm me, Carla, in a way no one ever has. And as far as bad memories go, they hold no power over me anymore. If my woman wants me to fuck her on my bike, then that's exactly what I'm gonna do."

The smile she gave me was pure beauty. "You settle me too. I don't know how but you've managed to bring peace into my world. Even with shit going on in my life, knowing I've got you by my side makes it all okay." My heart hammered in my chest at her declaration. Knowing I gave her that was everything.

I let her go and turned my bike on. After settling myself on the seat, I reached for her waist and pulled her on. As she slid her pussy over my dick, I groaned and shut my eyes for a moment.

Fuck.

Always ready for me.

Her hands circled me and she said, "Fuck, this is gonna be as good as I've imagined it."

I found her gaze again and held eye contact as we began moving.

It was just us.

Together.

In that moment.

Chasing.

Pushing.

Wanting.

I crushed my mouth to hers and we kissed while our bodies moved in a perfect rhythm. She opened herself to me and I consumed her.

Everything

I wanted it all.

Her.

She was all I ever needed.

"Havoc!" she cried, her nails digging into my back. "Oh, God... the bike... fuck... " Her voice trailed off as she surrendered to the pleasure.

I thrust harder and faster, moving her closer.

When she came I watched every second of it.

The way her eyes closed and her lips parted.

How she panted through the orgasm before her teeth bit down on her lip.

And the way her body shuddered right before a smile took over her mouth.

I'd been delaying my release but when she smiled I couldn't hold it back any longer. The orgasm rushed through me, filling every inch of my body with the kind of pleasure a man would give anything for.

She sighed and ran a finger across my lips. "This bike is magic," she whispered.

"Baby, *you're* fuckin' magic."

Smiling, she shook her head. "No it's definitely the bike. You should move it into your bedroom."

I chuckled and dropped my mouth to hers for a kiss.

When we ended the kiss, I said, "Marry me."

Her eyes widened. "Like for real?"

"Well I sure as fuck don't mean we should pretend."

She smacked me as a grin formed on her lips. "I don't know. You're pretty demanding with the blow jobs. I might get tired of that as I get older."

"Fuck the blow jobs. I don't need them."

"Well, shit. I thought you lived for your dick in my mouth at least twice a day."

"I used to. Not anymore."

"This seems very sudden. Give me one reason why I should marry you."

I could give her more than ten, but the one that meant the most to me was what I'd give. I reached for my necklace..

My yin yang necklace.

"My mother gave me this right before she died. She knew I had darkness in me and explained that the yin yang was a reminder to find the balance between the dark and the light. She prayed I would meet a woman who would balance me." I took a deep breath. "You're that woman, Carla. You're my light."

She stared at me and I almost held my breath. I wasn't sure she would say yes. And then, she smiled and said. "Yes, I'll marry you, but only if you agree to up your game when it comes to giving me your cock."

I grinned. This woman was completely fucking made for me. "What are you thinking?"

As she pressed a kiss to my lips, she murmured, "I'm thinking a little kitchen action while I'm cooking dinner might be nice every now and then, and also some washing machine time while I'm doing laundry would rock. You know, turn some boring-ass jobs into something I'd actually look forward to. I'd also like some sex in public."

"Done. We're getting married." I would have agreed to anything.

"Carla Caldwell. It has a nice ring to it, don't you think?"

I fucking loved the sound of it and couldn't make it happen fast enough.

I'd never seen her coming.

We hadn't been in each other's plans.

We collided and as much as we fought it, we were destined to be together.

Because sometimes life worked out differently than the plan in our head, and that wasn't always a bad thing.

Sometimes it was the best fucking thing in the world.

Epilogue
Carla

3 Months Later

"Mum, this party is amazing. You didn't have to go all out like this. Havoc and I really just wanted to come home to see our families."

She wiped her hands on her apron and gave me a look. Not just any look, but *the* look. The one she reserved for when she was exasperated with one of her children.

"Carla, a mother lives to see her daughter happy in life, and part of that is to see her marry the love of her life. You took off with Havoc three months ago with not a word, or even a suggestion that you would get married while you were away. *You eloped.* And I missed out on my opportunity to fuss over you, and help you choose a dress, and see your face light up when the man you love told you he would look after you forever." She took a deep breath. "Today I get to fuss. Today I get to give you the party I would have given you if you'd married Havoc in Brisbane. Please just let me do that."

Tears welled in my eyes. I didn't often cry but my mother had a knack for causing emotion to take over at times.

I reached for her hand. "I'm sorry, Mum. I should have thought of you."

She shook her head. "No, I'm not saying that. You should always live your life the way you want to. But you should definitely let me throw you a party whenever I want to."

Wiping my tears, I laughed. "Okay, you're on. Any time you want a party, you just tell me."

Her face lit up and she wrapped me in a hug. "I can see he's making you so happy. And that makes me happy."

When she let me go, I nodded. "He really is."

My gaze drifted to where Havoc stood laughing with his Storm brothers. Even Nash laughed with him.

Three months away had been good for us. It had given Havoc and me the chance to strengthen our relationship away from the interference of well-meaning family. It had also given us the freedom to figure out things as we went along. Havoc loved life on the road and being by his side, I was able to witness that. My work hadn't suffered at all and I'd quickly developed a good routine to ensure I managed to finish all the projects Jack set me.

"How long will you be staying in town?" Mum asked. We'd only arrived in Brisbane two days prior. I'd given her plenty of notice, though, so she'd had the time to plan this party. Not that I'd known that was her plan, but I loved the chance to catch up with everyone.

"A couple of weeks. We want to spend time with you and with Havoc's dad. Then we're gonna head up the coast and possibly make our way to Darwin."

Mum's gaze drifted to where Havoc's dad stood deep in conversation with Madison. "Al seems to be doing well these days. I've had him and Yvette over for dinner a few times."

Al's gaze met mine as we talked about him and he winked. "Carla, get your ass over here, little lady. I want to ask you something."

"Like father, like son," Mum said with a shake of her head. "He's so damn bossy."

Laughing, I agreed with her. "Yeah, he is. And dirty like his son too. Will you be okay if I leave you to go and chat with everyone?"

She shooed me away. "Go. I've got the food under control."

I left her and made my way to Al and Madison. However, Nash cornered me before I reached my destination. His hand landed on my arm and he said, "You got a minute?"

"Sure, what's up?"

He pulled me aside. "You look good, babe. Happy."

My mouth curled up in a smile. This was a lot for Nash to admit. Mainly because for him to say this meant he would have to acknowledge Havoc. "I am. Life is good."

"You didn't have to run away to get married, though. I wouldn't have stood in your way."

"I didn't run away, Nash. Havoc asked me to marry him before we left, I just never told anyone. And when he asked me what we were waiting for a couple of weeks ago, I didn't have a good answer for him, so we did it. I feel like I am exactly where I'm meant to be."

"The fact he makes you this happy is enough for me. That's all I ever wanted for you. Dad screwed you up in ways I'm sure I don't even know and I spent my life trying to make up for that. Knowing that Havoc keeps that smile on your face makes *me* happy."

I reached up and laid the palm of my hand against his cheek. "You've carried that burden for too long, Nash. I love you for it, but you have to let it go," I said softly. "And as far as Dad's concerned, I've decided to see him."

Nash's eyes widened. "Why?"

"I need to do this for me. To forgive. Not for him, but for me. Like Mum said, holding onto the bitterness and hurt and anger only causes *me* more pain. It's time to let that pain go." I'd started to work through all this old pain and I knew the next step was to see my father. I didn't want anything to do with him, but I hoped talking with him would help me on my journey.

"I'll go with you if you want," he offered.

I smiled again. "Always looking out for me." I stood on my tiptoes and kissed his cheek. "Thank you for being the best brother anyone could ask for."

Al interrupted us at that moment. "Carla, you coming?"

"I've gotta go," I said to Nash. "Havoc's dad is bossier than him sometimes."

Nash grinned. "So is his fuckin' sister. I've been subjected to her at dinner a couple of times, and fuck me, I don't think I've met a woman like her." He jerked his chin in Al's direction. "Go."

I headed over to Al and Madison. "What's up?" I asked.

His eyes glittered with mischief. "Madison here was just telling me that her husband spends his hours trying to get her pregnant. It got me to thinking. Are you and my son planning on blessing me with a grandchild anytime soon?"

Havoc's deep voice boomed from behind me at the same time as his hand slid around my waist. "Dad, I told you when you asked me the same question that it was too soon for that. Don't harass my wife about it."

My belly somersaulted at the use of those two words. *My wife.*

He didn't use them often but when he did, I melted.

"Did I hear the words Madison and pregnant?" J asked, joining us. I watched as his gaze found Madison's and they exchanged a smile.

She slapped his hands away as he reached for her. "God, Al, why did we have to get onto this topic? You've started something now. J will be all over me for the rest of the day." Although she grumbled, you could hear the affection in her voice.

Nash wandered over. "Babe, J's all over you every day. Today's no different."

Madison sighed as she finally allowed J to wrap his arms around her. "True."

I looked up at Havoc and found him watching me with the look he reserved only for me.

Love.

"I love you," I mouthed.

He bent to whisper in my ear. "How much?"

Heat shot straight to my core. I knew what those two words meant.

"Where?" I asked.

He smirked. "Angel, we just arrived at your mother's, I don't think it's appropriate for me to fuck you in her house while everyone's here for a party."

I smacked him and dragged him away from the group. "You're playing with me. You only use those two words when you want me to show you how much I love you. Those two words get me wet and you know it. And since when do you worry about how appropriate you are?"

He snaked his arm around my waist and ran his hand over my ass. "I *am* playing with you. Recall this morning when you refused to suck my cock?"

"That was because we were running late."

He dipped his mouth to my ear again. "Baby, I don't give a flying fuck if we're running late for something, if I ask you to suck my dick, I want you to wrap those pretty lips around me and suck. My goal today is to get you so turned on and ready for me that the word no isn't even in your vocabulary tonight. I want your pussy so fuckin' wet that you're dripping from my chin when I eat you later."

Oh, God.

My dirty biker.

I loved him and his filthy mouth more than I ever thought possible.

As Harlow flashed past us with cake, and Madison and J laughed with Al, and Scott and Nash joked with Griff, and my mother happily buzzed around her kitchen making food with love, I smiled up at him.

Thank God my life plan had been fucked up because otherwise I may never have taken a chance on the man destined for me.

HAVOC PLAYLIST

Take Me To Church by Hozier

Art of Love by Guy Sebastian & Jordin Sparks

Drinking Class by Lee Brice

When She Says Baby by Jason Aldean

Wheels Rollin' by Jason Aldean

Easy Lover by Phil Collins

Stay With Me by Sam Smith

Lonely Eyes by Chris Young

Whatever She's Got by David Nail

Let It Go by James Bay

Craving by James Bay

If You Ever Want To Be In Love by James Bay

Stitches by Shawn Mendes

Rolling In The Deep by Adele

One and Only by Adele

Smoke by A Thousand Horses

FOAD by Kid Rock

City In Motion by Ron Pope

Piece by Piece by Kelly Clarkson

ACKNOWLEDGMENTS

This book was a labour of love and could not have become the story it is without the following people.

My editor, Becky Johnson from Hot Tree Editing – we've only just started working together, Becky, and I have loved the work we've done so far. You've taught me things about my writing that I didn't realise. I am so grateful for all the work you did on Havoc. Thank you <3

My assistant and friend, Jodie O'Brien – To say I am thankful you haven't decided to write books about appliances is an understatement. (If you ever do decide to do that, I will still love you and pimp you!) Havoc is our sixth book together, babe! And you haven't sacked me yet. I love you for this alone. But I love you for so much more too. Here's to a kick-ass 2016! PS I particularly love your messages in shouty caps that say "YOU WIN AT LIFE". They rank just after the messages you send me that say "I'm not feeling Nash on this. Rewrite that whole chapter."

Becca Dawn – I love you. That is all. No, wait. There is more. Thank you for your medical advice for this book and for beta reading it. I truly appreciate the time you take from your busy days to respond to my messages. And for your help getting my characters and plots right. But more than all of that, I adore the hell out of you for being my friend. For checking in on me, for making me laugh, for taking the time to ask me about E and for sharing stories about your family and life with me. I can't wait to meet you in person one day!

My beta girls - Mara, Diane, Shaz, Becca HM, Malia & Drue. Thank you so much for reading my work and offering your thoughts and suggestions. You help me see the things I've missed and offer some awesome ideas to make my stories better. Love you ladies!

My cover designer, Letitia Hasser, and my cover photographer, Sara Eirew – OMG this cover! This cover is the bomb! It is my absolute favourite cover and I owe that all to you two amazingly talented ladies. *blows kisses* Thank you so much!!

To my Levine's Ladies – thank you for your beautiful friendships. I know I say it each and every book, because it's true, I treasure our group. LL is my favourite place on the internet and I am so thankful for you all. Thank you for reading my books, loving my characters, sharing your lives with me and for telling your friends about my books. I love you girls xx

To my Team Levine girls – thank you, thank you, thank you!!!! I am always in awe of you ladies. It means so very much to me that you spend time promoting books and sharing your love of those books wherever you go. I really don't say it enough – I am so thankful and grateful for the hours you give up to help me and other authors <3

To my readers – I remember publishing Storm and wondering if anyone would read it. The fact that many of you are still on this journey with me, reading and loving my Storm books, blows me away. In fact, if I was to go by the messages I receive from readers, most days it feels like the love for Storm just keeps growing. Havoc won't be my last Storm book. In fact, let's just say it now – until you hear otherwise from me, the Storm MC will continue on! Wilder's book will be next in this series. And if you are also reading the spin-off series (Sydney Storm MC), I think Nitro's book will be one of my next releases. Thank you for loving dirty alphas as much as I do!! And thank you for reading my books and allowing me to keep doing a job I absolutely love <3

To Natalie Gayle – thank you for being a wonderful friend and for checking in on me regularly. Neither of us have lost the plot yet and I thank you for helping me with that lol! Love you, babe xx

To my author friends – thank you <3 You know who you are – thank you for your support and encouragement. In this crazy world, just knowing you are there is all I need. I love you for that.

To Dan – thank you for sharing your wife with me. She's the Levine in all this. You've welcomed me into your family and I am so thankful for that. Especially for the car park in your driveway. It's mine now ;) xx

ABOUT THE AUTHOR

Dreamer.
Coffee Lover.
Gypsy at heart.
Bad boy addict.

USA Today Bestselling Aussie author who writes about alpha men & the women they love.

When I'm not creating with words you will find me either creating with paper or curled up with a good book and chocolate.

I love Keith Urban, Maroon 5, Pink, Florida Georgia Line, Bon Jovi, Matchbox 20, Lady Antebellum and pretty much any singer/band that is country or rock.

I'm addicted to Nashville, The Good Wife & wish that they would create a never-ending season of Sons of Anarchy.

www.ninalevinebooks.com

Also by Nina Levine

USA Today & International Bestselling Author

Storm MC Series
Storm (Storm MC #1)
Fierce (Storm MC #2)
Blaze (Storm MC #3)
Revive (Storm MC #4)
Slay (Storm MC #5)
Sassy Christmas (Storm MC #5.5)
Illusive (Storm MC #6)
Command (Storm MC #7)
Havoc (Storm MC #8)

Sydney Storm MC Series
Relent (Sydney Storm MC #1)

Crave Series
All Your Reasons (Crave #1)
Be The One (Crave #2)

Printed in Dunstable, United Kingdom